Forevermore

Alpha

Wendy E Sanderson

May we all find courage, strength and love and find care for every
human being and our Mother Earth.
And for my husband, Christopher
For his love and support.

Christopher, you are my Forevermore.

Prologue

There was a time of Darkness. The time of Nothingness. But the Nothingness stirred, it did not want only Darkness. It became more. Now there is the time of Creation. But the Darkness would grow ever resentful of Creation. It would seek revenge on Nothingness. It would always strive to undo all that the Nothingness had begun when it rose from the Darkness, Creation. Creation is light and life, Darkness is Oblivion. A war that is eternal.

If you seek answers to why you exist then you are merely a fool. There is only Creation. Of Birth, Life and Death. The Great Wheel of Creation; a Life-Force that is ceaseless and eternal.

If there is a Creator, God or Gods then those made of Creation have never stood before that ultimate and supreme First Creation. There is only one eternal prophecy. From Nothingness came Creation and all that is created returns to Nothingness, to be reborn. Some will remember all their lives, the immortals. For those of the mortal realm we are spared the eternity of lives remembered.

Why we are is a question that will never be answered. Those who spend their gift of life, seeking the answers to life and creation waste their gift. Those who seek power and sacrifice their Soul to the Darkness waste their gift. For the Darkness offers such sweet mortal pleasures. When Death calls to your mortal soul, the Darkness will devour your soul to the Oblivion. Oblivion is your soul's price for such a mortal existence in the embrace of the Darkness.

Those that embrace life, embrace the wonder and expect no explanation, that live in Balance will find joy. Those that stare in wonder at their new born child, the grain and fruits that feed them. That see the endless beauty of Creation, the endless heavens but seek no reason for it all, will find joy.

Creation is born of two worlds, those that are born of the immortal realm, The Forevermore. Created by The Fates, to serve them always. Those first born of The Forevermore will suffer many lives or choose to become mortal and forget. There is always choice for the immortal. Their soul, their lifeforce continues even after their physical form dies. They remember all their forms; they are The Watchers, and The Mother and The Father of Realms. But even the immortals do not know The Creator or know why they exist. They live both in the mortal realms and in The First Garden. They are the Guardians of Balance, The Warriors of the Fates. It is in their hands that we, mortals, live or die. They bring destruction to those creations that leave The Balance behind seeking self-worth, glory and mortal immortality.

Then there are the mortals, The Nevermore. Their soul, their lifeforce returns to the golden life-force. All memory of their mortal life gone, all sorrow gone, all pain gone. Their lifeforce finds peace and returns to the sanctuary of The Nevermore. To be reborn, pure and innocent in whatever physical form the universe creates. It is the immortals that suffer their past, suffer their sorrow and pain for all eternity so do not envy them or covert their existence. Immortality is not a gift it is given as a duty to The Fates, a duty to The First Creation.

But as in all creation there is chaos, and in that chaos is purity. And there are those mortals that will always find the Darkness. The Darkest Force that Creation wars with in an eternal battle. The Darkness will seduce the mortal. The Darkness offers the powers of Gods, the sensual pleasures of the flesh.

The Darkness will always take more than it gives. Its realm, the Oblivion waits for all those that have made bargain with the Darkness.

Of all the immortals and mortals there are The Three Fates. Taking no physical form, they live in their energy form. They never confer, they never reveal. They are The Past, The Present and The Future and the cloth they weave, wages war with all creation. The Balance is all. There cannot be life without death. There cannot be rebirth without death. There cannot be light without dark.

Within this Chaos we are all born.

What cloth The Fates weave for us – only the fool would spend their gift of life seeking the answer.

The Trinity – The Forevermore, The Nevermore and Oblivion.

Creation and The Fates at the Centre.

So is life, so is death.

So be it.

Amy

The cold seeped into her bones, waging a constant war with her young body. Cold had staked its ground and set siege to her very soul. Her teeth chattered and her body convulsed trying to find any warmth from the dark, damp stone chamber she had been entombed in. They very air she breathed was chilled and moist. She tasted the salt and iron that permeated the air. Iron-bound, her captor had been clever. Iron was poison to her kind. It stole away her magics. This deep penetrating cold became pain. A constant torment raking over every inch of her body. A savage beast with ice claws tearing away her life force. Never satisfied this ferocious ice beast was intent on devouring her morsel by sweet tasty morsel. How long she could hold onto life; she did not know. Slipping into darkness and closing her ever-sluggish mind was her only escape. But always the clawing, bone chilling creature that called itself Cold roused her. Mocking her, it always brought her back to her reality.

Chains bound her to a stone slab which rested on some ancient crypt was also intent on its share of her diminishing body heat. The rough stone scraped her back. Each shudder of her body ground the unyielding rock against the thin skin of her spine. Her thin linen nightdress offering little protection against the grinding rock. Maybe she should surrender to this beast. But always she fought, knowing she needed time. Time to protect her destiny. To stay alive if only to send her tormentor to the purgatory he so richly deserved. The pitch blackness added to her torment. Moving around her, crushing her. Unable to see, unable to move, she had lain there for what seemed like an eternity.

But she knew this was only the beginning of the war. This first battle she must survive; he must be stopped. She must play his game. The Mother was alone, slowly giving over to despair and our beautiful Earth mourned with her. She rested now in her child. She had surrendered her heart to her bloodline and then returned to her spirit form. Lost and alone without The Father, our Mother Earth had slipped from the mortal realm. And now her child, a child that now must survive and carry The Mother's Heart within her. Just as her own mother had, before passing it to her. Generation after generation. Each generation carrying all hope of redemption for Humankind. A child that must out run time itself until Father returned. Love and hope must never be surrendered. Earth, Mother and Father were bound as one. Amy knew balance lost would create The Fall. Who or what had taken the Father and for what ends she could not fathom, so she continued her fight to survive these days here alone deep within the earth?

Her preternatural senses connected to the decaying corpse that lay beneath the slab on which she was chained. The ancient stone tomb had been torn open, desecrating the ancient burial. She sensed the iron that had been cast into the tomb. Whoever had been laid to rest had been of her kind and now iron burned away the magic that was part of that ancient ancestor's burial. Another poor soul had then been entombed alive, mouldering, screaming in terror. Praying for an end to their purgatory. Their wretched soul forever trapped in this dark place. This tortured soul which was trapped beneath her she could not reach, could not help. The power that had bound the soul to this ancient place was too dark for even her to break. When her magics reached out the iron snapped and bit and her magics retreated in terror. How she longed to release this soul, send her to her eternal rest, but she could not. Was this her fate? Was she to join this soul? Her mind swam with endless thoughts. Her emotions ran rampant. Love, hate and despair. All mingled into one – survival. Just as she could not break the chains that now bound her, she could not break the chains that bound this pitiful soul to this pit. But she would find the way.

Outside this pitch-black chamber where she lay were so many more souls, bound in terror. Too many to count had been enslaved in this subterranean lair. For what purpose she could not comprehend, nor the Evil that permeated every damp corner of this place. A place so ancient and a place once of light, now turned over by him, The Priest, a Cardinal of the Church of Rome, to the corruption of darkness. She sensed the light of all her ancient ancestors trying to regain this place. But his power held the light at bay.

As her frail body shuddered the chains rubbed and tore away the flesh at her wrists and ankles. Iron teeth gnawing her flesh to the bone. The one consolation was the blood that slowly seeped from the ever-deepening wounds was warm. She was sure she would soon die, if not by the slow caress of the endless cold but by the hands of her captor who would ensure she would leave this Earth in pain and agony. But her secret was safe, her child and what she carried within her would not be revealed. Words she could now never speak bound to silence by the spell she had cast upon herself. He would never find or know of her child and what she carried within her. She closed her eyes and allowed the darkness to swallow her, allowing her body to begin its journey into the beauty of oblivion. If this was her final battle then so the Fates had decided. She would fight for every last minute, each moment allowed her child to slip further away from him. She felt her child's life force moving ever further away from her. Every moment she slipped away.

Her sluggish thoughts drifted to her mother, so little did she know of her, her long obsidian hair, black as night, her green eyes, all blurred images. Just memories glimpsed in a childhood mist. Taken as she was, murdered by the very hands that now held her. Did she die here? Jed had said she had been sent to the flames. Had it been a lie? To protect her from the horror that one of the soul's here was her mother. That she was not free of Earthly life. Jed would not lie, no that she knew. Her uncle was true. And surely, she would have found her mother's soul if she was here. She would soon be with her. This gave her peace and the courage to fight on. The Earth and their life here soon a distant memory. She filled her heart with the love of her mother and of Kydan, a being that had her heart and the burden of protecting their child.

'Soon I will be home.' She whispered into the blackness and slipped into her fractured, tumbling memories.

She remembered the nightmare of her capture. Sleeping in her warm soft bed oblivious to the men slowly making their way to her home. A sly fox, creeping silently to the chicken coup, hungry for blood they crept to her home under the dark night sky. Only a snowy white Owl, high in the branches above them, watching their silent progress, curious but soon disinterested. After all they would not fill her empty belly, so she continued her search for the small creatures that dared to venture out into the terror of the silent dark night.

Her uncle Jedediah and aunt Elizabeth across the room, deep in their own peaceful slumber, blind to their approach. The Wards that would have warned of strangers passing their land boundaries was blocked by the Evil that came in the night. The small farm cottage quiet, the fire banked down, gently glowing. The reassuring creaks and groans of the timber structure as it also seemed to settle into the night. All at peace, unaware of the approaching danger.

The sudden deafening crash as the army of God burst through their door. Her aunt's screams. As her uncle Jed tried to speak, one vicious soldier lent a blow to his face. The crimson blood pouring down his face and onto his nightshirt from a broken nose, now bent and twisted by that blow. He neither acknowledged the blow or the pain. Aunt Elizabeth dabbing at the blood with her own linen nightgown as they clung to each other. Jed wrapping his thick muscled arms around her aunt. Peg their lively sheepdog growled and backed into the corner. White teeth barred, fur rising down her back.

'Take the crib, take it now, safe in the barn!' the otherworldly voice entered the dog's mind. Suddenly she launched herself at the soldier that had hurt her master and bit deeply into his calf. Ripping soft calf tissue. Slicing through veins.

'God's teeth, damned animal!' the soldier yelled and kicked Peg in the belly with his other foot. Peg yelped and ran out the broken cottage door and into the dark night. As she bolted for the door the sheepdog grabbed the small crib of woven reeds into her mouth that lay beside Amy. The other soldiers too focused on the injured, cursing soldier to notice her swiftly grab the small bundle. Amy knew Peg would find shelter in the barn with the other animals and her child would be protected by the fearless dog.

The other soldiers snickered. 'Shut up or by Jesu I will ensure my pain will become yours!' the soldier grumbled as he examined the vicious wound to his calf. 'Good thing that beast buggered off. I would have gutted her!' he spat at Jed.

Jed turned to her as she watched in horror, his eyes told her that her fate was sealed.

These images moved across her closed eyes, reliving that fateful night as she lay, shackled in the dark pit.

'Keep thy peace child, hold fast with Our Lord,' he spoke gently to her, the sorrow immeasurable in his voice, 'Hast thou said thy prayers this night, for thou will need all thy strength little one?'

'Aye, all is bound, all has been said....'

'Silence, speak not one more word Witch!' the voice boomed through the one small room they lived in. 'I will not hear one word from your Hell spawned mouth, speak once more and I will ensure you never speak again.' Cardinal Charles de Gosse, The Priest! His face appeared from the gloom of the night, his red cassock flowing around him, ethereal, as he calmly walked into the room. His Angelic beauty, soft blond hair that curled around the red cardinal cap, sky blue eyes and a strong powerful nose led to pale pink lips that were smiling sweetly at her that belied his true heart. A heart of darkness and power. Jed had warned her of this man, but this man before her should not exist. She felt the air change, it sensed the power of this so loved Man of God and she knew that power, as dark as the night itself. It swirled around him, drawing on the evil that he was. His words bellowed through her very soul.

'Why do I have to leave the warmth of my carriage? What takes so long?' The Cardinal glared at the injured soldier. He said nothing. All the soldiers cast their eyes to the floor not daring to meet his gaze. 'Then can I be assured that this scrap of a witch will soon be in the wagon? Or do I have to drag her there myself?' The chill in his words roused the soldiers to action. All not wishing to provoke The Priest as he was known to all.

They dragged Amy from her small cot in the corner, where she and her aunt and uncle were forced to their knees by the soldiers in the middle of the now preternaturally freezing room. She knew she was seeing death before her. His very words crawled over her skin, like the slow crawl of a spider gently creeping over you in the dead of night. Waking your most primordial fears.

As The Priest turned to leave their humble home Jed spoke, his voice thick as his nose was now blocked with blood.

'How in Jesu, how can it be? Thou has not changed Priest, nor age touched...' Jed's voice halted as The Priest brought another blow to his face. Jed knew the man before him was exactly the same man as he had first encountered him, but he had not been touched by time. 'Not possible.' Jed thought confused by the image he saw before him. He was looking at the same young man, but how could that be? Not possible, but Jed would never forget his face or his voice which chilled the soul. But his last encounter with this Evil he had been merely a soldier, not the powerful Cardinal that stood before him now. All his instincts had been right. This man he had seen at each Sunday mass was the very same soldier. Jed had watched him from the back of the church. Head bowed, listening to this young French father give mass. He had been sure they were one and the same, but Elizabeth and Amy had disagreed with him.

'How could it be the same man?' They had both said. Amy in her tortured nightmare remembered all Jed had said with them. But then Jed had finally agreed with them. They may be of similar likeness, but no soldier could rise to be Cardinal. And that soldier would now be in his fiftieth year! But now that smile, the voice. Jed knew, beyond doubt, that he was one and the same and Amy knew the truth of Jed's conviction had been right. Evil was at play in this land and this Priest was at its very centre.

'You cease Jedediah or do you wish to join your niece.'

'No, please my Lord, please, it is me you want, let them be. I beg you.' She had beseeched, her voice near hysterical.

Her memories remembered the horror, the cold fear that her aunt and uncle would suffer her fate. That could not be, this was the fate of her bloodline. A bloodline that stretched far beyond the rise of this Church, far before man ruled this Earth and would endure long after this cruel Church of Christ. Humankind are The Nevermore. This Church would never understand how its power would fade to time and memory. The spell she had cast that night, her prayers her uncle had so carefully asked earlier had been said, binding her tongue. No matter what she would now never reveal The Nevermore or her child.

The night replayed in her mind's eye, showing her home pulled apart until he found their book of shadows, his smirk as he caressed the tooled leather that bound centuries of spells, incantations and hundreds of years of their history. She smiled in her mind, how little did he know, this power-hungry man of God. Read as he may, cast as he may the book would turn on him. The book knew Evil, would read his grim intentions. He would try and master the book, to control it, little knowing that the book can never be mastered. The memories faded to the final memory of being dragged from her loving home and seeing Elizabeth and Jed's heartbroken faces as they pushed her into the prison wagon to begin her journey to what she thought would be a quick merciless trial and the torturous death that all her kind faced, the fire.

But she never expected this to be her destination, never would have known how far down the path of the Dark Arts the Priest had come. She understood why Jed had been so confused by his appearance. This man that had snatched her mother twenty years ago had not aged. He was still the youthful man that it was impossible for them to be one and the same. But his features were so memorable to Jed that he was in no doubt that he was one and the same. He may have changed his name, but it was the very same man that had come for her mother. The memories continued to be played in her minds-eye. The Cold becoming angered at her distraction, needy for her attention it continued its hungry pursuit of her life force.

'Another hag for the fire!' The driver of the wagon muttered to his passenger. 'Seems a right many in these parts these days. Guess that's why he be here then, I suppose.'

Amy shivered in the wagon as it made its way along the rutted road, listening silently to the cheery driver. Happy that another of Satan's children had been caught.

'Just do your work and get us to the Manor House,' the soldier grumbled, he was in no mood for idle talk. His calf throbbed something terrible, 'Just get these old nags moving.'

'Aye, Sir.' The driver nodded. 'Only trying to be polite and all. Nasty wound you got there. Hope the fever don't take you. Nasty wound that is.'

The soldier said nothing, the throbbing pain was getting worse. That dog was a witch's bitch. Maybe it were a demon. Maybe its bite carried sickness. His head ached. He felt hot, even in the cold of the night. He'd ask the Cardinal to bless him. To protect him from Evil. He'd seen many a soldier die from a lesser wound. Turning putrid, rotting the body away until they hacked off the leg or arm. Still few survived even after taking away the stinking limb.

'Why we going to the Manor? Should be going to the town jail, shouldn't we?'

'Not your business, do as he instructed and shut up. For heaven's sake be quiet!'

The memory faded from her mind and the wagon slowly moved through the night. Amy did not see the soothing mist moving into the barn where Peg had taken refuge. Or how Jed and Elizabeth had to endure a sleepless night knelt on their cottage floor while the soldiers systematically ransacked their humble home, hoping for hidden coins or silver. They found none. The only thing they were blessed with in the breaking of the dawn was a curse upon their souls. All would die in poverty, their suffering in this their mortal life payment for the injustice they served on a family more ancient and more powerful than they could ever imagine. The mist kept watch that night!

'Ssh child, sleep now, all is as it should be, sleep.' The mist crept through the barn, carrying the soothing words and the child slept.

The snowy white owl silently glided to its perch high in the rafters of the barn. Its belly full after a good nights hunting. As it settled for sleep also it curiously noted the strangers in its home. In a far corner lay a sheepdog, quietly watching the night and diligently guarding a small bundle of soft downy wool. The child inside slept. That night the snowy owl and watchful dog pondered over the tiny child that slept so peacefully in their barn. But both knew all was well.

Kydan

He had watched over her bloodline throughout time, but he could do nothing now. His duty was to the child, not to Amy. Protect the Mother's heart was his sworn duty and her child now carried that legacy. He and his army were bred purely for this. They were the warriors, sworn to protect Her, the Mother of Earth since the universe began. Brothers born of the first fires of creation, fierce, unyielding in their duty. Until the Father returned, they must protect the bloodline so her heart would one day be reunited with her spirit and the Father.

But how could he watch this Evil growing in this unsuspecting town, built around a church so powerful. He saw it spreading. Wealth and greed surrounding it, corrupting all that once lived in this sacred land of the ancient Celtic Britons. He found Humankind a strange creation. They discarded their magics. Discarded balance. Embraced Gods, and allowed the few to rule in greed and terror. A creature that embraced suffering.

'Kydan, my Brother,' Michael's deep voice shattered the silence, 'my Brother, she is lost. She will return to The Forevermore soon, her ancestors are waiting.'

'Why must she die so? Why must we watch, knowing her pain, her suffering?' He brushed his hand over the silver orb that he was staring into. Michael stood beside him as the vision of Amy vanished. The Hall of the Eyes was peaceful. The white immense hall stretched before them. The towering walls of sparkling white marble led to the open skies, millions of stars slowly moving on their ceaseless journeys across the vast universe passed over the open roof. The Verse of the Immortals, those born of The Forevermore stretched before them, teaming with life. Some waiting for their next calling. Others resting after battle. All allowed in the First Garden, to see its wonder and live in its paradise. Kydan raised his eyes to those stars and wished that her Fate could have been different. Thousands of orbs floated silently in the Hall. Each one connected to a realm and bound in the Hall by the Fates. Others were there also. Quietly watching over their charges – The Watchers. They slowly and silently left, the many forms they all took reflected the diversity of the Verse, but all here had one charge; protect The Balance, keep the Darkness at bay. Protecting all the realms throughout the Verse each Watcher was charged with that one tenant. The silver orb drifted away. Soon joining the others, floating calmly until called again by its Watcher.

'It has always been this way; the Verse has no mercy. It does not judge, it simply exists. Even the Mother and Father cannot change the laws that nature laid down on creation. The Fates do not allow us the grace of the knowledge of the future and we must live by the tenants that they have laid down since creation.'

The Three Fates, taking no form but light. Past, Present and Future never ceasing in their work. Weaving the vast energies of the universe's life force into the essences of creation. Their imagination having no limits on the forms of life they created. They wove their cloth of life. Vast energies merged into life, and destroyed in an instant. No creature created had ever come to know why. They were silent in their task. Creation, birth, life and death seemingly a tangled, but beautiful cloth. But also, their tangled weave was black and dark, filled with pain and suffering and the terror of death and what came after. And those few born as Forevermore, immortal and granted the right to be here in their Garden. Watching, tending to their realms. And destroying at their command. Watchers often spoke of their own Fate, the price of immortality. To see worlds created and then watch them grow, and betray the Tenants of Life. To betray life was to betray The Three Fates and they showed no mercy. Humankind seemed to be on this path.

Michael stood tall and unyielding at his side. The leader of The Watchers, one of the oldest and most powerful of them all. Never breaking his vows, a solid mass of power that followed the path that The Three Fates laid before him. The Destroyer of Worlds, Warlord of The Three Fates. Kydan, young in Michael's lifespan, still carried the compassion and empathy for the creations they watched over.

Michael would often look into his eyes and laugh at his youthful, untarnished view of life. 'You will soon become stone as I, young one. That or you will not survive.'

Kydan often wondered if he would one day stand next to his Brother with the same coldness. He hoped not. But that was for the Fates to decide!

'I know, but she is beautiful. I hear her heart, it fades with each day, with each pain he inflicts upon her.' His heart heavy with the burden. The burden that is love. His courage would hold, even if his heart broke. He would not break his vows; he would not break the law of The Watchers. But he knew the pain would never leave his soul. He wondered if this was how Michael began his journey into stone? Had it been love?

'Kydan, her fate is sealed. We protect the child.' With that Michael left Kydan to his thoughts. He knew how Kydan felt for this young female humankind. He knew Kydan loved Amy and he knew his secret. He would hold his peace, would respect his brother's pain. The other Watchers sensed Kydan's love for Amy but through the eons of time, each had their secrets. With each new world they watched over they all had lapsed, fell in love and carried the wounds that it inflicted. All creations were born from the Verse; how could they not meet their Forevermore Spirit. The creations of the Forevermore were drawn to each other, bonded by a light that only they could see. Love had found them all and all had paid. Michael's only concern was that the child was safe. Amy had cast so she could never to reveal the truth of The Nevermore and more importantly The Forevermore to this Human that sought out a power that he could never control. The existence of the child must also be kept from him at all cost. The Mother's heart and bloodline must endure. Amy had accepted this and her Fate. She was one of two of the Forevermore left on Earth that had survived and were destined to protect the Mother and Father. Hunted and murdered, they had become the hidden. Humankind were Falling, it would not take many of their centuries if they followed on their current path to destroy their home realm. He cared little for these ever-growing selfish creatures. He would gladly order his warriors to wipe them off the face of the Earth, he had cleansed many planets of such creations. Once they were gone Earth would flourish again in the Mother and Father's care. Kydan would have to bear his pain, as Amy had accepted her Fate and carry out his sworn duty as a Watcher and warrior of the Earth realm. He headed for the garden. He always took time to walk through its pathways, drinking in the heady scents of the flowers, trees and all manner of plants that grew here. It was his way of understanding why they did what they did. This, The First Garden, was what they protected and all the gardens of all the planets that life flourished on. Life in balance. Taking only what you needed for life. Shelter, warmth, clothing if your form needed it and food. To cherish life and to create life with care. When Death called you home to The Nevermore, the gift you gave to Creations was to leave no mark on your realm, only your bloodline. If Humankind lost the balance and destroyed all wonder and beauty of their home realm, so be it. They would simply be another species that could not protect and love all that creation and the Verse had given them. As a Watcher he had seen so many species do the same and would never hesitate to destroy every single one of them if required.

'How is he?' Raphael spoke as soon as he came close to Michael. He always knew where to find him. Michael now stood looking out across the vastness of the Verse above him, leaning on a huge tree trunk that towered above them. Raphael stood beside his brother, plucking a small purple fruit from the tree's branches. 'Why do you always choose this tree?'

'Because you cannot resist the fruit, and so I know you will always gravitate here first.'

'And therefore, I find you! You conspire Brother. Soon I will need four wings to get off the ground!'

Michael smiled, Raphael could always find humour, even in the most desperate of times. 'Kydan's heart breaks, she is his Forevermore Spirit. He will have to bear the pain.'

'Do you think he will intervene?'

'No, to alter the course of her Fate would...'

'We do not always think rationally in such times, my Brother. That we both know all too well.' Raphael chuckled, 'We have all...strayed. How I remember Sharkaria when Mars was home world in their verse. What a female, I don't know how I survived. But she is gone now, but when Death comes to this lifeform and my soul takes journey to The Forevermore, we shall be re-united. Ahh what times we shall have. I shall build a garden such as this and the nights!'

'I know. You will no doubt plant a garden filled with these trees!' Michael smiled and looked towards the vast skies; the Universe spread before them. Each world in their guardianship. His eyes fell on the Universe of the Earth Realm. 'I pray the Father will soon be unbound and the Mother return. So many souls will be lost if we cannot find him.'

'Lucifer has much to answer for, it is a pity we could not have destroyed him,'

'We cannot destroy a Forevermore, you know the price if we do!'

'Still a pity.' Raphael whispered; Michael agreed but the price would be too high. A Watcher is bound in the vast energy that is The Forevermore. As all born of The Forevermore are. Eternal spirits. His eyes fell on The Forevermore, its blue light shone, a beacon in the dark vastness of the Verse. Amy would soon be there, all pain gone. Her family would be waiting and one day Kydan will be allowed to go to her. He thought of Shepshu. Would he too be reunited with her? 'Come brother, leave Kydan. We have a new charge to watch over.'

'It is a pity the Humankind do not remember the ancient laws. To lose their magic will be their journey to Oblivion. They slowly depart from Balance. They tip towards their hunger with each cycle of their Sun.'

'There are those who still watch over the Balance and draw on Earth Magic. But most have lost all sense of their ability to draw on it. Every day those that practice the old ways are taken and destroyed because they are different. Or this new Christian God decree's them Evil. They are simple minded creatures who prefer to bow to a God in their own image than see the wonder of their Earth. They destroy everything the Earth brings to them. Greed over care, power over kindness. One day The Mother will return and seek out The Father, then humankind's fate will be decided.'

'It would be a pity to see them vanish, they do have so much kindness.'

'And so much darkness,' Michael's tone was harsh, 'that they may lose their very home because of their hunger for power and wealth. This Church of Christ grows ever more powerful and the new faith in the dessert lands also begins its journey away from The Balance. These two religions of their one God already in conflict, will draw them both into darkness. Maybe it would be for the best to end them now, allow the Earth realm to begin again.'

'I think you may be right, but for now....'

'We protect the child.' Michael stated, Raphael turned and walked towards the armoury. Michael continued to watch The Garden, his eyes resting on The Great Tree. Its huge branches reached to the heavens and each of its precious fruits gleamed in the light. It was said that if you watched the golden fruit, one by one, they would vanish. It was said that each fruit contained the seed of life and left to meet a new Mother and Father who would seed a new realm. The seed of all creations were said to come from those fruits. Earth had been seeded so many thousands of years ago in this way. One Mother and one Father planted and tended that fruit into life. Then humankind arose from their garden. Earth was in their hands now. If the Father remained bound and unseen all would be lost. Lucifer will be found and he will be made to release him, Michael swore this oath. No Forevermore being could bind the Father from sight forever. Nor would Lucifer be able to hide, he would rouse him from his deception and put an end to this madness. Without both Mother and Father how could Balance be kept? He outstretched his huge wings, his claws and fangs lengthened at the anger boiling inside at his Brother's betrayal. 'I will find you Brother, that I vow and I will send you back home!'

Amy

And so, she was brought here. Not to the Keep Moat jail by the castle in the town centre. This place she knew must be near the Manor House, St Mary's Croft. She had heard the soldier tell old George so while she was driven here. Was she under the Manor? She had no knowledge of such a place as this. Ancient, deep underground. So many steps she had been dragged down, deeper and deeper, the cold ever growing. Dank smells of mould and earth changed to the smell of death, that cloying sweet smell that tore at the back of your throat, clinging to all living things, reminding of what all flesh became. The screams and pitiful moans that swirled around her, unable to see those who pleaded, begged for release, her eyes made blind by the rough sacking they had thrown over her head that her other senses formed pictures of the poor wretched souls trapped in this forsaken tunnel, long and winding until she reached this tomb. Then placed in this chamber, water seeping down the walls. There they had removed the sacking giving her sight back. The torches they carried sent shadows bouncing across the small round chamber. The soldiers had forced her onto the stone, chaining her.

'This place, like the Devil's pit itself. Heathen words burned into the stone itself, and those poor buggers!' one soldier grumbled.

'Keep quiet and hurry. I want out of here as fast as I can!'

'Aye, no place to linger is this. The smell of those poor wretches!'

'Do not have any concern for those children of Satan. Do you think he would put them here unless they were guilty of sins of The Evil one?'

'Nay, I would think our good Cardinal knows what's best.'

'Aye, and it's best we keep our tongues in check or it will be our mouldering corpses that will be paying a visit down here!' the soldier said and both quickly left, pulling the screeching ancient door closed behind them.

As they left, she saw the ancient runes on the walls and as she read those ancient markings, she realised she had one chance to stop this man.

'Of all that is in the heavens, dear blessed Mother and Father. He plays with such dark magic. Souls of the dead. So many. Why, why does he do this?' she thought. 'There was no purpose in drawing the souls from The Nevermore!'

'BONE TO STONE!' The souls whispered in the pitch dark, breaking through into his iron bound cell, 'BONE TO STONE!'

She understood as those tormented souls whispered into her magic senses. She knew what they asked of her and knew it was a dear price and she did not know if she would have the skill or be able to draw enough power to carry it out. But she had to endure, she knew not what he was doing, but she must stop him. He wanted The Nevermore for what it contained. 'Why?' she had not the knowledge to understand what his mind was about. It would take a Mage of immense magics to understand his path. She knew he was not searching to gain access to The Forevermore. She was in that moment sure he had no knowledge of The Forevermore. He only saw power and darkness, blinded by it, not seeing the true light of The Forevermore, seeing only what he could gain by opening a portal to The Nevermore. What that gain was she could not comprehend. What could be gained, souls passed into death, souls waiting for their next life, bound never to be human again. What could be gained by entering The Nevermore, a swirling mass of pure energy. The Grimoire, their book of shadows, had shown her when she began her lessons when a mere infant. A place of blinding pure light, a place where all souls travelled once their Earthly human flesh had failed them. A place to be judged and sent either to the Oblivion or to travel to the next mortal existence. This priest needed her alive, it would give her time to cast. He had magic, but needed more, something he knew she had. She was his key.

'You could not break her, could you?' she spoke into the dark, 'my mother was too powerful for you. But you waited, waited all this time. Waiting for me.' She smiled. 'That my dear Godly man is your mistake. I have all her power and more. It grows with each generation. Foolish, weak Mage!' She laughed into the dark and her previous doubt left. And so here somewhere in the small town she had visited on market day he had made his lair, waiting. She would ensure it was also his prison.

'BONE TO STONE!'

The words rang through her mind. And so, she began, but to her despair she found her cell bound by powerful Wards along with the iron. She could not draw in the Earth magics she would need; she could not reach the Grimoire for its ancient power. Sadness swept through her and she wept. Defeated and forlorn she thought of the town's folk of Tickhill, simple, kind that had no knowledge of the Evil that they had invited into their mist in the guise of this holy man. All good God-fearing folk. All striving to stay alive, to feed their families, to make a good simple life. All looking to this priest, this Cardinal to guide them, to save their souls.

'Your Soul is your own. Owned by non. Your choices of light and dark your own. Neither sold or bargained for, your soul was yours.' She whispered, opening her heart to The Forevermore. Reaching out to the Mother and Father. 'I make my choice blessed Mother and Father. Guide me in this path for I am Forevermore and I will never surrender to the dark path. I will bind him in his own Evil until you return and tear the darkness from his heart. I will sleep in cold embrace binding him until I can return to my beloved Kydan. Blessed Mother your heart is safe, my daughter now carries it away, and my bloodline will carry it down through time until you rise again. I am Forevermore and one of the Immortal Souls'

And so, she kept her vow, weakened but she threw out her power to reach for the Earth magics she needed. Each time more weakened. Each time despair pouring over her. Each time failing.

Soon she lost all sense of time in his underground pit. Guards never spoke when they came, placing morsels of bread in her mouth and then pouring water into her mouth before she could even swallow. Some smiled, others had nothing but pity in their dead eyes. One took the time to slowly roam over her young body, reaching beneath her thin nightgown to squeeze and pull her small breasts until his breath quickened and his release came in ragged breath.

She separated her body from her mind. Her life on Earth soon became her dream time and her mind lost itself to the Immortal realm. She would never be released from her memories; they are the curse of the Immortal. Jed, her patient and loving uncle had spent so many times talking of this curse.

'My young one, remember well. I am mortal and I only carry Earth magics as does your aunt. Her sister and your mother, she was cursed with The Forevermore….'

'Cursed, how can it be a curse, uncle?' The young Amy had puzzled. Amy smiled now at her memory. 'So young, such wonderful days.' She remembered.

'A Forevermore is an immortal soul. Living life after life as The Fates deem and remembering all their lives. But sweet child, you are a First Born Forevermore, so have no understanding of the price of immortality. Your mother was not First Born. She remembered three past lives. You must heed my words, not all lives are filled with love, comfort and joy and so those memories which are of lives lived in pain, fear, persecution and war are all remembered. Mortals are gifted with innocent re-birth; immortals carry the curse of all memories. Your dear mother, taken by that creature, betrayed by her own father when he found that his beautiful twin girls were of the magic. Aunt Elizabeth saved as non could prove her guilt, but your poor mother. I was so young then....'

'Aunt Elizabeth, she is not Forevermore?'

'No child, she is of the Mortal Realm. But is of Earth magic as I am.'

'I do not understand, why she is of mortal soul and mother was of immortal soul?'

'And you will never know. The Fates cause our path. You must accept this, learn all I can teach you. How I wish your mother was here, for she could show you so much more than I can of your realm.' Jed said, his heart filled with sorrow for all that his niece had lost when her mother was taken from her.

'Uncle, please do not be sad. I will be good and learn. I promise.'

Jed looked at the Raven-haired, amber-eyed young girl. Her innocence glowed. He knew that that innocence would soon be lost. He had not even spoken of The Mother's heart that now rested in her bosom. He and Elizabeth could only protect this Child of Light, or as best they could.

'She grows wiser each day, does she not?' Elizabeth stated and looked up at Jed as the young girl scampered off to play with their boisterous sheepdog.

'Aye, wife. That she does.'

'Those days at home with Father seem such a distant memory now....'

'A babe out of wedlock. Whore, Satan has lured thee woman and what man has put that sin in your belly. Tell me daughter, tell me now!' Her father's rage had gone beyond all control. He stared at her growing belly, now swollen with the daughter that she carried, Amy. Her mother cowered with Elizabeth in the corner of their kitchen. 'How could you, your mother is to blame, indulging you both and you were always the wilful child. Elizabeth always the dutiful daughter but you, WHORE!'

'Aye Father, whore I be. But this child was born of another world. You foolish, down-trodden man. You know nothing....' Her bitter words silenced as the huge rough hand of her father lashed her cheek. Tears stung and her teeth sliced into her tongue. She tasted the metal of her own blood. Her mother began to weep. Elizabeth

stared in horror at her foul words. Poor Elizabeth, poor mother. What could they do now to save her? They kept their place and hid their birth-right of Earth Magic. If she spoke now then she would betray them too. Her father, his loyalty to the Crown and Church was unquestionable. The Crown brought wealth, being the Sherriff of Nottingham and the Church brought pious social respectability.

'You will be confined to the attic. This, this child that grows in your belly will be born. I have this day betrothed Elizabeth to Jedediah, of Holme Farm in Tickhill. Not the best match, but she will be away from Nottingham and the babe you spawn can go with her. Jedediah has agreed….'

'And my fate, dear father?' Her mother spat

'Oh, you daughter will be turned over. Suspicion already abounds about my errant child.'

'No, husband, no please…'

'Hold you council, Mathilde. If you defend this child of Satan you condemn yourself.'

'It is you that is of Satan's blood. You would hand over your child and your wife to those soldiers. Was it him, that perfect blond creature that whispers in your ear? That you find need of council from him in the dark of the night, Father?' Her mother had known of her Father's meetings with this beautiful soldier and it was not mere council that her father had sought. Her father had been silenced in that moment. For in his world, the world of Crown, Church and moral-society his love was an aberration. A thing of Evil. A love exposed

that would see his standing in the world obliterated and his mortal body turned over to the mercy of his Church. To Amy's kin love was love in all forms it took.

'I will accept your terms dear beloved Father on one condition, that my babe lives and Elizabeth as you say, is married and allowed her life with Jed. And my mother is left in peace. If so, I will hold my tongue in my confession and you can continue with your nightly 'council' with that snake that you so covert. I will see you in the next life dear Father and I will seek my revenge then. I fear only the pain that death will bring, but I do not fear beyond the realm of death. It is you that should fear, your hypocrisy, your fear of Crown and Church. Your soul is as black as a moonless night. But I will hold my peace and die by your and your lover's hand if you hold your words and swear on that book you so love. Swear our terms on The Holy Bible and I will go to the doors of death by your command.'

'So be it.' And her Father had taken their family bible and swore the oath. Elizabeth had told her that her mother hid herself away until the day she was born. Elizabeth had wed Jed the day after the oath taking and left to begin her life with him. Unbeknown by Elizabeth then, her and Jed would live a prosperous and good life at Holme Farm and that Jed was of their kind too. The Fates had smiled kindly on them on their marriage vows that day. Kydan had carefully watched over them and then their babe, Amy. Once Amy had been weaned and was able to be cared for by them, her sister's babe was sent to them. Her sister, her beautiful mother, Angelique had been

taken by the soldier and their Father's lover. That soldier knew not of Amy, none had known. All kept the babe a secret. Jed had simply told of a cousin who had passed and they had taken the babe, Amy into their hearth. As for her mother, Angelique. She confessed all and passed through the searing flames, that burnt her flesh to the bone into the next realm. To Amy the tale was told as warning to her, to Elizabeth it was a tale of horror and never-ending suffering. Her Grand-Father had passed over in pain and suffering and found The Oblivion awaiting his treacherous soul, as his body rotted with the whores-sickness, his debauchery, duplicity and unfaithfulness repaid in full. It is best not to betray those of Earth magics! Elizabeth had said her mother shed not one tear at his passing and took a small cottage by the coast. To pass her final days in solitude and in the grace of The Mother.

And so, with her body separated from mind, she paid little heed to those that came, but each time they came they brought light and she used it well. Memorising the runes that were carved into the ceiling, piecing them together to understand the form of the Wards he had created. She vowed she would turn them on him. It kept her alive. Kept her despair at bay. The fear of failure fed her resolve.

He had not been, not yet, leaving her to her dark tomb, to lie in fear. She was afraid, that was his first mistake. Fear was not defeat, fear was her power and strength. And she embraced it. Jed had taught her that to embrace our fear was to conquer it. Fear was only powerful when we ran from it. She was Forevermore. She was young but Jed had taught her that her female line carried The Forevermore. Jed was a powerful Warlock but was bound in Earth Realm magics and was Nevermore. He had warned her of such humans as this Priest. They chose the Dark, for it was enticing. Offering earthly power and dominion. It was the Great Deceiver. Feasting on your darkness, gaining power. For all his skills, his dark knowledge he could never know the power of the magic that he played with. With each new power he gained he gave away his soul to the Oblivion.

Her dreams, scattered thoughts vanished. He was here. She heard the wretched pleas for mercy from those souls still left alive in the dark tunnel outside her prison, the hollow sound of his heavy, confident footsteps crawled into her mind. He was coming. The cold turned into ice cold fear. Calm, control the fear. Use it! She could not know how long she would have to wait until what she would do could be undone. It would take someone more powerful than her to finally end this man. She would find a way to break his Wards and bind him. Until that day of release, she knew, no matter how many years she would have to wait she would one day belong to The Forevermore and be joined with her mother's soul and all her ancestor's. Kydan would be there to welcome her home. Remember this as you leave this mortal world, binding yourself to the Darkness that would take the Priest with her. Remember She is safe, soon to be far away in a distance land where this church has never reached.

She is safe. The fear left. She would be returned home. She would be Forevermore. He and his Church may have declared war. But her kind would gladly meet them on the battlefield. 'Come priest, come. Let our game of battle begin. The board is set. Make your move.' Fear, despair, savage rage, use all. Jed had drilled her, emotions controlled are our strength, our weapons. Earth magics feed off our emotions, it feels our intentions as does our ancient book. It will turn away from the Dark but will be your greatest ally when your intentions are allied with The Balance.

'It knows.' Jed had said of the Earth. 'Never try to control it, never try to oppress it. It gives freely. You cannot take.'

The ancient cell door screeched on its worn hinges as the guard wrenched it open. The desperate pleas became deafening. And for a moment Amy felt the full force of all the ancients trying so desperately to break through his Wards. She quickly drew on the moments of connection to the Earth and it gave freely. Earth magics poured into her soul, steel against iron, light against dark. Her armour had been given. Her weapon had been given.

'Bone to stone, bone to stone! Child of light we are here. Child of war we are here.'

'I see you have been made comfortable, sweet little Amy.' His voice washed over her like needles piercing her soft flesh, the light from the torches that the guards quickly lit blinding. Her eyes desperately trying to adjust to the light. A soft gentle hand ran up her leg, it seared her flesh, it was the caress of Evil, of a man bound by the dark arts, a man who thought he was all powerful, but he was Nevermore and his power would engulf him and the Earth, for the Darkness could not be controlled only kept at bay by the light that shone in all life, the binding energy of the universe.

'Priest, do thy will, for I know nothing.' Her voice rasping, parched from lack of water. Her lips cracked open and bled as she spoke.

'Oh, little one I think you do, and I am quite sure you will tell me all I need to know.' His voice soft and gentle. 'I am so sure of it, soon you will tell me all that you know of your craft. I think it is time to meet another great craftsman. A true master of his craft. And I am sure you will soon agree!'

The huge dark hooded figure that walked in was the Death Master. His craft was the extraction of confession. He was infamous in these lands. He was fear itself. Those he greeted would simply spill forth all they knew and all that they did not in order to be released to death rather than feel his craft upon their mortal body. Soldiers grunted behind him, dragging in a brazier and a heavy leather bag. Soon the coals were burning bright. All the while the hooded figure stood silent. He was a man of strength and patience. He was a man of pain. But Amy saw something beneath, fear and goodness. He truly believed those he extracted confession from, were the children of Lucifer. But his spirit wavered as he stood silently, waiting. His simple mind in confusion and also in despair.

'Master, shall we begin. I have little time.' The priest grinned, his eyes burning with desire. The hooded man simply nodded. The soldiers retreated to the entrance... 'You stay, it will inspire you to see such a craftsman at work. This man here, is truly exceptional. Pray that you never meet him in his work!' The soldiers remained; the priest smiled. Fear was truly the ultimate power.

The iron seared her flesh. The pain flashed through her. Her body convulsed. She smelt the burning flesh. Her flesh. But still she could not give answer to his questions.

'Tell me child. Tell me how to open your book?' his face so close to hers, his warm breath on her cheek. The smell of his expensive oils masking the odour of her own roasting flesh. 'I can take away all your pain. Set you free.'

She simply stared into his pale blue eyes, the eyes of an Angel.

'Tell me,' he hissed, 'and I will see your life ended here tonight, quickly. I do not understand why you do not speak, we have your book, all I need is the key to opening it. Give me the words. What is it to you now?'

'I can....not!' and she could not, no words opened their book. It chose to open to whom it chose. It was not of this realm; it was not of mortal construction.

'Why, what stops you. Maybe I will bring the last of your family here, maybe their pain would release your tongue.' He raged. 'Have you ever seen some wretch after they have had the pleasure of a Scavengers Daughter! Our Death Master has made this a true artform of merciless pain. They tend never to rise and walk again. Their lungs collapse, their spine ruptures. But dear child, they do live. And I am most certain will curse you to the end of their wretched days'

The steel hoop sat by the door, ready. Waiting to embrace the unfortunate creature it would slowly crush. Their hands tied around their knees as if in fervent prayer. And at each rachet turn the steel would tighten, inch by bloody inch.

'I can....not.'

'I lose my patience child. Give me the key and I will end your miserable life now. The freedom of death awaits and not the torturous flames.' He left her vision and walked around the chamber. 'This is a Pagan site, did you know? That is why the Church chose to build here, to erase the old place of worship. You feel it don't you? Those ancient races, you feed off their magics. That is why we cover them with the Holy Light of God.' He was speaking more to himself as he walked around and around her. 'So, your Evil kind can be destroyed. God will show you mercy, tell me the key and you can grovel before His throne and ask for His forgiveness for your pitiful female soul.'

The two soldiers guarding the door glanced at each other. Their priest seemed fevered, barely controlling his emotions. His usual serene demeanour gone. They barely recognised the fraught man that circled the room like a caged animal. They looked at the Death Master. He stood tall and silent, seemingly unmoved by their priest's sudden change. One thought it was this place. An ungodly place if there was ever one. All those creatures hanging outside, you could hear their screaming in the walls. All Pagans that the priest had found and brought to the grace of the Lord. The soldier wanted to leave, to run from this place. He felt the cold sweat pouring down his back. Was he going to be infected by this place? And this woman, a beautiful child that he had guarded these past days. Was she truly a witch?

'TELL ME!' The priest screamed and the soldiers both jolted in surprise which turned to horror as the once peaceful man grabbed the hot iron from the fire and aimed the white-hot rod to her amber eye. A huge hand grabbed his wrist, pulling his hand away with brutal strength. The tip glancing her delicate face leaving an angry red line of blistering flesh.

'Father, she knows nothing.' The Death Master's deep voice spoke as he held fast onto the wrist of the priest. The soldiers fear mounted. Fearing both the Cardinal and the torturer. This Death Master was known throughout this land. His methods renowned and his success un-rivalled. Both men now facing each other. One holy and pure, one shrouded in his black hood and death. 'She is merely a simple farmer's daughter. She could not withstand this. She would have confessed!' Her torturer's voice bellowed at the priest. His anger at the Cardinal now plain. But he was not listening to him, the Death Master knew by the Cardinals fever.

'Release my hand!' The Cardinal hissed. He knew what she was, he would not be swayed by this hooded creature.
But she could not speak of it, could not say anything. The knowledge was sealed within her. It did not stop her pain though, she only wished for the release of death. She had little strength left to create the trap and now death seemed to draw ever closer. Hope left her heart with each minute that passed by. She hoped Kydan was not witnessing her death. Their love was for The Forevermore, for another time and place. 'Protect her my love, leave me to my fate.' She hoped he heard her prayer.

'Hold fast, soon peace will come. Hold fast. Do not abandon us, we will be ready. We are here, child of light, hold fast.'

The whispers caressed her, a soft warm breeze around her torn and broken body. The priest had lost his grip on the Wards; the ancients were breaking through. He was right, this was an ancient place. For all the Darkness he brought to it, the centuries of ancient worship fought against his dark powers. Tears slipped down her face, stinging the open wound on her cheek.

'We are here. Separate mind and body.'

She looked at the two men that stood beside her. The priest slowly regaining his control. The other holding fast to his wrist. No one moved. The two soldiers motionless.

Silence!

She looked into her torturer's eyes and saw the pity in them. She knew those deep brown eyes; they were so familiar. James! Through the mist of pain, those eyes of her gentle suitor struck her. His face covered by the black cloth of a Death Master revealed nothing of his identity, but she knew those eyes. James, son of the blacksmith in the village. Those doe eyes that followed her everywhere, his stammering and blushes whenever they met, in church, the market and on the rare days when their families came together to dine and celebrate a birth, wedding and the wakes of those that had departed this troublesome life. She pretended never to see his intentions; her intentions were not to marry. Her heart was gone, Kydan held her love and they would both be bound apart until they could meet in The Forevermore. No, no, not James but Samuel, his father. The Death Master who stood before her, whose eyes were filled with grief and pain was Samuel, not James. Samuel had kept his secret well, she doubted even his wife and son knew of his dark work. She could not hate this man, obedience to the Church, to this vile Priest was without question. Samuel loved his God. To question would mean death to him and his family. To support an accused of the Church was to condemn yourself and all your kin. He believed in the Church of Christ, he believed in its power, the power of their Pope as the voice of their God on Earth. He knelt as all knelt before this power that had risen from the ashes of a fallen empire. A power that had taken a simple man's words and used them to rule the world.

'I do...' her voice came is short rasps as the pain continued, 'nothing.'

'Continue!' the voice of the priest was now calm. 'Continue!'

'My Lord, Cardinal. End this now.'

'Again, or do I find a better man than you?'

Samuel took the hot branding iron from the grasp of the priest. His hand trembled as he placed the iron into the brazier. The iron soon regaining its white-hot heat. He feared for his soul. God would not forgive him for this! This child was no witch. He had dealt with many over the years. All confessed.

'It is Lucifer that fortifies her. Do not be deceived. His dark power holds her tongue!' The priest bellowed. The soldiers cowered like beaten dogs.

'He must be right; he was a man of God.' The Death Master thought as he stared into the blazing brazier. Their small town prospered under his watchful gaze. His family had paid for the new church, nearly complete. A glorious edifice that looked over the castle and mound. But there was something. He had been blindfolded before coming to this place. He knew not where he was, deep underground, aye, but where. Somewhere in the town for he had not travelled long to get here. The moans and screams that came from beyond this dark pit made his soul turn to ice. If it was not for his presence; he would swear on the Holy Book itself that he was in Lucifer's pit.

'Very well, my Lord.' Samuel spoke quietly. He feared that his strength of will would leave him. He feared for his soul. He gripped the iron, its white glowing end radiated heat. He lowered its burning heat onto her stomach, the flesh blackened, smoke rose from the searing, blistering flesh. Her scream vibrated around the small chamber. His heart broke. This was not the work of God, but the work of man.

'The Nevermore, tell me?'

'I...do...know...nothing!'

'She is dying.' Samuel knew she had little time, he prayed that it came quickly. He had seen Evil women, seen their vile craft. Their debauchery. He had little pity for them. He had taken his duty seriously, obeyed the father when he was called to do the work. These women of Lucifer's must be eradicated, their infection stopped. He never took the gold the father offered once he had extracted their confessions; he saw it as his duty. But he knew Amy, her family. They were good farmers, always said their prayers. Amy had been a light in Jed and Elizabeth's childless home. Amy was beautiful, both physically and in nature. Never conversed with the never-ending young lads that would find some excuse to visit the farm. Only went to market with Jed or Elizabeth. He had hoped that she would have taken to his own son, James. James was a good lad, strong and had his trade as well. Good blacksmiths were a good catch. Always had a good living. His son was pretty set on her. Jed thought it would be a good match and had conspired with him in the tavern only last month to bring the two together at the Harvest Dance. Now this, this would be his last service to God. No more would he serve this man, for he was no man of the cloth. He saw the darkness in his eyes. His questions to little Amy. The Nevermore, tell me how to open the Grimoire. He searched for something, but it was not for Lucifer's children. He knew what a Grimoire was. Why would he want to open such a book, filled with the vile works of the Devil himself, that was what they were. 'My Lord, she has little time. She must be taken to the square to meet her death. The town must witness her death!'

'Guards!' He yelled. 'I will not tolerate your squeamish, pitiful attempts to extract the confession.'

Two guards posted outside the door marched in. Pushing the two soldiers aside. Their distaste at the pitiful sight of Amy showed in their eyes, but they kept their peace. The Cardinal paid well. 'Take him home, he is of little use to me anymore, his stomach fails him.'

The guards covered Samuel's head with the rough sacking bag and marched him from the dark pit. Covering his hooded head, blinding him to the passage out of the cell. Samuel remained silent;

he prayed that Amy would soon be with God. By tomorrow evening his family will set about plans to be far away from this town. He would leave to go to his brother in York, he would leave this horror behind him. His brother prospered there and had sent word that his family would be welcome and more so their skills. The cathedral caused for much wealth to be made as its towers grew ever towards the heavens. They would go there. His mind flitted to all those he had extracted confession from; were they the same as Amy? Simple women folk, healers? The thoughts burned through him and his unease grew at all that he had done. He would pray every day for forgiveness and never would be a Death Master again. He thought of Amy, the tears fell silently as the guards led him out of Hell.

'Do not weep for me, soon I will be free. Go in peace gentle Samuel, know I will love you always. We are safe!'

Amy, her voice filled his head. She was dead. He knew and he knew as her soul journeyed to Heaven's embrace, she had forgiven him. For only she ever called him her 'Gentle Samuel'. His heart soared, and peace fell over him. She is free and he thought, 'rest in peace, my beautiful girl.' Jed and Elizabeth had already left; he knew not where. Jed had met him last evening to ask of Amy. Samuel lied; said she was being held in the Keep Moat jail. He knew Jed knew he was lying, but he simply said that they were leaving, that they were going to a land that the Church had never touched. Samuel had not understood but he promised he would make sure Amy's body would be claimed and he would see her buried in a quiet place. Even that now would never happen. When the guards pulled off the sacking, he sucked in the cool night air. His hood came with it too, but these guards knew him well.

'Go home Samuel, never speak of this.' The guard spoke quietly into the night, not even looking at him. 'May God forgive us all this night!'

'This night has damned us all; Lucifer will be eagerly awaiting us.'

'Aye Samuel, aye I thinks you are right.' Both guards turned and walked away. Samuel looked up at the bright full moon and felt the soft rain that began to fall. 'Even the heavens weep on this night.'

It was but a short time after that fateful night that they were closing up his home, settling all debts and packing their cart, that his family were beyond the limits of the town of Tickhill on the York road.

James

'Is she truly gone, father?' James' voice was bereft and he never raised his head. The soft rain still persisted into the morning, James was soaked, but did not seem to feel its touch. He sat beside him on the old carts bench. The two heavy stallions slowly walked along the muddy, rutted road. Their few meagre possessions stored in the back. Martha, his wife sat quietly at the other side of James. Her cloak wrapped tightly around her to ward off the rain.

'Aye lad, I believe she is. I am sorry son, so very sorry.' James knew little of his work for the Cardinal, he had never admitted he was the infamous Death Master so feared by all in the Shire. He had told him only the bare truth of his actions as aid in the riddance of Satan's Children for his Church. He knew James would not understand as he saw only good in all people. His heart was always prepared to understand, to forgive. But now, now he saw the change. The hardness creeping around him. Soon his son's heart would be stone as his had become over time. He must never learn of his part in poor Amy's torture. How could he tell him what he had done, even his ever-loving wife would not understand? So much pain had he inflicted on those wretched creatures, at the instruction of the Cardinal. He still loved his God, loved his Son, but the Cardinal, doubt now plagued him. But he must carry the burden as the Ox to the plough. He would accept his judgement before God on his knees. For the rest of his pitiful days that he had left he would live by the Grace of His Light. Maybe mercy would be granted. He could only hope forgiveness would come as Amy had forgiven him. Maybe!

'James,' his mother's voice soft and gentle. 'James, listen to me. You must not speak of her again; it will be dangerous for anyone to know that your father aided in these things, even though it is righteous and Godly work. Even more so that we were friends of a witch!'

'SHE WAS NOT A WITCH!' Anger seethed in his voice; James spoke through clenched teeth. 'How can you say this, HOW! She was gentle, kind. Did you ever see her commit the sin of the craft? No mother you did not...'

Samuel saw the shift again in his son. Something moved within him. Burning rage, but something more; power. He son seemed un-Earthly!

'Son, beware your anger.' Samuel spoke sharply, trying to calm his son. 'Your mother speaks truth. Amy was no witch, that we all know. Why do you think we leave, to begin again, but your mother is right! We must begin again. I left word with old Mathew that my brother has taken ill and needs us in York to keep his smithy alive. He has seven daughters to keep, by Jesu help him!

'Samuel!'

'Sorry mother, but seven daughters! But James lad, keep Amy in your heart only. Treasure her memory, treasure all the times you stuttered and stammered around her. By the Lord you were red as the beets your mother grew in our garden!'

'Mother, I am sorry for my anger.'

'Beloved son, your heart breaks, do not fret. We must do as your father says. Keep Amy in our hearts, remember her.'

'Was I that bad around her?'

Samuel laughed and his mother began to smile that turned to laughter as well.

'Oh, my son, you were as bad as that simpleton Edward around her!' Samuel felt good to laugh as James punched him in the arm. And then James began to laugh. As they travelled along the muddy road to York, they found their peace. York stretched before them and they carried their joy of Amy with them. Not knowing at that moment, they would never work on the Cathedral that Samuel's brother had talked of on the rare occasions he came back to his birth home of Tickhill.

The Fates had other plans for James, plans that would take him on a journey into a far distant future.

Kydan

The dawn began as it should, the sounds of the natural world just waking him from his deep slumber and gently rousing him into the early light, but that was soon to change. His body ached from yesterday's training.

'I am getting old; my bones groan with each new morning.' He grumbled to no one but himself. Stretching in his simple cot set against the stone wall of his humble cell. His tall, muscled frame carried many scars. His long beard now silver-grey but always neatly trimmed. His long hair the same, now matted from the night's sleep. And in a craggy, wrinkled face, bright blue eyes still shone with intelligence and humour. Gideon, was a man who could easily fine mirth and cheer many fearful Brother on their road of strife and battle. He lifted his aching body and placed his feet on the stone floor. 'Ah, at least the floor is warm.' He sighed, thinking that those Roman's at least knew how to keep a warm house. The ancient warm air under floor heating system continued to warm the abbey as it had warmed the ancient villa that stood on these foundations centuries ago. The monks sensible enough to rebuild their quarters on the old system and keep the indulgent heating system to warm their simple dwellings. Their God would forgive them their one simple indulgence! Suddenly his cell door blew open, crashing against the wall. 'What in all of the heavens!' he bellowed.

'Kydan is here!' the young acolyte screeched into his chambers, still trying to arrange his simple, rough weave robe, his hair unruly and his face unwashed. He raised his hand to the young man, forgetting his name. More signs of his passing years. His ears still ringing from the door smashing into the wall and his brain trying to take stock of the young monk and his look of shear-terror as he delivered the news to his now very wide-awake Master. Gideon trying to decide whether to laugh at the red-faced young monk or admonish him for his most discourteous entrance, raised his hand at the young monk.

'Ssh, are you sure that Kydan is here, now in the abbey, my young man?'

'Of course, I am here, Gideon. Would this young warrior cause such a disturbance to your much-needed slumber?' The deep voice boomed into his cell.

Gideon laughed, while the young acolyte turned white and pressed himself into the wall to allow Kydan entrance. The Watcher hunched over in his small cell. His wings touching both sides and trailing on the warm floor. His huge torso bare. The apron and leggings straining from his huge abdomen and thighs. Gideon thought that the young monk would be more than happy for the wall to swallow him whole. He had gone quite pale! 'Kydan, you do not usually hold your manners and wait outside my door.'

'Perhaps I wish to preserve your dignity. Shall we meet in the temple?' The Watcher's eyes filled with mischief as they looked over his old night shirt and soft woollen stockings. Amused at Gideon's night attire. These creatures found human frailty amusing.

'Nay, perhaps the dining hall would be better, those of us who need to eat can break fast while you give command.' Gideon replied, laughing at the acolyte who looked on with horror to think that someone would speak so to a Watcher. 'And the socks were made by a concerned lady-friend, and God's teeth my feet are cold in the night!'

'Brother, I forget that you have ...... needs.' Kydan smiled. He would often forget that these frail humans had to eat to survive, and had to make other bodily functions. Watchers needed no food to survive, taking food and of course wine for its simple pure pleasure. He was also grateful that he suffered not from other bodily functions.

'Aye that we do and my other needs also need tending to.' Gideon's jibe was to end the conversation; his bladder would not hold out much longer. Curse of the old as well.

He had finally dressed himself, David, the young acolyte who had burst into his cell, was incapable of doing anything but stutter and fumble around. Gideon had finally dismissed the lad and told him to go about his duties. Now washed and dressed, his dignity preserved he made his way to the hall. It was obvious that Kydan's presence had soon passed around the Abbey, hushed voices echoed around the ancient corridors of the living quarters, part of the complex that made up Roche Abbey. Gideon had retired South leaving his command in York to a younger man. Roche Abbey was small. It was one of the most ancient of their strongholds but to the outside world it was a simple albeit wealthy abbey. The world knew nothing of their order. Even the persecutions had failed to unveil their true purpose. Warrior Knights of the Forevermore, now all in hiding. Many murdered. But they were here still, never would they be broken. Gods and Empires came and went, they did not. Down through time they had had many names, but only one purpose. Preserve the balance, serve The Watchers.

But he was puzzled why Kydan was here, he would have thought he would have made command to his new charge in York. His unease grew the nearer he came to the hall. 'Why would he be here?', he thought to himself, his expectation would be command from York or London now that he had taken his last post due to his advancing years. He may have lived over 200 years now, but time always beats a door to old age. Gideon had not expected to see Kydan or any of The Watchers again. He stood before the closed refectory door. He could hear only silence from the room. He guessed that everyone had decided that breaking fast could wait this morning. He pushed open the old door, it creaked in protest and seemed all the louder because of the lack of human presence in the area. As he walked into the room his eyes fell on Kydan. It always took his breath away to see him. He would never be without awe of him. He radiated power, supreme physical strength. But it was the fear that fell over him when first seeing him. It would never leave him even after all this time, but it was a fear born of many years knowing the Forevermore Watchers, knowing them was to always fear them. They may fight for justice, to preserve the Earth and humankind but that would not stop them from tearing a man limb from limb, piece by piece if it served the higher cause. The Forevermore was all to them. He shook off the feeling, marching to the table where bread and cheese and cold pork was laid out. He filled his plate, filled a beaker with the weak and bitter third brew beer and carried them over to the scarred rectory table. Kydan had somehow manage to fit his huge frame on the bench, though he thought, looked rather uncomfortable.

'My Brother, are you seated well? You look....' Gideon smiled

'Perfectly fine.' Kydan smiled and the room filled with a warm glow. 'I forget how small humans are!' Their constant bickering was a sign of their enduring respect and love for each other. They had fought, wept and prayed for the Earth Realm. The knowledge they shared had been passed down through generations. The Watchers were immortal beings, The Knights were endowed with long life spans but were part of The Nevermore and returned as all life did when their time on Earth was done. Gideon had always found peace in knowing that he was mortal. The Watchers did not have that final mortal ending. Kydan said they ended their existence with their spirit whole. Their memories intact. The mortals passed into the next life, leaving behind their mortal memories. Finding eternal peace in The Nevermore. To be reborn in a new mortal existence. Some would not return. Those whose evil had permeated their spirit. The Oblivion was all they would find. Their own horror, their own immortal purgatory. Death was known to the Knights as The Return. The Return to the prior state before mortal existence. All life, existence was circular. The Wheel of Life, always turning full cycle. He had talked endlessly with Kydan, Michael and Raphael about existence. With age The Return was hope. He knew he would become reborn. Michael had, after sampling the delights of Earthly wine, loosened his tongue. He had told that some spirits were intertwined with each other. They found each other again and again. He had said that he believed that they could never be undone. And as Michael's head hit the table in drunken stupor he had said no more.

'We are the perfect fit for this world!' seating himself easily on the creaking wooden bench. 'Kydan, we are old friends. You come early, no announcement. The abbey falls into chaos at your arrival. The Father?'

'No, we still search, but still cannot find no trace. It is not why I am here. You know of the town Tickhill?'

'Yes, of course. The town thrives, the old fort has fell but the new church brings wealth to the area. It is much talked of and that of the new Cardinal.'

'The Cardinal is fallen...'

'Are you certain? We have seen no signs.'

'Yes...'

'I will call to arms; the Brothers will deal with him.'

'No, you must not. He must not know of us. The price is too high for your people.'

'I do not understand; the Brotherhood has always dealt with these aberrations.'

'He has knowledge of The Nevermore...'

'How? DAVID...' Gideon bellowed down the hall. David footsteps could be heard racing down the corridor, he almost fell into the room. 'Call council immediately, all present and I mean ALL!'

'Yes, my Lord Commander, I will call the summons immediately.' His high-pitched voice, still not fully mature disappearing down the corridor as he ran to call the abbey to council.

'Gideon, this Priest, this Cardinal. We must be careful. He has gained vast power from Lucifer. He works to his goal.'

'What would that be? Wealth, power are humankind traits, not Forevermore.'

'Lucifer's rebellion against the Verse has condemned him to this realm. He would destroy your Mother and Father, hold dominion over all the Earth realm. He sees your need for Gods, your need to kneel to this one true God and uses it to his advantage.'

'This Cardinal then, the one who holds domain over the village, what his is purpose in this?'

'Darkness, Lucifer uses this man's hunger for power, guides him. Opened his eyes to the dark magics of your realm. This

Cardinal's greed for power blinds him to The Balance, a useful tool for Lucifer to exploit. Lucifer feeds of the darkness now, but that is for the Forevermore to deal with, it is your realm that now lies in peril!'

'I cannot see how we have missed this darkness, are we failing, does our power fade?'

'No, but you have lost so many recently. The day the Pope struck out at your Brotherhood sent many to their deaths. It is only now, hiding in their own places of worship that you can begin to regroup. It is simply that you are distracted by the brutality you all faced and so few survived.'

'Aye, the loss of de Molay was a bitter blow to us all. Your warning saved many, we see such a dark age before us, but to miss the rise of this man and so near to our watch...'

'We digress, watch this man but do not intervene. Learn what you can, what he wants from The Nevermore. We must not allow Lucifer to know we have identified his emissary on Earth.'

'Aye my Lord. By your command.'

'There is a family, Jed and Elizabeth of Holme Farm. They need safe passage to the new lands. They hold a precious cargo in their hands. They had taken refuge in the caves at Creswell, but they are now on their way here. At all cost they must be taken away to safety. I have sent for all the magicians to come to the Abbey to aid your journey. Can you ready your ships quickly?'

'Aye.' Gideon said, puzzled. To call upon all the magicians was dangerous. They hid from sight, keeping their craft secret. He knew the Holme Farm family; they had hidden their origins well for he had had no word that they were of the old bloodlines. 'This family had a child, would be a young woman now?'

'Beyond our reach.' The pain in Kydan's voice struck at the very core of Gideon's heart.

'The Mother!' Gideon's heart faltered. Suddenly understanding the true identity of this family. To have lost the Mother now would mean all Balance on Earth would be gone. The Father's disappearance was causing waves of imbalance. Without him the dead were not gathered at Samhain. Without him to guide them into the Nevermore they were lost in limbo. The humans were already slipping into darkness. Gideon knew the loss of the Mother would mean Earth realm would fail. The Watchers could not locate The Father, they had tried since Lucifer had bound him well from their sight and embrace of The Mother. Her heart torn and broken she had retreated into the oldest bloodline of the Mages. Leaving her heart in their care. Leaving the Earth in the hands of humankind. Bereft of their care humankind had soon found other Gods to worship, selfish, cruel Gods that cared only for glory, adoration and power. Lucifer hid well in this realm, his whisperings slowly corrupting all of humankind. The words of Jesus and Mohammed now his weapon. During the Crusades he had witness the hatred. Meted out in blood. The Brotherhood had come together as the Order of the Knights Templars in hope of influencing the Christian realm and they had failed miserably. And then only to feel the revenge of a cruel, greedy Pope and a power hungry but poor French King. It was a shame they had to bear. They failed to broker any peace in the desert lands and the two faiths. It seemed to Gideon that the two faiths had drawn their battlefield lines and would always now be sworn enemies...

'Safe.' Kydan interrupted his thoughts. 'Protect Jed and Elizabeth and see their cargo gets to the new land.' Kydan stood and stretched his wings. His huge frame rippled with anger and Gideon saw the soft white feathers on the huge wingspan begin to change. A change he had seen on the battlefields so many years before. Only the Brotherhood and magicians could see the Watchers. Arch Angels as they were known to the new Christian faith. Most humans only sensed their presence, like a watchful gaze of some unknown creature lurking out of sight. All but a few in the race of humans had kept their magics, the ability to see a Forevermore, they were perhaps the unlucky ones he thought as he watched Kydan; seeing the true form of a Watcher, claws lengthening, soft feathers turning to the razor-sharp blades that formed part of his armour. His skin glowing in a radiant blue light, the eyes red and long lethal fangs were a sight that turned blood to ice. Kydan was a preternatural force. Those that believed in the angels, guardians of their God's Heaven would never recognise the fearsome creature that now stood before him as one and the same. Those wings would slice a war horse in two, the fangs would rip a man's throat open and their last sight their eyes would see would be the Arch Angels of Heaven feasting on their blood and death.

'Kydan!' Gideon said, standing before the towering angel, twice the height of a normal man, feeling the power radiate off him, spoke calmly. He knew when not to provoke, their anger was not to be tangled with. 'Kydan!'

'There is one more thing,' Kydan hissed and he turned his red eyes down to meet Gideon's gaze. 'On the road to York the blacksmith family travel to his brother's. Go to them, take them with you to the new lands once you are prepared for the journey. Their son James, make him your Brother, for if you do not reach this family in time they will be slaughtered by the priest's soldiers.'

With that Kydan vanished, not waiting for Gideon's answer. Gideon felt the power leave and sucked in a breath of air. Not realising he had been holding his very breath at the rage that came from Kydan. He would do as instructed but his unease grew. Darkness was at work here. He looked down at his unfinished meal, not feeling hunger anymore. He turned and left to go to the temple.

This would be the last journey of the Brothers of Roche Abbey. In the centuries to come the disappearance of these Brothers would become a distant mystery which would fade as the stones of the abbey crumbled to dust. It would be a very different world the Brothers would return to.

Amy

In her dreams Amy drifted on a soft downy cloud, soft blue light surrounding her. No longer did she feel the biting cold, the fetid stink. She felt so warm, so safe. The pain gone from her body, briefly she thought of what she had endured. Feeling the iron burn away at her cold flesh, heat then daggers of such immense pain that raced around her young body, her mind fighting the onslaught. She remembered Samuel leaving, the Cardinal sneering at his lack of will to continue. And as all life faded from her sight, the Cardinal's soft whisper 'Perhaps we must find another way to extract all that you know from your pretty head!' and then the dark wrapped around her, soothing her pain, taking her on her final journey into oblivion and freedom.

'Ssh, rest now.' A soft voice whispered in her mind. 'Sleep child.'

And she did, allowing herself to accept her death, she embraced its comfort and hoped that she would now begin her journey to her ancestors. Peace. Her tortured mind relaxed and embraced the peace. Slipping into that comforting darkness of sleep, where we are safe. Where we are free.

The young woman placed the cooling cloth back into the mint water. The girl had stirred, but at her soft words she had slipped back into unconsciousness. She had been summoned in the dead of night to come to the Manor House, now as morning light began to appear, she had done all she could. She sat on the edge of the soft bed and reflected on the night that had just gone by. Her Pa had been angry at the disturbance but had thought better of disobeying the Cardinal's commands. Her charge to come immediately and care for a sick relative. How she had paled at the sight of her charge. She closed her eyes, fatigue and fear washing over her, as she relived the long dark night.

'My sweet Lord,' she muttered, 'by all in Heaven, who has done this to you?'

She quickly set to work. Trying to remember all her mother had taught her. Rushing around the kitchen, boiling water, adding mint to one bowl of water and lavender to another. Seeking out the salve that the housekeeper swore by. Clean cloth strips, a sharp knife and the harsh soap were added alongside the bowls of steaming water, all placed on a large serving tray.

'Don't think,' she muttered to herself, 'just get on with it.'

But she was panicked. Her heart beating loudly. Thumping in her ears. Carefully making her way back to the attic, praying that he would not be around. The attic was warm but she banked the small hearth and lit a fire. Carefully she began to tend to the mutilated form lying on the bed. Cutting away her foul nightdress and casting it to the fire to burn. She bathed the poor girl, carefully and tenderly removing the filth that clung to her body. Washing her long black hair and combing out the tangled tresses. Then carefully cleaning the horrific burns that covered her stomach, arms and legs. The lavender water would help to sooth and she hoped that the housekeepers salve would heal the blistered and burnt flesh. She held little hope, but she would try. The girl was fevered, and she used the mint water to soak a cooling cloth which she placed on her charge's fevered brow. Then she had prayed, prayed with all her heart. She knew what it was to be a woman in these times. Her Ma and Pa had told her about how a woman who showed any signs of rebellion, outspokenness would soon catch the attention of a man such as the Cardinal. Poor old widow Smythe had met such a fate. She had had to watch the poor woman; already half dead meet the flames. Her Pa had made her go. Said if they did not, they would arouse suspicion. The flames had burnt away the flesh on her legs, as she screamed and screamed. Those screams would never leave her dreams. As her flesh blackened and melted from her bones, the widow had mercifully succumbed. All of the town had stood in the market square watching as flesh turned to ash and blackened bone. The ash settling on them. The sickening roasting smell of human flesh and fat permeating the air. The Cardinal's eyes roving over all the towns folk. Looking for any signs of sympathy for the poor old woman, who had refused to sell a small plot of land to her neighbour and had had the finger of witchcraft pointed at her. Finding strange herbs and bottles filled with potions in her well-tended and valuable cottage had been enough to seal her fate. Now all her land in possession of the church, and soon to be sold to her neighbour!

'See Sally lass, this is the fate of a woman who makes herself known to the church.' Pa spoke as they walked home. 'Don't be misled by the Cardinal, he'll make money out of today and Thomas will have a rich piece of land by evening's end.'

'Aye lass, your Pa is right,' Ma had agreed, 'do your duty, keep your tongue in check. You'll soon be Wed and have the protection of a good husband. These are dangerous times.'

'Aye, I am sometimes fair glad we are poor and simple labourers, that I am.' Pa said, 'Ambition brings jealously to your door, and those who would soon crush you under it.'

She hadn't agreed, 'Why,' she had thought, 'was it wrong to want more comfort in your life?'

Looking down now at this poor woman, her body mutilated and forever scarred, she understood what her Pa had meant. Fear gripped her, her stomach in knots. In that moment she made up her mind, she would accept the marriage offer from Eric, their neighbour's eldest son. Eric was strong, hardworking and had just taken over the managing of the whole of Thomas' herd. Ma and Pa would be pleased and she would be safe. A married woman, soon with babes in arms and a good honest husband. And most importantly as soon as she was Wed, she would never have to set foot in this house again. She maybe a simple labourer's wife, but it would be safe and Eric was besotted with her and he was kind. A better fate than this poor girl. Tears silently slipped from her eyes. She neither understood this cruel world or understood the God that would allow such things to happen. Maybe it would have been better never to have been born to this world. But born into it she was and she would make best of it.

She quietly stood and left the room, closing the door of the small attic room as silently as she could. Her small feet hesitated at the top of the steep attic stairs that led down to the opulent manor house. She breathed deeply and quietly descended the stair way. Opening the lower door and walked into his palace. She had never beheld such things. Soft, thick strangely patterned rugs lined every corridor and room. Cloth tapestries and rich oils were hung along the walls. Some were horrific depictions of demons dragging poor souls to Hell. Strange objects were displayed on tables. Some she would not look upon, being so crude. He had caught her looking at one when she had first been engaged at the manor and he had laughed at her.

'They are Pagan. Fertility Gods. That is why their member is shown in such a way.' He said into her ear as he stood behind her. 'They are rather intriguing, are they not?'

'My Lord, sorry....' She had stammered, 'Such things, they are so ungodly. Should be burned!'

'No, Sally, no, no!' he had chuckled. 'You see they are reminders of our dark past. A past without the Light of our Lord God.

I rescue them to ensure we do not forget our ancient past. How lost we must have been.'

'Yes, My Lord. But they still give me the cold shivers.'

'Do not be afraid. You know Sally they only hold power over you if you truly believe they can. I see you at Mass every Sunday and you say your prayers every night?'

'Oh yes My Lord.' She had quickly replied, feeling hotter by every moment. He stood so close to her that day. She felt ashamed at the way she had reacted. Many of the young girls spoke of how masculine he was. Some even whispered about his manhood! She had rushed from the house that day and made confession of lustful thoughts. And now walking down this corridor she deliberately averted her eyes from those Pagan idols. She raced down the back stairs to the lower floor and to the back room which was now being used as the kitchen. The cellars were off limits and each day workmen would arrive and disappear into them.

'Sally, what on Earth girl. Is your charge well?' the housekeeper cheerily spoke to her. Judith had always been here at the Manor House, whoever lived here she had meticulously cared for. Her cooking was famed in the area, and her careful bookkeeping had earned her great respect of all the residents. St Mary's Croft without Judith would be unthinkable.

'Sorry, its' those things up there. They give me the wobbles. Like they are watching me!'

'Oh girl, don't be daft.' She chuckled. 'He told you about them didn't he...'

'Yeah, but they are...'

'Look there just lumps of stone with big man's didlies on.'

'Judith!'

'Well they are. I reckon those Pagan women made them to make their men feel...'

'Judith, my goodness.'

'Oh, alright lass, come on we've got midday meal to prepare. Those workmen, tch, well I never had to feed workmen before. But master is master and we does as we are bid. So, get a move on. How is your charge by the way?'

'Her fever has broken but she sleeps in fits, bad dreams plague her. Those, those...wounds. Well they seemed less angry now, they maybe healing with your salve. I don't think, I don't think she will live, she seems so weak. I can't understand why she has been treated so.'

'Look Sally, tend to her, do not look beyond that. These high-born men, well us women folk best keep out of their business. So, care for her and no more. You hear me. No more.'

'Yes Judith.' She stammered and set about laying the long refectory table with wooden bowls ready for the midday meal when the workmen would come to eat. Never speaking about their work. In fact, apart from their gratitude they never made any conversation. Sally always thought they looked haunted, and they smelt awful. She could not place the smell, but it hung in her nose so that even when she left for the day, she could still smell it. She knew who the girl was, but decided it best not to say. She was Amy from the Holme Farm. She had seen her odd times in the market. A beautiful girl with long black hair always platted neatly down her back, and dark golden eyes. Sally and the other girls were always sniping about how beautiful she was, but she could not help how she was made. Amy never seemed to notice all the young men whimpering after her like a stray pup looking for a home. She had heard that she was to wed James. Now not that she had not liked James, but Amy could have picked any young man, a rich one would be easy pickings with her looks and her quiet obedient temperament. They had taken her last month in the dead of night and folk said she was a witch, but Sally could not really believe it. But her family had disappeared, and the rumours continued. Now here she was caring for her and sworn on the Holy Bible not to disclose that she was being housed by the Cardinal. Judith was right, best for women folk to mind their business or end up like poor Amy.

The smell came first, wafting like the smell of the cow sheds on a hot summer's day. Then the slow heavy slap on stone of their heavy leather work boots on the stairs. The dirt blackened faces appeared in the door-way one-by-one. Sally's simple mind soon left behind the thoughts of her charge and diligently set to work serving thick soup and rough bread to the men. They greedily slurped down their meal and left as silently as they came.

'Thank thee, kindly. Mistress Judith does feed us all well this midday. Truly grateful madam.' The only words spoken from the charge-hand, the other nine men leaving without a single word spoken.

'Will they ever be done.' Grumbled Judith, her nose twitching in disgust at the smell they left behind.

'Do you know why they are digging a new cellar?'

'No, but I did hear one say that they will soon find the second burial?'

'Burial?'

'Aye, that is what I heard. But keep thy nose well out.' Judith tutted at her. 'I sneaked down there and I see no cellar being dug only another iron door like the one fitted there and locked. And the smell!'

'Maybe there's treasure down there....'

'Oh, sweet Mary-Mother. Child you hold that tongue it will fair see you in trouble one of these days. Now are you about to eat too.'

'No, my stomach has no appetite now.' Sally said as she now never ate at midday meal anymore, the acrid smell rolling her stomach, removing all thoughts of hunger. Judith and her round plump figure seemed also to be fading as she also lost all desire for the meal. Both left unspoken the thoughts of what those wretched, dirt laden men were digging for under the Manor. Both knew how to mind their female business in the hope of anonymity and survival.

The world of our Lord God had watchful eyes.

James

The horses plodded along the rutted road, the cart bumping through each hollow. They had spent the night huddled in the cart. Sleeping fitfully but at dawn eager to continue. It would be a long journey, the horses steadfast but slow and the cart heavy with his trade tools. Its passengers always silent, each lost in their own thoughts. Samuel bereft in grief at the memories of his duties as a Death Master. His deepening fear of the Cardinal. Cardinal Charles de Gosse had arrived in the town to take over the ministry of the new church. Rumour had it that it was his family's money that had paid for its completion. The Norman invasion had vastly increased the family's wealth down the centuries. A favourite of the conquering King his ancestors had profited well from the lands they had acquired. It seemed their fortunes outweighed Kings and even the Vatican. The Earl of Lancaster had personally seen to his placement, most likely for a good sum of gold, Samuel mused. The castle was in much need of repairs after the siege and the town had suffered greatly. Gold would have been welcomed! He remembered that first mass. The women folk swooning at this angelic man. Tall and surprisingly muscular for a man of the cloth. And young! Everyone was expecting to see an obese, greying Cardinal, sent here perhaps under some cloud. Sent to end his days in this town, pushed far out of sight of the Pope John XXII. Samuel had heard his personal guard often discussing their master. One night after extracting a confession from the widow Smythe, Samuel had sat down with the watch. It was only now that their tales of the Cardinal began to form a dark picture of Charles de Gosse.

'Good night Samuel?' the young soldier greeted as he walked from the cell, now quiet. Even the widow's tears had ceased, 'see the widow soon confessed to her ungodly ways. Tickhill will soon be rid of its demonic forces.'

'Aye, that they will. The Cardinal sweeps with new broom the Evil from this place.' Samuel responded as he washed away the blood and bile from his hands and face. 'You have served the Cardinal for a while?'

'Nay, he engaged our services in Southampton. Paid for a full cohort to journey with him to this place…'

'Nay, that's more an army than an escort…'

'Aye, but paid he did and has them housed at the Sheffield Castle apart from the twenty men that are his personal guard here.'

'Aye, strange one,' the other soldier quipped, 'I heard he asked to come here, to this backwater, I heard Pope John was hoping he'd become the next un after he met his maker, but he insisted he come here. God only knows why. Gud ave been swanning around Rome, adding more gold to the pot! But here's we are, and neva felt so much Evil either. So many witches and going ons as I ave neva seen.'

'Aye, Samuel's been busy a lately, earning good gold. Eh Samuel?'

'He neva taks it, seen with my own eyes. There's the good Cardinal handing out his gold and Samuel here, neva taks it'.

'That true, you never take the payment? Death Masters are hard to find!'

'Aye its true, I do the Lords work, be like taking Judas Silver if I did.'

'More like the Devil's...' the soldier muttered and returned to cleaning his blackened finger nails with a lethal looking blade.

'What is thy meaning?' Samuel retorted. 'I simply refuse the Cardinal's payment, what is thy implication?'

'Well, I heard that this Cardinal, well he's more than that. Tha he's searching for sumin. Some say he's knowledgeable on all those dark arts and such. An one of those tha came with im from Rome, tha young priest, Julius, says he's looking for Hell's Gate and he says that it's here, right bloody here. Summat about Lay Lines, old magic stuff like that and he says that's why there's so many of these witches here, demons an all he says.'

'Shut up, ignore the stupid bugger, Samuel. Hell's Gate, Lay Lines. Too much bloody ale, that's what.'

'Aye, but what about the book, tha knows, tha one he always askin bout. Gwim sumatt...'

'Grimoire!' Samuel blurted.

'Aye tha be it, Gwimoore.' The soldier continued his assault on his finger nails. 'Julius ses it's the key to opening the Gate, ses it's here. That's why he's got those stonemason's digging under St Mary's Croft, digging away in the cellar. Ses they found tunnels and things down there, old things, ancient things, likes before we were God fearing. Pagan stuff.'

'I am sure you're a halfwit! Pagan stuff. Be telling next there's human sacrifice and demons chewing on the corpses. Ignore the daft bugger, Samuel.'

'Tha thinks what tha wants, but that Julius has put in a request to go back to Rome as fast as his soft little Roman feet will carry him.'

'Well demons and witches aside. My bed and my lovely Martha, awaits also. I'll be more afraid of her tongue lashing for coming home at this hour than demons chasing my arse around the town. Just make sure that old bitch lasts the night, she'll be before the Sheriff in the morning and ready for burning on Friday. They soon repent once those flames lick at their fetid flesh. Where's old Satan then, eh boys. Likes to leave them to burn, so he does. Well God keep this night.' Samuel said and left the Widow Smythe in their care.

As Samuel recalled that night, he thought on what the soldier had said. The way everyone called the Cardinal 'The Priest', never speaking his name. His aura of power, him being appointed Cardinal at so young an age. Why would he go against his Pope's wishes to come here? The soldier had spoken about his search for The Grimoire, seemingly looking for one particular book. Samuel knew the old tales of this area. Some say that the mound was built over some ancient stones and there were tales of dark mists suddenly appearing around the mill pond, some even saying strange apparitions would appear in these mists. Most put it down to drunken men, belly filled with ale seeing things in the influence of liquor. Some talked of the strange caves, filled with drawings at Creswell. Old Pagan tribes that once roamed these areas, the Brigantes with their Pagan sacrifices to strange horned Gods. All these thoughts roamed through his mind. Soon he began to think that the soldier was not far wrong. The Cardinal was searching for something but Samuel was certain now that it was for no Godly reason. Cardinal Charles de Gosse was a fallen man, and whatever he searched for was far from the sight of the Lord. Hell's Gate! What he did know is that his stately house was always under guard by four of the strange men that had followed him here. Dark skinned, yellow eyed Nubian warriors. Mute but never left his manor unguarded and one always by his side. Those that had called on the Cardinal had said the manor house was richly appointed, filled with strange objects and books! Many books. His table was richly offered, strange delicacies from Eastern lands, but all said that they wish they had never set a foot over his threshold. The manor house seemed oppressive, dark and cold even though his hearths blazed with great fires.

'Samuel,' Martha interrupted his thoughts, 'Samuel are you well? You seem pale.'

'Aye wife, I am fine. Just daydreaming. How's James?'

'He's sleeping soundly in the back, how I do not know with this awful road.'

'He's exhausted wife, we all are. Soon well be in York and we can put these days behind us.' He said and wrapped his arm around his beloved wife. Only James now lived, four younger brothers gone. All succumbed to the fever that raged through the town a few winters ago. She had borne their loss, given all her love to him and James. He was glad to be moving on. Glad to leave the darkness that seemed to be engulfing his beautiful town. Even the rain was giving way. He shook off his thoughts of Cardinal Charles de Gosse, made a pledge to forget him. Not to dwell on what he had seen and heard. What good would it do? No common man could speak out against a Cardinal of Rome and one it seemed favoured by the Pope himself. If he was a deceiver; then let the Church deal with him. If he was at the Devil's work, well he would rather be far away. But he could not shake off the soldiers' words of looking for Hell's Gate. If he were in league with Satan, why would he search for Hell's Gate? Would he not know his way to Hell? 'No.' Samuel thought. 'There was something more to this man. He searched for something in the name of his Church. Better that we are far away.'

'Come on lads, tch tch. At the rate of your lazy plodding we'll reach York by next Whitsuntide!'

The two stallions snorted and grudgingly picked up their pace.

Amy

'Sally...'

The bowls fell from her hands and clattered across the tiled kitchen floor. Judith turned from her work table and glared at her. Dawn had not yet broken, yet he was up. She had not seen him yesterday and had been grateful. Being tired she raced home as soon as possible. Now, this morning, at this early hour he was up and looking for her. She felt hunted. A doe in the huntsman's hungry eye. Bow drawn.

'Sorry, I did not...'

'It is fine; it is lucky it was not the best plate ware!' The Cardinal spoke and smiled at her as she scrambled around the kitchen retrieving the various bowls that she had dropped. 'Sally would you come to the drawing-room; I would like to discuss how your charge is doing? It will only take a moment as I have to speak to the guard who are preparing in the courtyard. It is best not to keep our soldiers of God waiting, especially on this morn they have such an important hunt ahead of them. Ah, so much Evil in such a small town, do you not think?'

'If you say so My Lord, these things are beyond me. Pa tells me that these are not for women to be concerning themselves with.

Keep to our Lord's path that's what he tells me and to mind not the work of men and the Church and our King. And me soon to be Wed, it will take all my time to be a good wife and keeps his house.' she said confidently, Judith began to cough.

'Your father is quite right and I am pleased that you have found a good match, but not so for me. I will miss your diligence. You will make a fine wife and hopefully a wonderful mother.' And in gentlemanly fashion he lifted his arm towards the door and allowed her to leave in front of him. She walked quickly down the hall and turned into the drawing room. It was cold even though the fire blazed. She hated this room even more that all the others. Books, rolled up paper were crammed into every space. Even more strange objects littered every spare space and strange pictures that made no sense, just scribblings and coloured patterns were hung haphazardly all over the walls. His desk was cluttered with the same strange items.

'Please sit.'

She perched herself on a hard, wooden chair placed in front of his desk. Judith said he had the chair made like that so people would not linger. The hard wood soon numbing their backsides.

'So how is your charge? Does her fever weaken?'

'Yes, she still is fevered but it does not burn as much. The mint water I bathe her with cools the skin and helps. Her...injuries, they, well I am not sure. Judith's salve helps but it is a matter for God now.'

'Good, I am very pleased Sally and of course I understand that you have done all you can. The apothecary will be arriving shortly so you must not worry, he will take over when he arrives. You do seem to have a healers' touch though. Does it run in your female line?'

'No Sir, I have never cared for anyone before nor has any of my family, apart from when our own kin are sick. We have no money for the doctor, so apart from simple care we only have our prayers.'

'Well you have done a fine job and as you know I expect you to keep you vow. No one must know that this girl is here. Is that understood, it is so very important.'

'Oh yes my Lord. I have not spoken to anyone, apart from Judith, but she knows of her anyways.'

'Good, that is very pleasing to here. Now as I am so very thankful for all your help, I have put a small expression of my thanks in your earnings.' His smiled at her and handed her a gold crown.

'My Lord, no this, this is far too much. I only tended to her.'

'Sally, please. You have served me well and the young girl lives because of your loving care. Please I would be deeply offended if you would refuse my gift.'

She reached out and took the coin from his large hand. She had never seen one before. This would keep her family for a year. But it did not sit well in her hands. How would she explain it to her father! 'No please my Lord.' She said placing the coin back on the desk. 'My pa, well he would think I had been up to no good bringing this vast sum home. I, I,' she stammered, 'I do not wish to offend, but...'

'My apologies, forgive me. I was not thinking. I would imagine your father would be quite perturbed on how you acquired such a sum.' He rested his chin on the ends of his fingers as if in deep thought. The room became oppressive. 'I know,' he suddenly announced making her jump. 'I will give you a small pay rise and that way you may have my gift, but your father will not be needing explanation. Very good, that is settled, you may go about your duties.' And with a wave of his hand he dismissed her. Sally rushed out of the room, closing the door behind her. At least she would not have to explain the money. Aye it was tempting, all that money. She could have done a lot with that. But Pa would have beaten her and would have dragged her back to the Manor House to ask why the Cardinal was paying his daughter such money. Her Pa had no liking for the Cardinal. She'd put the bit extra in her Ma's hand and that way Pa would not have to know.

The huge Nubian stepped from behind the screen that stood at the side of his desk, silent as ever, waiting for his Master's command. The Cardinal nodded to the silent man. He remembered how he had met these four brothers. Sons of a great king. A king he had come across in need of much aid. A king plagued by fearsome tribes wanting to destroy his rich kingdom. He was a Mage then, a Shaman and with his dark magic he had turned the king's warriors into such fearsome killers they had wiped out all the king's enemies in one bloody battle. The brothers had asked to travel with the great Shaman, to learn of the Darkness and soon these four men had become more brothers to him than apprentices. He knew that one day they would wish to return home. They had taken some of the Darkness, just enough to increase their strength and battle-skills. He would miss these men should they ever choose to journey back home. But he would not hold them to his side, one does not chain brothers.

'Once the girl is recovered, the Sally girl will be of no use. She will soon forget her vow and will open her pert little mouth. Make sure it looks like a tragic accident.' Cardinal de Gosse spoke in his warrior's native tongue. 'Or maybe not!' He found this language useful, anyone eves dropping would not understand his commands to these his most trusted of men. The Nubian simply nodded. Soon poor little Sally would be found, perhaps having fallen in the mill pond. Better still. He smiled, perhaps the victim of another witch that would be found in this little town. It would be a convenient way of dealing with his housekeeper at the same time, he would miss her delightful fare, but sacrifices have to be made. His plans would not be unravelled by the idle gossip of simple women. Yes, that would nicely tie up all the loose ends. He raised is eyes to the ceiling, 'Yes little Amy, that will tie all the loose ends very nicely. Sleep well little one, soon we will begin again.'

Kydan

'You can leave me, David. Please prepare yourself and you have advised all to be in Atrium by midday.' Gideon smiled at the drawn face of the young man. Both had retired to the library after Kydan's untimely visit, to discuss his plans. 'Do not fret so, young master. All will be well.'

'Its, well my Lord. Well...'

'Come David, you have known me only but a few years, but am I such an Ogre.'

'Blessed be, Brother Gideon. Oh, my no, no. It is that I have never met a Watcher. I thought the tales were, well, over....'

'You thought them fantasy. That they were not as you have been told. As you have seen, they are all that you have been told and far more. The Watchers are a force of nature, never under estimate their power over this Earth. Even the new religions, Hebrew, Christian and the new Muslim faith have their version of The Watchers. Angels as they prefer. Their ideas are rather lacking in their true nature. Be warned, Brother, they have no love of our present state. And understand this, when the Mother returns and the Father is released, we will face judgement. And heed well young Brother, we will still be upon this Earth and we shall witness a judgment that even John, the bringer of The Revelation could never imagine.' Gideon knew his words were harsh but this young Brother who had to take the final vow must understand his duty. He had no doubt in David. He was strong, a good warrior and studious in all matters of the Earth Realm but he lacked Gideon's years of life. His years of watching humankind fall, of the slow loss of the Earth magicians and more so those of the Forevermore bloodlines, the true Guardians of The Balance. 'You will be endowed with centuries of life; it takes great strength to endure. I know for all your quiet gentleness, the inner peace you have found here, you Brother, are strong. No tales have been told to you. You have been taught the Warrior Code, given the truth and wisdom of the Earth. Now, on this day, you have seen the power of a Forevermore. Kydan is one of thousands. One of an army.'

'My Lord Commander, Blessed-be. I have no doubts. My eyes have been opened and I will serve with a true heart.'

'David, you are and always will be with us as Brother. Whatever guise we take down the path of mankind, we are the tree that bends in the winds of storms and that is never destroyed. Now go and prepare.'

'My Lord.' David nodded and left Gideon to his peace.
As he left Gideon sank in his chair. He thought of all the Knights here and throughout the many lands on this Earth. Hiding now after that dreadful Friday on the 13th of October, 1307. Many died, taking secrets to their grave. But far more survived. Most now far across

the great ocean. And it seemed now that all that was left would be following. And this land will be forever lost, of their watchful gaze and the last of the magicians would leave a land bereft of balance.

'Blessed Mother, Blessed Father. May we endure. May we serve under your guidance. May The Fall never come.' He stood and made his way to The Temple. War was upon them. Not great battles, not mighty warriors on bloody battlefields, but war all the same. He could sense the Earth, sense discontent in nature. It would seem mankind had pitched itself against the Earth itself.

Gideon set off down the steep worn staircase, he took each foot fall carefully, the steps could be treacherous after centuries of wear. He often pondered as he made his way down, the many that had followed before him. All those Commander Generals that had climbed down this narrow winding stair case into the labyrinth below. The yellow candles barely illuminating his path, rivers of wax falling down the walls from the stone niches that had been carved into the rock to hold the ever-dancing flames from the sweet-smelling candles. The wax forming grotesque shapes. The ceiling soot coated. He reached the final step and stood in the Temple gateway; three entrances carved into the buttery limestone rock face. Each doorway carved into a beautiful arch and atop each arch the symbol of the Watcher's. A strange pattern of geometric shapes that all formed a man with outstretched arms and outstretched wings radiating from its shoulders. All the temples were constructed in the same way.

Only the stone varied depending on the rock and stone that was in each land. Any one of the three archways would take you to the inner Temple, but only the Brothers would find the right path through the labyrinth. It would be futile to memorise your path as the walls moved with each sunrise. No one knew of the magic that created this changing stone edifice. No one ever asked, but he thought that, like him, many would have pondered this very same question. He stepped through the middle archway to begin the back and forth march through the dark passages. A true Brother simply felt his feet taking the right pathway. He allowed the darkness to swallow him and confidently began his journey to the inner temple.

'Blessed be, Brothers.' Gideon boomed into the central circular inner temple.

'Blessed be.' Came the response from the one hundred and twenty Brothers that were seated on the carved stone bench that wrapped around the temple. All equal, not even him above any other Brother. All called Brothers even though many were women. He admired his female Brethren. They hid their female forms, taking the guise of young men within the monastery walls. Always working in the dark kitchens or brewery so as to be seen as little as possible from the prying eyes of the constant pilgrims or travelling clergy that would pass through the abbey seeking respite from their long journey's. Here though in the Temple they were free to show their true identity.

He walked to the centre and climbed the three stone steps onto the dais. Again, he admired the beauty of the stonemasons' work that had carved the dais. A central circle of perfect cut stone. Three steps led to the raised platform. The upper circle bordered with an intricate border of exquisitely carved stone in the old Norse looped ropes, swirling round, under and over each other forming an astounding pattern. As he admired the border, his eyes focused revealing other forms that could be seen intertwined in the rope work. Wolves, dragons and other mythical beasts were set into the stone work, each a masterpiece to the stone masons art. The pentagram encased in the border was inlaid into the dais. Moonstone had been cut and polished then laid to form this most ancient of symbols. Gideon eyes took all this in as he stood in its centre. The domed ceiling above glittered. A star filled night sky reaching high above him and at the very centre a solid gold sun and silver moon had been inlaid. The Father Sun and Mother Moon. All around the walls, niches were filled with candles, the wax slowly creeping down the walls. As they flickered the crystals set in the dome caught the light forming a sparkling representation of the stars. The constellations swam around him. He bowed his head and his Brothers followed his lead.

'Blessed be the Mother, blessed be the Father. Protectors of our Spirit and keepers of our heart's desires. Hear our blessings, hear our voice. Brothers all, bound by vows made on our sword and blood in our veins.' The Brothers' voices filled the temple each opening their hearts to The Forevermore.

'We call upon The Watchtowers; we invite them here. Earth, Air, Fire, Water. We come this night to ask for guidance.' Each Brothers voice spoke in one chorus.

As they repeated their chant the room filled with the scent of summer, slowly at the four pentacle points a ball of light grew, forming into a bright glowing orb. Gideon took his position at the fifth point. The Watchtowers had arrived.

'Brothers' we are blessed this night; The Watchtowers of the elementals are here to guide us this night. We thank them.'

'Blessed be.'

'This morn Kydan came within our walls. This morn he gave command and as Brothers here, we are all sworn by solemn oath to obey his command. First, we must prepare for the Magicians, for they have all been summoned by Kydan to our Abbey...' as he spoke, murmurs went around the Temple. 'They are here to help us on a final journey to the new land, none will remain here apart from ten of you who will vow to watch over this land. I have this morn sent word for all our ships to meet at the home of our ancient Celtic brothers. We sail and will not be returning. The cargo we take must reach the new land.' He paused, looking around at all the Brother's, none showed any sign that they would question him. It was as he had expected from these warriors whom he had grown to love and respect over the two hundred years he had held command in these lands.

'Those few who remain I charge you as Watchmen. Cardinal Charles de Gosse is fallen...'

Murmurs now became gasps, like him they were all astounded that they had not seen the signs of a Fallen.

'Brothers, I understand. How could we have missed the signs, but Kydan tells of a man far down the path of darkness. Tickhill is his. He brings his gold, his Papal power and corrupts all. But we are not to engage him, Kydan forbids it. The ten will watch and wait. Gather information and Kydan will call upon you. That is his command. Jedediah, Elizabeth and their charge are our cargo, to be protected at all costs. Also, on the road to York there is a family, a Death Master, his wife and son. We must intercept them for their son must be sworn into the Brotherhood. That is our command.' Gideon paused. 'Brothers those who stay will be the last ten. For all the temples have been called to sail. I will not choose those ten, but ask for those who have the strength of heart to stay here. Ten Brothers, alone in a darkness that will not rest. Against all our warrior creed, to hide and watch. To be alone.'

'By his command.' All spoke 'We thank the Watchtowers for their light, we thank the Mother Moon and Father Sun. Blessed be.'

The four glowing orbs pulsed; light streamed from their centre. Growing, slowly engulfing the whole Temple in its beautiful light. Gideon felt the energy reaching into him, infusing every molecule with its radiance. A radiance that gave the Brothers their strength. Giving them prolonged life and vigour. A gift from the Earth for their service to the realm. Binding their souls to this Brotherhood and to the Mother and Father. Slowly the orbs dulled and then vanished. He felt his whole skin tingle with renewed power. He breathed in and allowed the energy to fill all his body and felt the euphoria that always came with it. All the Brothers were now ready for the times to come. Gideon left his position, command given and walked into the labyrinth, and his Brothers followed. At evening meal debate would begin about Kydan's commands. In presence of The Watchtowers none would question command. In the refectory hall much debate would begin and Gideon knew it would be a long supper. Command would be followed but each Brother had a right to question and to offer opinion, but by end the of evening all would retire, resolute to carry out all commands. In the weeks to come much had to be accomplished. He knew already that David would stay. He would take his final vow and Gideon knew he would travel down time, watching and waiting.

Amy

Amy stirred. She struggled to open her eyes. Her mind sluggish. Slowly from the depths of unconsciousness she returned to the world. Her last thoughts had been of her journey to her ancestors. She was not dead. She was not at home. It was no nightmare. But she was not in the tomb. The room was warm. She was on a soft bed. She was clean. She tried to move.

'Arrgh!' she moaned. Pain shot through every part of her body. Every joint ached. Every muscle strained with fatigue. The huge burns stretched and pulled apart, reopening the livid tissue. Her mind tried to close down, to return to the safety of the dark. She fought through the pain, the nausea that swept over her. Cold icy sweat drenched her body. She panted through the feelings. She wakened her senses and slowly everything steadied. As she lay, slowly moving her head to make out her surroundings she tried to remember. She had been cared for; why she thought? The room was small and sparse but clean and warm. Her bed was also clean and soft. She did not understand, could not fathom what was happening. She remembered that, the last time she was fully aware. Bathed in pain and cold, when she had recognised Samuel. The two soldiers covering his head. Leading him away. The other soldier taking up the hot irons. The insidious pain. The priest's insistent questions about the book. Then nothing but the soft voice of an Angel telling her to sleep. She searched her mind, trying to find answers. Had she been rescued? But how, and who would have come to save her; Kydan? No, he could not, he would now be charged with caring for her daughter. She was now of no importance to The Watchers and he could not risk their secret.

'Focus,' she told herself, 'you need to heal or you are lost.' She closed her eyes and searched for the book. It was nearby. There would be time enough to seek the answers to her present situation. She needed to heal. Without her strength she would be of little use to her daughter. She needed to give her a chance. This man, this priest had to be stopped. Time for her daughter was everything. Kydan had promised he would do all in his power to protect her, but the price was her abandonment to her fate. The Forevermore had blessed them with Arabeth for a reason. She wished for that summer. Meeting him, loving him and the blessings it brought. Those memories flooded through her. Reminding her of the fleetingness of happiness. Those few precious moments when joy was everywhere. Memories!

Heady scent filled the air, butterflies and all manner of creature busied themselves in the woods. Birds sang and the whole earth sang in the summer sun. She remembered her happiness of that day. The young creatures, born that spring played. Young rabbits, hares and deer. All played their games ready for when they became full adults, ready for their own journey of life.

'You look beautiful. You glow with motherhood.' Kydan turned to her and looked into her eyes. 'Why we have been granted this I do not know. But my love and happiness, is all in this moment. I will not question why The Forevermore has granted us a child.'

'That glow you see, is because I feel like Jed's prize hog. My feet swell along with my growing belly, Kydan. How can you say I look beautiful?' Amy teased him.

'Amy, you are and always will be beautiful in my eyes. Even when you are aged and wrinkled and...' he got no farther. Amy's eyes flooded with tears. 'Ssh, oh sweet Amy. I speak truth. I will be here with you always and I will see you pass over to the Forevermore.'

'It hurts, Kydan. It hurts that I will age and you will not...'

'But you will not pass into the Nevermore, we will find each other once more.'

'I know, but I cannot stop the pain that will come with each passing year as I slowly succumb to time and...'

'Amy, Amy! What is it!'

'Oh my,' She sat down on the soft mossy ground, 'Oh, I think we will not be waiting long to see our child. Get Elizabeth now!'

Kydan vanished, not caring that when he appeared at the farm, he could be seen by someone other than Jed and Elizabeth. He cared little that they knew nothing of Amy, her condition or their love. Amy had Cast a concealment spell over herself to hide her condition.

To all she was the same beautiful, innocent young woman. They had hidden their love well. Always he appeared as a man, hiding his true form as well. Their meetings had always been in secret. Even his fellow Watchers had no knowledge of their true relationship. She was the Mother's heart. He was her Watcher. But from the moment she had seen him she had seen his true form. She had stared at him in wonder on that first morning when her mother had passed from the Earth and the heart of the Mother had entered her. Such a tiny child, staring at him. No fear only curiosity. Over the years as she grew and he watched over her his love spiralled out of control. Then Amy, once grown into womanhood, had returned his feelings. Both knew the danger. But last autumn they fulfilled their love and their spirits had joined. They were bound as one. In the spring she had begun to bloom and they knew they had been blessed by the Forevermore. A new Forevermore was being born to the Earth realm. A new life filled with Earth magic as Amy was. A new guardian. It was then that Kydan knew Amy carried the Mother within her, passed to her from her dying mother. He knew then that Amy would pass this to her child. Arabeth would hold the Mother's heart and spirit. And their love would be lost in this Earth Realm. For his duty would be to the new born Forevermore who would carry the Mother's heart until she would pass it to her daughter or the Mother would be reborn. He did not speak this to his beloved Amy, but he thought she knew. They would find each other again, when The Fates granted them both the Final Rest in the First Garden. He had to have faith that this tale of a

Final Rest, joined to your Forevermore spirit was true. That their final immortality was one of love and peace.

'Push, push now!' Elizabeth yelled at Amy, 'all you have girl, now push this child into the world.'

Amy summoned all her strength, and pushed. Holding in her need to scream, fearing someone would hear her in the late afternoon sun of the woods. Suddenly she felt the child come from her womb, into the heady summer air.

Then it began.

The air changed, clouds gathered and thunder rumble through the air. The Earth magic rose up from the ground and shook the very soil Elizabeth and Amy rested on. The blue magic swirled around them; the very air crackled with power.

'Elizabeth!' Amy screamed

'Amy, take your daughter now. Take her.'

Jed appeared from the woods, Kydan behind him. Elizabeth had sent them away, too fraught to put up with Jed's anger at his niece and Kydan. The trees shook, the black clouds above raging. Pain shot though Amy then euphoria. She saw all. The universe. Arabeth. She saw the Mother, weeping at the loss of the Father. In her moment of despair, Mother had released her heart to Amy's bloodline to hold until the Father returned. As Amy now passed that heart to her daughter; she saw all worlds, all life as one in that one moment and the Mother's heart left her and passed to her daughter. Arabeth was life, she was the bloodline that would stretch into time itself and she was the hope of all creation of Earth. She saw all, all that was life. She filled with joy and peace.

Arabeth!

As these memories flooded her very soul, she found strength. Those lost, chained souls from her prison rose up again and spoke. She could feel their hope in her and her daughter.

'We are here, we wait, we will have our revenge! FIGHT HIM, BIND HIM. BONE TO STONE!'

James

The two dark skinned warriors stood silently in front of ten mounted war horses, who snorted and stomped their huge hooves on the cobbles. The soldiers mounted upon their backs silent in the misty dawn. The rain now beginning to dissipate. Each man eager to be after their quarry. Born to blood and battle they had been bored in this simpleton town. Idling away their time and pay in the Carpenters Arms or seeking out more dubious activities with some of the more willing young females. They had found a ready supply of young girls who soon became enamoured of the muscular battle worn men that had arrived in town, with stories of valour, foreign lands, strange exotic customs and pockets full of gold. It was a simple task of whispered promises of escape to these foreign lands and adventure that lured the simple girls to their beds. But these hardened men soon became tired of the naïve town girls, soon blood and gold, was beginning to itch its way under their scarred skins. And at last a decent hunt, no mercy and all spoils to them. The Cardinal had also promised to add his own gold to ensure that the hunt was successful.

'Why are we waiting, sat here, our bloody arses soaked!' one particular soldier grumbled

'Quiet, he wants to talk to us before we leave, say a prayer over us.' The soldiers' commander hissed at the rebellious soldier. He was annoyed at the wait, wanting to be out of town before first light. Their quarry had a good start on them and they were not sure of the path they had taken.

'Humph, say a prayer,' the soldier muttered, 'don't see how that will do us any good. Blood and death that's all were good for.'

'This is God's work and the Cardinal will bless us and as such we are forgiven of all our sins. We kill for our Lord.' The commander hissed again and turned to glare at the insubordinate soldier. He understood their impatience. Since coming to this flea pit, they had sat on their arses, getting fat and bored. It would feel good to be at God's work again. Killing with the blessings of the Church. He loved it; they could carry out their butchery with impunity just because they had the blessings of the Church. He smiled. He loved the Church. Sin free killing, sin free gold! Soon he would be a rich man and could retire. His long years of bloody battles had acquired much gold. Soon he would be buying his own farm back in the rolling hills of Somerset. He'd find himself a fat young bride. All his years had taught him that a man was best served with a nicely rounded wench. They were grateful for the attentions of a man and grateful to find one that would marry them and especially one that could provide the means of a good farm. Aye a nice plump one, good for carrying babes.

A door slammed and his horse lurched and snickered. He's here he thought, his horse always got skittish when he was around.

He would be glad when this tour of service was over. And those dark fellas, never speaking. He shuddered. He also feared them. He had never in all his days seen such warriors. Their strength and might lent to fearsome men, who did not even fight for gold but to be warrior, to be pure strength and might.

'Good morning to you all. You have your Papal orders. These people you hunt must be found and must not survive to reach their destination. No word must leave this town of the demonic forces that are at work here. We must purge this place.' The Cardinal's voice swirled around the court yard, the early morning mist seemed to darken and become cat like. Creeping and crawling. The Cardinal spoke to the Nubians in a strange tongue and they simply nodded. He stood before them all and bent his head in prayer and hidden from view he smiled. He began the incantation, silently mouthing the ancient words, his head bowed they could not see the dark magic he worked. They would think him in silent prayer.

'Dark Lord, Darkness called. Mists follow, mists flow. Hide all from view. Dark Lord, Darkness called.' He felt the Dark magic form, feeling it pulsate though his body. It rose up from the cobbled yard, warming, up higher to his groin. He held in a moan of pleasure. It rose higher to engulf him. The euphoria spread and he channelled it to his hands.

'Dark Lord, Darkness called. Mists follow, mists flow. Hide all from view. Dark Lord, Darkness called.' He released the energy into the early morning mist. He saw it bend to his command. Now as these savage soldiers rode out, they would be invisible. The soldiers' prey would not see them; they would be cut down before they even saw their assailants.

'In the name of the Father, the Son and the Holy Spirit, go in peace.'

The stewards opened the court yard gates and the Nubian warriors began to run, setting the pace for the soldiers to follow. They never rode but ran, never seeming to tire. Silent and relentless to their aim. The soldiers seemed not to notice the mist surrounding them, keeping them enveloped. Those that were awake at such an early hour, would later speak of hearing the sound of many horses, a clattering of armour but when they turned saw nothing but a thick early morning mist that seemed to pass by. The York road would often be talked of in hushed corners of this strange mist and the sound of an army passing by. Perhaps some said it was the soldiers from the doomed siege desperately trying to find their way home. Some said it was just another sign of the demonic forces that surrounded their town. Just another mystery like the two missing families and later, the sudden disappearance of most of the monks at the abbey.

The Cardinal watched the soldiers bolt out of the court yard. He knew they were hungry, restless for blood. He gave them the prize. Samuel, the finest Death Master he had had the pleasure of knowing, after leaving the burial ground seemed defeated by Amy. He had been suspicious of his future intentions, so he had sent his Nubian warriors to watch him. His suspicions had been well founded. They had watched as Samuel had quickly packed all he could into his aging cart and started on the road to York. He knew Samuel's old carthorses would be slow and he had held back until morning light to send out the hunters. Samuel and his family would be out of the town's boundaries. Blood spilled would not find its way back onto his pretty little town. He needed time to open the burial chamber further. He knew that the ancient one who was interred there was protecting the Pagan temple. The men excavating now, drew every closer. Soon he would find the stones, set thousands of years ago. A place where he could open the gateway. He needed no witness to that night with Amy. And there would be none. He would make time. He would not be stopped.

James jolted awake, something deep in his subconscious woke him from his deep slumber in the back of their cart. He shivered and rose up to peer out towards the back of the lumbering cart. All his senses were suddenly on fire, something was near and they were its prey.

'Da, somethings coming.'

'James, you awake at last lad, been sleeping like the dead!' Samuel said and turned to see his son staring into the semi-dark lane behind them. Samuel saw the cat like stance of his son, watching, listening. 'Martha, take the reins!'

'Samuel, what's wrong?'

'Don't know, but you keep these old buggers going, don't look back.' And Samuel jumped into the back with James. 'What is it son?'

'Don't know, but that mist, down in the valley, it's not...right!' James whispered. 'See how the mist moves. See how the trees on the narrows move and bend away. There's something there, Da! Something bad. It's coming for us, Da.' James head darted to the left. 'Something in that copse too, but don't sense it being bad.'
To Samuel it seemed as if his son was talking to himself. Seeing something he could not see.

Samuel peered into the early morning gloom, the shallow valley behind them was filled with mist, but, then he saw it, it moved, like some living creature. Then carried on the slight breeze, the pungent smell of many horses and the faint sound of metal against metal.
'James, get out anything you can to use as a weapon. I think my master does not intend for us to leave. Do it quietly, don't alarm mother!'
James quietly moved to the back of the cart to the old worn trunk that carried their smithy tools. He quietly pulled out two large hammers. Not much good against swords and trained soldiers, but it would give them some fighting chance. He did not feel any fear, just the steady thump of his heart. He should be terrified; he had never fought in his life apart from the odd childhood fight with his late brothers or local boys.

Samuel saw James, but it seemed not to be his son. He had ripped off his thick over shirt, and he saw his son like he had never seen him before. How had he missed the huge frame; the thick veined arms now clutching two 30lb hammers like they were feathers. His son's torso rippled with layers of muscle, toned by working in the smithy. His eyes glowed bright blue. How could he have not noticed the son that had become the immense man that now crouched in the rumbling cart. The very air around James vibrated. James remained still, watching both the rear and left side of their cart. Samuel selected the large axe he used for splitting logs. It was newly sharpened and its edge gleamed in the morning light. He crouched beside his son, silent and watching.

James breathed slowly and everything slowed. The air seemed to thicken around him, he felt energy tingle over his skin. As he raised his head he saw through the mist. Soldiers, many soldiers wearing the cross of Christ and two enormous dark men running before them. He felt their blood lust and knew that his family was the target. All this he saw and sensed in an instant. And then he saw the others coming from the left. He knew his Da was beside him. He knew what was coming and he knew he would kill them all before they came near the only family he had left. The very Earth seemed to talk to him. It seemed to push energy into his body. And those to his left, they were not the ones to fear. All this he knew, how, he would only begin to understand when this battle was over. He would not surrender to death this day.

Amy

Amy felt their rage, felt the vengeance of those wretched souls he had trapped in Earthly torment, awaiting Charles de Gosse, Cardinal and now she realised a Dark Mage. She opened her eyes; sweet memories fading from her mind as those souls pulled her back to her reality. She still lay in the small attic. She must have fallen into a deep slumber again. The fire had been tended. A small wooden table had been set with buttermilk, rich honey mead and small shortbreads. This fare would mean a house of means. She must be in his very lair. Her mind pondered. St Marys Croft, the new church and the ancient crypt. He had built his opulent home on their ancestor's site and the new church. He was truly clever this priest. Not only had he covered an ancient burial ground, there must be another chamber. A natural cave where her ancestors would have come to practice The Craft. The cave would be infused with centuries of their magics. He was binding the magics with iron and Dark Wards. Containing it.

'I must be the fox.' She thought. 'I must play the game he has set, but I must heal. Strength is all.'

She reached out and sought their Grimoire. Where she was mattered not, that she was alive was all now. She would have her vengeance, just as all those bound souls would. Together he would feel the power of the Earth. But the Darkness is sly, cunning and is an adversary not to be taken lightly. Those that Fell, who succumbed to its wonderous erotic power are the most dangerous. They seek only power and do not respect the Balance or life itself. The Darkness allowed you to take all you wished, but the debt mounted and would be paid back three-fold.

The book answered.

'Yes, yes, I understand your dilemma.' The Cardinal answered and fidgeted in his desk chair in his study. The Mayor was beginning to irritate him. His pungent aroma annoying his sensitive nose. His oily skin and rippling fat showed a man of over indulgence and greed, that turned his stomach. How could a man show such wealth with his gluttony? As these poor peasants scratched and scraped at the earth, this man swallowed enough food in a month to feed a family for a year. He kept himself trim. He indulged in fine fare, but in moderation. He had lived many lives and watched the hate of the starved masses at these pigs as they drowned in food and wine. Did these creatures not see? To rule you must be loved, feared and respected. Had their prophet, Christ not been a humble man, but how his words now ruled over nation after nation. He saw the gross indulgencies of the Catholic priest-hood. He had seen how The Vatican wallowed in grandeur, indulged all their perverse predilections. He had no fault in their vices, life was short and should be lived. He answered to his true nature but he made sure that his purse flowed. His soldiers, servants were always well paid and well treated. They lived in his fear but none turned away. Power and control were all. Control was not acquired by repression but done by fear and gold. Enough gold and they would love you. He adored this new Church. It had surprised him, the ingenuity of the Catholics. How that simple, gentle prophet's words of love, kindness and hope had been taken and used. The power he had gained in joining this Church of the One God. The fear came from the endless purgatory of Hell, a masterstroke. To follow God, you must obey his tenants, perfect control. To fail to obey your Pope, God's very voice on Earth meant denial of the ultimate, Heaven. Genius!...... The Mayor's babble woke him from his thoughts....

'But Father, all these trials. The townsfolk are living in terror. Some say that folk merely accuse to simply seek revenge for some past disagreement. You can understand Cardinal, surely. I cannot allow this town to become a place of false accusations followed by quick trials. The widow Smythe caused much consternation. All knew Thomas wanted her land. Now he has it...'

'Mayor, are you accusing the Church of culpability in this matter?' He smiled gently at the gross and port-bloated face of the ranting Mayor. Simply mention the idea that they were accusatory of the Church and.... 'Ah the power!' He thought as he felt the Darkness creep around the fat, grotesque body of the Mayor. Feeding.... 'Enjoy.' His preternatural thoughts whispered and he also felt the erotic, sensual caress of the Darkness. His body roused, full of energy....

'No, No.' Stammered the Mayor, sweat beading on his forehead. Charles inwardly smiled. Idiots, all of them. One tiny threat and they all shut up.

'Then I suggest you leave these matters to the Church and tend to your duties as Mayor.'

'Yes, of course. My apologies.'

'But, my respected Mayor, I assure you that if I ever find that any accusations have been falsely made, I can assure you that I will see the wheel brought back into service. Our European friends find it....shall we say....a most suitable deterrent for those who falsely accuse. We live under our Lords watchful eye, sir. As you well know, Mayor, I offer no rewards to those who bring information to the Church's ear. I believe it is a sworn duty for all God's children to root our Lucifer's Evil. But with that in mind I understand that this town has suffered and I will, out of my personal wealth, ensure the full funding of the hospital that you and your council men have been discussing. I will ensure that Nuns will be brought into your town, to bring comfort to your town's sick folk. I will also ensure a suitable dowry for its continued care so those who have no coin may receive the care and love of our Church and of our wonderful brides of Christ. Of course, those of means would be requested to make donation to the dowry, but a good Christian enjoying a more comfortable life would only be too happy to help those of no means!'

'Oh, Oh. Cardinal. I, I cannot express my gratitude. The Duke of Devonshire has granted title to The Manse and now, oh my. We can now begin. The Tickhill Hospice will provide such a Christian service and our folk will have such comfort of its charitable Christian works. You truly have blessed our small town, Sir.'

'It is merely a Christian duty. If our poorest prosper then do we not all prosper? Both in wealth and more so, in our souls.' He smiled at the now humble and pacified Mayor. He would leave filled with pompous power and no doubt take credit for opening the Cardinal's purse for the hospice.

The room suddenly changed temperature.

'You may go now, and be assured the Church intends to weed out all these vile creatures from your mist. You will also see how your town will prosper once it is sin free. Fare thee well Mayor.'

The mayor rose from the hard wood chair and groaned. His arse would be numb to the bone! As soon as he had closed his study door Charles studied the room.

'Well, Well. It seems as if we have a visitor!'

He searched the room, peering into every corner.

'Ah, there you are!' he smiled as he noticed her book had unlocked. 'At last, little Amy is awake.' He walked over to the stand that held her families Grimoire. The clasps he had tried so hard to open now unlocked. He touched the leather binding. He quickly pulled his hand away as burning pain shot up his arm. 'You are very well protected, but I will find a way into your pages. Now little Amy what are you about.'

Amy chanted the words to unlock her family's book. It was dangerous but she needed the healing spell. She knew every page and soon felt herself falling into the book. Spell upon spell, incantations surrounding her, the runes glowing bright blue with the power of the Forevermore. She had to be quick.

'Blessed Mother, blessed Father lead to the path I need'

Soon she could see the page in her mind's eye. Each spell and ward written down eons ago. The book's soul reached up to her. She saw the spell appear and began the cast. The book freely gave her the spell. You could not command it only ask for its help. Soon she felt the Earth magic rising. It entered her body. Finding her injuries and healing them. Repairing charred flesh. Bruises vanishing. The energy restoring her weakened body. As the spell dissipated, she relaxed and thanked the soul of the book. She felt its warmth. The book had become a life form over the centuries. The Earth Magics had given life to its pages. And it would protect itself against those of darkened hearts. Earth Magic was not power; it was Balance and had one tenant.

An do no harm, do thy will.

In his study the silver claw like clasps on the Grimoire closed over the pages. The claws opened and reached into the locks embedded in the heavy back cover and clicked into place and relocked themselves. He watched, intrigued by this, tome. He could almost see it breathing, alive. Power. More Power than he could imagine. His way into the Nevermore, to all those dead souls.

An army of souls!

For a moment, a memory glanced into his mind. Dark silver wings, cutting down creatures. Red skinned dragons. Gone.

Charles raced to the attic. His cardinal robes annoying him, the pompous symbol of his power. For the joy of his past lives. Not having to wear these confounded robes of office. To be the soldier, merciless. Cutting down the heathens and the new army of Allah. Blood flowing, blood lust as he cut all in his path down. Leaving bloodied corpses to rot. He climbed the steep attic stairs to her room as silently as possible, holding his breath. Silence! He opened the heavy door; it made no sound. He made sure it was well oiled.

She lay on the small bed. Sally had banked up the fire so the room was pleasantly warm. Her eyes were closed, her long black hair fanned out on the pillow. She was a true beauty, the most beautiful creature he had seen. He felt a surge of passion run through his whole body.

Memories assaulted him; he grasped the door handle. Memories of a passion so consuming, so beautiful. She, the pale red dragon. No name. Who is she? What is she? Such love! Her skin covered in soft warm scales, glistening in the red sky. PAIN! Blinding pain. He fell to his knees, his heart burning with pain. He saw the bloodied blade in his hands. PAIN! Beyond all his imagination. Blinding hate. POWER. REVENGE...

The memories faded just as quickly as they had assaulted him. He pulled himself up, straightened his back and quelled the fear and pain. Slowly his heart settled, but deep in the back of his mind the memories lingered. Moving silently through his mind. Memories or visions! He had no comprehension of what they were. Was madness taking him?

'Fool, take hold of yourself. Childhood nightmares, that's all. Take hold.' He whispered to himself. All that was important were his plans. Power was all that mattered. This Church would see that his vision of the world would take place. Humankind had to be controlled, their path was an all-encompassing journey into Oblivion.

He would control them; he would save them and they would raise him as they raised the Lord Jesus Christ.

His control returned.

Amy lay motionless on the small bed. His memories flooded her mind. Then something more powerful than she could imagine locked them away. The memory of the red creature lingered in her mind. But also, the love that was so locked away in this man. It was the same love she had for Kydan. She had found the weakness. She had found a path into this man's mind. For he had found love once, as she had. He was not completely given over to The Darkness. She could use that to break into his mind. To find his true purpose.

Kydan

The wailing echoed through the Abbey, its pitiful yells going unanswered by the one it sought comfort from. Elizabeth cradled her gently, holding her close but she could do nothing for the babe.

'Let me take her.'

Elizabeth started not daring to look up. Knowing who was in the monk's cell with her.

'Please, I mean no harm. I am her father!'

She held the child to her breast, not wanting to raise her head, not wanting to hand over the child to him. 'I know and I know what you have done could mean the death of this innocent child. If the others find out this, they will come for her.'

'She is the Mother's heart! No harm will come to her. She will be protected at all costs.'

'That, that is not possible...'

'Your niece was not just a Mage as you are, she is a Forevermore!'

Elizabeth sucked in her breath, she always thought Amy was... different. Her Quickening had come early. Her control over the elements soon learned. Her understanding of their Grimoire had been so easy. But a Forevermore. No that could not be, there were no humankind Forevermore left. They had been hunted down and murdered for their strange abilities that had seen them return to the Forevermore leaving only the few Earth Mages left alive to protect the Earth from the Darkness that was set to engulf all of the realm. Soon Lucifer would hold dominion of this realm.

'There were two left on Earth. One your niece now in the clutches of the Cardinal. One I endeavour to bring here. And now, this one, our babe, the hope of all humanity.'

Her tears fell on the soft woollen shawl that wrapped around the babe. 'She has not even a given name!'

'Arabeth! We chose her name before she entered this world.'

'Will the Mother ever return; can the Father even be found?'

'I believe so Elizabeth. In your life years that I cannot foretell. But I believe in humankind, I believe Lucifer cannot hold sway over all of your kind. There are those, not of magic, but those who still feel the light, feel the Balance.'

'She loved you Kydan, loved you so much. I told her your love would be doomed, but our kind know so little of your realm. But I know if she is Forevermore then you will be reunited?'

'Yes, one day. If The Fates allow.'

'At least then she will find happiness, and Arabeth?'

'We do not see the future Elizabeth; we can see glimpses of possibilities but nothing is set.'

'Can you tell me of your world?'

'Yes, but time is against us. Once Arabeth is safely on her way to the new lands I will come to you and tell you of our realm. But know this I have no understanding of the gift of this child. I have no understanding of The Forevermore. It is just...there....and will always be there even if the Oblivion engulfs the universe, it will always be there. It is love, balance, empathy, and most of all hope. Hope in the just, the good and there will always be those who find a path to it.' Elizabeth stood and lifted her eyes to him. Her breath snagged as she gazed up into his blood red eyes. Blue light danced around him. His bare torso rippled with muscular strength. His huge powerful legs and lower body covered in thick leggings that seemed to be scales. Heavy metal like scales covered his arms, Manica's that seemed of the same make. Like the old tales of Merlin and the dragons with impenetrable scales of skin. His wings folded behind him trailed to the floor with soft pure white feathers. Soft brown hair surrounded his strong angular facial features. Only the eyes unsettled. Red as blood. He towered above her and as he bent to take the child, she nearly yanked the child away. But he was so gentle as his large hands lifted her from her arms. His eyes never left the tiny child that he held in his arms.

'Arabeth!' he whispered and smiled. 'What a miracle you truly are. I give you my oath I will protect you with all the power of the Forevermore. I will watch over you, and watch all your kin to come, for your bloodline carries the Fate of all humankind. My daughter!'

The child closed her eyes and slept and he gently handed her back to Elizabeth just a Jedidiah walked into their borrowed room in the Abbey.

'Kydan!' he roared; anger emanated from him. 'You dare; you dare to come here after all you have caused...!'

'No, Jed, no.' Elizabeth shouted and stood between the two of them. Kydan stretched his wings as far as he could in the cramped room. His fangs lengthened and claws emerged from his fingers. 'Both of you be calm. You wake Arabeth and both of you will be banned from her sight.' She could not believe what she was saying. As if any of her magics could stop Kydan or Jed come to think of it, especially in the temper he was in. Jed blamed Kydan's interference for their misfortune.

'Have your kind not done enough. Elizabeth and I did everything in our power to protect her sister Angelique's child.' Jed's voice a mass of anger and pain. 'Was it not enough for Angelique to sacrifice herself to the flames. Never knowing if her daughter, her beautiful Amy, even endured.'

'Jed, Amy is a Forevermore and the little that we know is that they could not stop finding each other. They are spirit bound.' Said Elizabeth.

'Amy was Forevermore! How, that bloodline was wiped out when Lucifer defied the Verse. Humankind hunted them down and eradicated them'

'Angelique was gifted Amy. Angelique knew the danger, knew that this new Church may seek her out. That is why she made the pact with your father, Elizabeth. She hid away, birthed Amy, weaned her and gave her up to your care. Angelique submitted to the fire so the soldier that had so enticed your father could not get to her or know of Amy. This Cardinal, one and the same as that soldier, has now found the bloodline again in Amy, not knowing her true nature or knowing her true kin. Again, we sacrifice your blood and must again keep Arabeth a secret, he must never know of her birth.' Kydan knew he was speaking of things he should not. A Forevermore was born out of light and gifted to a realm. They were sent to protect a realm, to be the spirit guides of those species that held dominion on a realm. Powerful magics flowed through them. 'A Forevermore is gifted to your world. Amy was born of light, sent to Angelique in the hope of restoring magics to Earth...'

'Kydan, I saw Angelique's belly swell with child. Our father raged at Angelique to give the name of the boy that had filled her belly with child. She never gave a name...'

'She could not, there was no humankind father! No father as you would understand'

'My head spins.' Jed slumped onto the cot.

'Only two Forevermore born can create a new Forevermore, but only if it is gifted by The Fates. Amy was gifted to Angelique, and we were gifted with Arabeth. The reasons for this, is not known to me but Arabeth must survive, nor, before you ask, do I know the

Forevermore father of Amy. Arabeth now carries our Mother's heart, if she dies then with the Father missing, lost to our sight Lucifer will hold dominion over all humankind.'

'Leave us Kydan, leave us in peace. We will do as you command and go to this new land. But leave us in peace. Whatever games you play,' Jed waved his hand to the heavens, 'leave us alone. Have not all the Mages paid the price? Lucifer is winning and he will wipe us out, soon all humans will have no recollection of Earth magic. Maybe it will be for the best, then we do not have to suffer the games that these Fates play.'

'Jed, you can no more run from your gifts than I can leave Arabeth unguarded. In her is the Mother's heart, the only hope for your kind to survive. I believe that humankind can find the path of The Balance again.' Kydan gently placed a hand on Jed's shoulder. 'You are just the first step in the journey that follows.'

'And if line does not survive?'

'Lucifer will rule this realm and The Fates will abandon the Earth realm as it has abandoned many realms before.'

'Destroy you mean!'

'That I cannot know.' Kydan snapped and taking one last look at Arabeth, he vanished.

Amy

She was just like her mother. He had been hiding as a lowly soldier then when they took her mother. Not the high-born man they thought he was now. It was easy to intercept Charles de Gosse on his way to the Vatican. The pathetic creature, begged on his knees for mercy. He had taken his time taking his head. Enjoying the sheer pleasure of slowly hacking at skin and bone of his pale white neck. His sword was lethally sharp, but he took his time. Seeing the horror in his victim's face, slowly drowning in his own blood. Finally, as his prey's life ended and his eyes dulled, he cut through the neck bones. Looking at the lifeless head, he knew he had chosen well. They could be blood brothers. He and his Nubian warriors had slaughtered his entourage, burning their bodies to ash and bone. Assuming his identity and taking his place had been simple. He placed on the robes of God and carried on to Rome. As Charles de Gosse he brought wealth and no family left. He was welcomed warmly, even more so his purse. God had granted him so many favours and the Pope so grateful for the gold and lands he had dutifully turned over to his Holy Father. He had had little use for the wealth of the de Gosse family. His own private wealth far out-reached this puny French Aristocratic family's. This Church would lead him to ultimate power, gold was not his aim.

'Good morning'

Amy pretended to startle awake, trying not to show her discomfort at the visions she had just witnessed. His murder of the real Cardinal. It seemed their magics were connecting in some way, sharing thoughts and memories.

'It seems that Sally certainly has the healers touch or maybe it is more other worldly powers she has.' He said as his eyes roamed over her body, smiling at his veiled threat to Sally. The almost transparent linen slip clearly showed her pale skin and he could see none of the burns or bruises that he had inflicted upon her. Her skin was perfect. 'Was that you just a moment ago? It seems you found what you required to heal yourself.'

Amy pulled herself up and stared at him. He was angelic. And muscular. All that a priest should not be. But she saw the darkness around him. She simply stared at him.

'Come, come child! Let us not play games. We are kin. Both from the same ilk are we not? And, so like your mother. You should be careful to hide your thoughts too!'

'We are not. I am nothing of your kind.'

'I was born from a line of Mages, just as you are. Hunted and misunderstood...'

Her puzzled expression said a thousand words, 'Who are you, more Sir what are you?'

He began to softly laugh, and sat down on the edge of her small bed. She pulled her knees into her chest not wanting to be near this vile man. A man it seems of her kin, a man that had hunted his own kind down and mercilessly tortured and murdered them. Her mother included. She could not comprehend this man. Following a Church that mercilessly set about to destroy all her kind, taking many innocents in their relentless desire to rid their lands of their ancient past.

'The Church, oh little Amy.' He snorted. 'They are the route to our power. To my power. With the rise of Islam; they battle to rule the world. They seek to make all men kneel before the same God. I see this true power of the Church and I will ensure all men kneel before God and my will.'

Amy saw the hunger in his eyes. 'Using dark magic to conquer man, is that your plan? To have all mankind live in fear, to kneel in your edifices to the glory of God. While you plunder the earth, filling your Vatican with gold! Is that what you seek Priest?'

'More, much more. Lucifer challenged the power of God and was Hell bound for his sins. I do not challenge God but seek to make every kingdom, to see every man bow before this one God. To live by his tenants...'

'While you rule over them...'

'Someone has to be their shepherd.' He chuckled.

'So, you use your birth right against your brethren, we are born to protect, to heal and to guide. We are not born to rule.'

He stood and paced across the small room, clenching his hands, trying to control his anger. He turned towards her, 'Do you think we are meant to live as servants, NO. We are meant to rule. We know Earth magic; we know its power and yet we are supposed to grovel in the dirt.'

'Once all humans had the gift of Earth magic, once they felt the wonder of this world...'

'You are pitiful, just as your mother. She was the same. Help them, show them The Balance! But little child, man should rule his domain and if that means that this Church brings them to kneel before me then I shall bring every man to his knees before the altars of Christ. They will see the power of a Church, a God that will bestow all the riches of the realm on them.'

'Lucifer uses you well, Priest. You neither understand the power you use or the cost to you and mankind. Your Church will enslave you all until it destroys all of mankind and this Earth.' Amy saw his rage and thought of what she must do. She must play this game, manoeuvre him. She needed to know who he was, where he was from. He was truly old, that she knew. 'But how old?' she thought. She sighed and he turned to her as she sat upon her small bed.

He saw her dark gold eyes, her night black hair and soft feminine features. He saw questions in those eyes and curiosity. 'Could it be a way to her, could he find a way to make her his ally?' these thoughts passed through his mind as she stared at him. If she could understand why he did what he did. If she could understand why he wished to open the Nevermore. The Church could rule the Earth, all man beholden to one God. How their kind could rule over them, restored to a rightful place. Not grovelling servants, healers. He had no hatred for women. But this Church feared them, knowing how most women healers held power over the illiterate and simple towns folk. Magic had to be eradicated, superstition erased. Once these old pagan rites were vanquished the Church would hold ultimate power over the people. He would be there to see that happen. He would be there with the rise of this Church; a Dark Mage and he would have power over all of the Church. She could help him. She knew The Nevermore. Her family's book was one of the oldest he had ever found. He had seen so many empires fall, and seen the rise of the words of The Carpenter. Seen how His words had inspired so many. One God, vengeful but benevolent. All forgiving. And the church with its Pope had the power to speak for this one God, to forgive all sin. To order armies to murder all in their path in the name of their God. Righteous, pure!

We are here child, we wait. Bone to Stone. Play his game. He knows not who he is!'

'If you truly are an ancient one, why do you destroy all our kind?'

He smiled, curiosity. Her innocent curiosity was rising he thought. Use it. 'Sweet child, in all wars there are victims, those that are simply in the way or those that have to be sacrificed to win. Did not even the Son of God give up his life? To save us, to give us his words. Is not that the ultimate sacrifice, to serve your master. To die for others to rise?' He stood and walked to the blazing fire. 'You know I cannot remember when or where I came from. Umph, I have always been. Travelling through time, watching mankind grow. Watching and waiting.'

'And now you have your perfect method of control. The word of God...'

'Yes, and it is so sweet, child. So very sweet...'

'And yet you know not where you were born, no memories of childhood or family? Do you wish to know, to know that maybe you were born of love, born of family?'

'No. My path is set.'

Amy thought, 'But pathways change.' I will find your memories; I will find the love that is buried so deep within your soul.

Two Mages, one battle. Both moving the chess board in a game for the soul and survival of all humankind.

James & Kydan

'James, James!' Samuel yelled at his son as he jumped from the back of their cart, 'James what in all of Heaven are you doing?' James paid no heed to his father's pleas. All his senses focused on the creeping mist that was approaching and the shadowy figures that were shrouded in the very same mist. His blood boiled, he felt power feeding into his body from the soil beneath his feet. Strength surged through him. He felt no fear. He was ready to fight for their lives. The soldiers before him meant death, those moving towards them from shadows on the left would surround them. He could not discern their intentions, but felt no threat from his flank and focused on the rear. He breathed. His hands gripped the heavy blacksmiths hammers. His perception of his reality had shifted. He was part of this Earth and the Earth knew him well.

'Stay back father, protect mother!'

'Son, come back.'

'I see them, they are the priest's soldiers and two of those strange mute men. I see their intentions Pa. They mean to kill us...'

'James, you cannot fight them all!' Samuel yelled at his son, bemused by his behaviour and the air that seemed to swirl around him. Blue light danced off his son's skin. The air smelled like lightening had struck the ground. He could hardly breathe. He could see only mist. How could James know who or what was coming.

'He is a Forevermore!' Gideon's voice boomed through the gloom as slowly his men appeared around the cart. Martha screamed. Samuel stared in disbelief; his throat dry. Out of the morning gloom there appeared twelve huge war horses and mounted upon them in full armour and bearing the red cross of the Knights Templar were huge warriors. The same blue glow around them, dancing and swirling. The horses snorted and stomped the ground. The Knights staring into the very mist that James was watching so intently. Silence, Samuel was suddenly aware of the whole road and that no sound emanated from the trees or brush. It was as if their small world had held its very breath. His skin tingled. Then four hooded figures walked from the undergrowth. Monks he thought, from Roche? What in God's name were they here for? Each walked with a staff, long and twisted wood, strange carvings along the shaft. At the tip woven into the preserved roots there seemed to be stones. Beautiful blue stones, gleaming and singing. Yes, a soft hum, like Martha at her evening sewing.

'No fear Samuel, we are here for James, but it looks as though his Quickening has begun. And it seems we are just in time.'

Samuel stared at Gideon, speechless, his whole body filled with fear. Martha had slumped in her seat in a dead faint. He reached over to her and pulled her into the safety of the cart. Gently laying her down. He thought at least she was spared this. What ungodly sight it was. These Knights he had heard of, ruthless killers, rich beyond measure and it was said that they had been cleansed by the Church for their ungodly worship of idols. Yet here before him were the very same. Appearing out of nowhere, inhuman! And they came for his son. A Forevermore they called him! So many questions ran through his mind. His thoughts raced trying to make sense of all he was witnessing.

'Stay with your wife. Move forward!' At Gideon's command the mounted soldiers took position behind James and drew their swords. The figures clad in the coarse hooded robes so their faces were hidden moved to both sides of James, and began to mumble strange words. The earth seemed to shudder, the trees and plants seems to tense. The same blue light rose from the ground up around the mounted men. The mist cleared. Two huge dark-skinned men emerged from its murk, sweat glistening on their naked chests, strange markings covering every inch of their upper torso. Soon the soldiers of God emerged behind them. Fierce, hardened soldiers with blood lust in their eyes. Their bloodlust faded when they saw the Knights before them. Samuel thought he saw fear. On the York Road all fell silent, no wind moved grass or leaves. No sounds came from the birds. The world stood still.

'Kill them all!' the commander of the soldiers of God yelled. They forced their spurs into the sides of their mounts. The horses lurched forward at the command. The two Nubian warriors, silent, ran at James.

'Hold the line.' Gideon boomed to his men. Fools, the pathway ahead of them narrowed. They would be bunched together.

'What about James!' Samuel yelled.

Gideon turned to Samuel, 'See what your son is, Samuel. Watch and see the true form of your son.' And with that he turned his attention back to the soldiers racing towards them. The horses snorting, their hooves thundering into the earth. James did not move. He watched the two dark warriors. As they charged towards him, he readied himself. Seeing each move. Feeling the power radiating around his blood. The first Nubian to reach him fell in one blow. James swung the huge hammer. He felt the impact. The man's jaw shattered, his cheek bones disintegrated into shards of pulverised bone and tissue. His eye swept from its socket. Such was the blow that James struck with. Blood, teeth and bone showered over him. He felt nothing. As the crushed boned expanded into his brain the Nubian fell to the ground. He was dead before he hit the rich brown earth. Samuel stared in horror.

'By Jesu, what in the name of God...'

'He is a Forevermore Samuel. This is his destiny unfolding before your eyes!' Gideon yelled. 'Here they come men. As soon as they hit the narrow path attack. Fools, they will be caught in a net!'

'What about James!' Samuel yelled

'I think he can take care of himself.'

Samuel saw James facing the second dark skinned man. The blue light glowing around him. He had never felt such fear. Yet he felt the power that emanated from his son.

'Come you demon, come face death.' James spat at the yellowed eye man before him. 'I see all the Evil you have done. Come!'

The Nubian hesitated; he had never seen such ferocity. Power surrounded him, more powerful than his master. He launched himself at James. His curved blade ready to slice thought his gut. James saw the move before it came. He turned away and swung the hammer into the base of his opponent's spine as the dark warrior passed his side. He heard the bones crack and shatter in that one blow. As the spinal cord was crushed the Nubian fell forward. He would never rise again. He knew in that moment his life was ending and never felt the final blow that James lent to his skull. The back of his skull shattered, blood and pale brain matter exploding with the impact, spewing out onto the roadway. Only Hell now waited for his soul.

Horses raced past him and a hooded figure came to his side. A gentle hand was placed on his shoulder.

'Be at peace brother. They came for your blood. They failed.' The voice from the hood was distant, as if a ghost. James dropped the hammers. He stood in silence watching the melee unfolding in front of him. The soldiers had not judged the narrowing path way.

Their horses were forced together and began to panic. As they did soldiers could do nothing but push their animals through. Gideon and his Knights waited as one by one they punched through the tightening pack of horses. The soldiers yelled and screamed at their mounts, some breaking legs in the crush and crying out in pain.

'Ready men, pick them off. No mercy. No one left alive.' Gideon said, holding back his huge war horse who snorted and stamped his hooves. It tossed its massive head, the vicious spike on its armour plate ready to strike. His horse was much a warrior as any man and would not hesitate to crush a man under hoof. Bite and tear at flesh. Gideon had seen his stallion lower his head in a charge and rent a man under the spike and armour plate and in a crazed blood lust trample him as he fell. That was a true war horse, warrior and killer. No mercy for man. No pity.

'Steady!'

Three of the soldiers burst through the narrow path. Gideon spurred on his stallion. His huge blade ready in his hand. The horse charged. Gideon picked off to the left man and swung at the commanding office. Already bloodied from the crush he stood no chance. He saw the massive horse coming towards him.

'Knights Templar!' He stared in horror. 'You cannot exist!' The huge blade that Gideon wielded swung down and cleaved the commander from shoulder through on downwards. The commander saw his shoulder and arm fall away as cleanly as butcher cleaves meat from the carcass of the Ox. His last thought was that he would never see Somerset again. Gideon swung again and took his head cleanly. Blood and tissue sprayed over his horse. He did not wait. His horse turned on instinct and as the commander's headless body fell from his mount and his stallion trampled his body into the earth. Each Knight carefully picked off the soldiers. Gideon found his next target. His mount rammed his head and spike into the other horses' side. It screamed in pain. Gideon swung his blade cleanly through the man's midsection. The body cleaved in two. The upper half fell away into blood drenched earth. His horse ran in terror, the lower half of his body still in the saddle.

'Holy Mary, Mother of God.' Samuel stared in horror as the bloodied horse raced past the cart. His passenger a bloody stump. Mercifully Martha was still lying prone in the cart. Samuel had inflicted many pains onto the poor prisoners of the Church. But he had never seen battle. He saw in true horror all that battle brought. The path before him was filled with cloying black blood. He saw limbs and all manner of innards being trampled in the foray. The Knights cut down every soldier in their path. No mercy. Their white tunics drenched with blood; it ran down their armour. He saw James watching. His face held no expression. The hooded figures stood beside him. All that he had heard of these men was true. From the tales of the Crusades to the battlefields that raged in far off lands. All was true. Their strength was unnatural. Their horses; beasts of war. It was a horror unimaginable, but now a reality.

Silence fell over the York Road.

Amy

After their morning conversation he had left her in peace. His final words that he would send Sally with suitable dress wear and that she would join him for Midday meal. But her freedom to leave the attic came with a warning. He had said that she could leave her small room, wander at her pleasure around his home and gardens. He said she could read all the texts he had accumulated, but again he warned that his Wards would stop any Cast she thought to use. He also warned her that his Manor was guarded and protected by powerful Wards. Should she be able to escape his Wards, his soldiers would soon hunt her down and he would be most pleased to return her to the crypt once more. 'See yourself as my guest, not my prisoner. For are we not the same? I am sure you have many more questions for me?' He had said, sweetly. She felt the threat though. And he was correct. She craved knowledge of him. It was if she was bound to him in some way. And what good would it do to run. The whole town now believed she was a witch and would soon turn her over to him. Time here would be well spent. Time to plot, to find a way to trap him.

'Mistress, but you are all but healed!' Sally stared at Amy. The expensive but plain dress still clutched to her chest with the soft slippers perched on top.

'I think the wounds looked far worse than they truly seemed. And your care has prevented a much worse outcome. I thank you and bless you for that care.'

Sally placed the clothing on the bed beside where Amy now sat, glowing in health. Her mind raced with questions, but she bit her tongue. She wanted to know, but decided best not to. Last evening her betrothal had been made. Bands would be read and within the month she would be a respectable married woman and away from this place. Her Pa had given his mother's cottage to them as dowry and his mother had agreed to take up residence with them. Grandmother was a kindly woman and loved both her daughter-in-law and treasured Sally so it was no hardship for her to come live with her son. And see her only grandchild take up married life in her cottage. She had even given Eric's Pa a purse of silver to complete the dowry. Eric's Pa was impressed and happily betrothed his son to her.

'You have questions?' Reading her confused face and the puzzlement betrayed in her eyes.

'Aye, but think it be best not to ask.'

'Sally, don't fret. It is simple. I am accused of The Craft, just as my mother was burned for the very same when I was but a small child. You must make sure you do not contradict the Cardinal....'

'Contra....'

'Do not disagree with his conviction of me....'

'But you are no witch....'

'That is my point, Sally, you must never say that. You must say that the Cardinal is led by God and he would know a witch when he sees one. That he is a man of the true faith and that his judgements are made in the light of God in which he stands. Never, never give him reason to doubt your faith and obedience to the Church. Promise me, please I beg you.'

Sally looked at the young girl she had grown up with. She knew that Amy was good and kind but the fear she saw in her friend's eyes as tears filled them, she knew what she said was truth.

'I promise Amy, though it will sit ill on my very conscience that I cannot speak for you.'

'That I know that your heart is with me is all to me, I bless you for protecting yourself and be sure you protect all your kin.'

'Aye, though many in town are grumbling at the accusations, especially about the Widow Smythe. Those potions were nowt but pickles and bottled fruits. Many a folk in Tickhill went to her for those jars, which she gave away at Christmas Eve. She always said that the gifts of Autumn were the treasure of a winters table.'

'This man, Sally, he is so very dangerous. Keep your peace, live a good life with Eric and have many babes. When you are wed go to our farm with Eric. Under the barn floor at the rear, lift the boards that are loose. There is a chest. There is table ware, fine lace cloth, and two fine silver candlesticks. They are my gift to you. Light a candle for me each winter solstice.'

'How do you know I am to wed Eric...'

Amy laughed. 'The whole town knew you two were sweet. Those furtive glances in the market, Eric bright red when you spoke.'

Sally smiled. 'Aye, took his bloody time though. Two years of fluttering eyes and sweet smiles. But I can't take those things.'

'Jed and Elizabeth are gone. I will soon be....gone....too. It would please me to know that you have them and will treasure them. A remembrance of our family.'

'Oh, lass....' Sally flopped down on the bed next to Amy and they hugged. Through sniffles Sally said she would go and that they would find the chest. And that she would remember her and her family and light a candle every Sunday Mass for them. Both shook away the sadness and smiled at each other. Amy had to get herself prepared for Midday meal.

Amy dressed in the fine clothes. Deep sea green velvet with a fine but simple lace collar. Soft doe-skin slippers lined with the same velvet. Sally had brushed her dark hair and plaited two sides and pinned them to the back of her head, holding back her waist length silk black tresses. Sally said she looked a true maiden and beautiful. Amy accepted her compliment and in a final hug Sally left. Amy knew she would not she her friend again. Her preternatural foresight saw nothing of the future of sweet Sally Briers. But Amy hoped that she would have a simple life filled with the blessings of the Mother.

Later that morning, just before midday struck, she walked down from the simple attic into a world she could not have imagined existed. She recognised all he had collected, she felt the magics that reached out to her from each ancient object, and the books and scrolls he had acquired. She reached out beyond the walls, her magics were repelled back. Even his newly built Manor House had been Iron Bound. His warnings to her returned. He was containing Earth Magics. Her bright intellect was intrigued by him. Her need to explain the enigma that was Charles de Gosse grew, as she padded down the rich rugs laid in the halls. It was tempting to peek into the many rooms on the second floor but she thought better of it. He would have no doubt placed Wards on the doorways and would know who entered each room. So, she resisted and walked down the curved stairway to the lower floor. The staircase ended in the hallway. The wooden floorboards still carried the scent of fresh timber and linseed oil. Heavy dark dressers lined each wall. She was again tempted to take up his offer and explore more, but was suddenly interrupted.

'Err-um.' Judith stood at the far door. Eyeing her with deep curiosity and what Amy perceived as distaste. Amy thought that Judith may have found it distasteful to have an accused witch in her domain. 'The master will be hear shortly. Please.' And she pointed towards the door behind her. Amy walked in front of the large woman, barely passing her large bosom. The indignant stare emanating from the woman, who obviously thought she was mistress of this house, confirmed her thoughts. Amy walked into a large dining room, a large fire blazing to one side. Tableware had been laid for two. One at the head of a thick oak table and one to the side. Jailor and prisoner. This room was plain, with dark wood panelling, a huge oak dresser, candle holders but no more adornments. It was a room meant to convey wealth but also piety. Obviously, the Cardinal had a sense of deception. He made no display in his public rooms of wealth. He made sure his guests were made aware of his humility. A far cry from the other rooms, rooms that few had been in but rumoured that his vast wealth was patently obvious in his private quarters. Judith it was said provided fare that was renowned in the county. Many wealthy land-owner had tried to lure her away in the hope of dining on her sumptuous cooking. But none had succeeded. Amy presumed she enjoyed her status in the town. She had seen

Judith on market days. Bartering with the traders. She had nodded greeting to her family and had often purchased their wares from the farm. Judith would be as all the townsfolk now. Distancing themselves. Many hoping that Amy would not confess of the secret blessings that Jed had whispered over their fields, or the visits by the womenfolk for aid in their pregnancies. All would now condemn the family. All would look away.

Amy cared little; one certainty was that they would not see her burn. Of that she was certain. Her plans would spare her the jeering crowds of once friends that would be glad to see another witch murdered and banished from their town. Some would still not believe, but would join the braying crowds for fear of the finger of God pointing to their doorstep!

'Good day, and may I say how beautiful and radiant you look. I see the colour suits you perfectly.'

'Thank you, my Lord Cardinal.' She was aware that she was on public display, no doubt Judith was lurking nearby, ear to the door. It was now vital that she play his game. Everything she said in these public quarters would be retold and more likely talked as a tale of conspiracy and the good Cardinal offering his mercy to a waif born into a bad family. Trying to save her soul, before cleansing her body and soul to the flames.

'Please, come be seated. I have asked Judith to prepare a simple meal. If that meets with your approval.'

'Any fare that Mistress Onsworth serves I am sure will be far from simple. Our town speaks of her unrivalled culinary skills.'

'Ah, yes, I am afraid her skills are truly unrivalled. I am often indulged in some of the most exquisite delicacies.' He stood by the table with his hands on the side chair in a show of chivalry.

She sat and he carefully slid the chair underneath her small frame. 'But your stature is most cared for, it seems you manage also piety in your meals?'

He laughed at the game, and thought her wit most charming as well as he knew his house-keeper would have ear to door at this very moment. Her comments no doubt for that very same ear. 'Yes, I manage. Judith provides small portions so I may partake but also refrain from becoming as....prominent....as our good Mayor.'

Amy stifled a laugh. 'I think you are too kind to our Mayor, sir. I think even Mistress Onsworth would struggle to feed that hog of a man. And her fare would be wasted on one intent in stuffing himself like a Yule Tide goose rather than seeking the pleasure and enjoyment found in taste.'

He sat and laughed heartily at the beautiful and intelligent and outspoken woman. He thought that she was going to be his most interesting challenge he had had in so long a time. It was a sheer pleasure to meet one of his intellect and nature. He even pondered who would win this battle. It pleased him.

A sharp rap at the door and Judith came in with the Midday meal. It seemed it was to be a simple soup with fresh bread. But she also laid out various fruits, including grapes in a show of opulence. Amy had never seen grapes but now she would taste them. Judith served two bowls of her rich rabbit soup, laden with fresh cream in beautiful porcelain tableware with silver spoons. The bread was perfectly white, soft on the inside with a crisp crust. It was the most delicious food she had tasted. How could a rabbit be turned into something so rich, and had the touch of herbs to enhance the flavour.

'She is truly a master?'

'Yes, my Lord. I could never have imagined that so simple a dish could be made into this.' Amy smiled and pointed to her almost empty bowl.

Her amazement of him grew as he took both his and her empty bowls to the dresser and brought over a platter with cheese, apples and grapes. He deftly cut the apple, cheese and grapes and placed a small plate in front of her. 'The cheese is from the milk of goats, I gave Judith our Italian recipe and said it was for her sacred book, that I most assure you of no one has ever seen.'

His undertone was perfectly obvious, he was also referring to the Grimoire. 'And I can most certainly understand. Some books are sacred are they not?' She did not wait but quickly pulled off one of the red fat grapes and placed it in her mouth. It burst with such sweetness. It was like eating the sun. She closed her eyes and savoured the marvellous taste. When she opened her eyes, he was watching her with such intensity and smiling that she could only smile back.

'To see such pleasure from so simple a gift from the soil. Ah, one moment.' He rose quickly and went to the cupboard under the huge dresser. He pulled out a bottle which contained a honey liquid. And two glasses that must be Roman, they were so fine and clear. They were so delicate and he handled them carefully and then tipped the golden liquid into each glass. 'Now, mademoiselle, take a little of the cheese then….'

He handed her the glass. She did as he bade. The cheese was smooth and soft with a slight bitter taste. Then she sipped the liquid. It was quite thick, but it was pure sweetness.

'It is a Roman sweet wine. Over fermented that produces a pure sweetness that enhances the most delicate of cheese.'

'I thought to die from its pleasure. I never knew such fare or drink could be so wonderful. Thank you, my Lord Cardinal, truly.' And felt the flush of the sweet wine reach her cheeks. She did not refuse when he refilled her glass once more. Judith returned and cleared away the dishes and Amy thanked her for such a wonderful meal and that she had never tasted anything as fine and that she would never again, even if she were to marry the King himself. Judith blushed and smiled at the young woman who now had a glow about her cheeks which she put down to her good food.

They both now sat in his study, she had seated herself by the roaring fire. Her head woozy and staring at the room. Some of the books were other Grimoires and Books of Shadows. Others even older, written in the script of the Woden peoples. Some were covered in strange text and others had columns of glyphs, birds, animals and other strange pictures. He had travelled down time, and amassed a magical knowledge beyond her comprehension. She sat in deep thought of him. He had said he had no memory of childhood, or family. It was intriguing. She wanted time, time for Arabeth to leave, time to know this man, time to learn and to plan.

'He is filled with curiosity, feed his need. Let the book guide you. Remember Bone to Stone.'

That was his weakness, knowledge. She saw him reel from forgotten memories when he had first entered the attic room, she had seen those memories. She had felt his hunger. He was so much more than

Mage, more than Magician. Had he seen so much of the horror of man that it had forever changed his view of them? She had to know him. How could she judge him, when she knew so little of him? A man of cruelty and power, but what of this man she had seen this day. Was there another, one that had compassion, could know love? Was she the prey; or was he, hers? Thoughts tumbled through her mind. There was more to this Mage than she could ever imagine, but it was buried deep in his soul. Could she release those memories? Could she see into his pain?

'Seek, Child of The Forevermore. Seek! Bone to Stone.'

'How can you not know of where you were born, raised?' she said sweetly. Hoping to find every tiny morsel she could about this strange enigmatic Mage. Some words he spoke rang true, but to murder all our kind to gain ultimate Earth magic and rule all mankind? That was not their credence. Their magics were gifted and to be used wisely. Not to rule. Not to kill. There had to be balance in all life. So, her mother had spoken to her Aunt Elizabeth. Elizabeth had been born of magic, but not Forevermore, but was still a creature of the Earth and understood her mother and over time had begun to reconnect to her magics too. She had protected her. As had all their line down through time. Keeping the bloodline secret. Once their kind had been welcomed. Healers. Wise women. Now hunted, cursed, mutilated and murdered. And so many by the hands of this Mage. All was puzzle. There but hidden. She must open this book.

'If I was born and raised as you ask, I have no memory. Glimpses of nightmares, but no memory of childhood.' He continued to stare into the flames, avoiding her curious gaze and at that moment Amy's heart stirred for him. Could he be right, should our kind rule mankind? All they did was take, building stone upon stone, crowding and breeding together. Towns filled with filth and disease. So many starving, chained to their Lords while they revelled in gluttony and power. Is that why Mother had retreated? Why the Father no longer walked the Earth.

'Beware sweet child, beware!'

'I have business to attend. You may wander the house and gardens at your pleasure, as I said previously and no doubt with keen interest, but this room, has many treasures, treat them wisely Mage and I will know if you enter.' He stood, reached for her hand and gently lifted it to his lips. 'I will be watching, always!' He marched out of the small warm room, the coldness in his voice now returned. She knew she had seen but a small glimpse of the true Mage, but she felt the hate and malice return. It was a beginning, a small crack in his armour. She quickly followed out of the room.

'Beware sweet child, beware!'

James and Kydan

James stood silent, blood and death surrounding him. The massive blacksmith hammers that had fallen from his hands, lay in the thick gore and mud of the road. He saw his bloody carnage, crushed bone and flesh. Murderer. A sin he could not be forgiven for. Power flowed through him. But in the silence, it slowly left and sank into the bloody earth.

'James.' His father's voice breaking through the rage in his mind. 'James. By Jesu. Son.'

'Let him be Samuel.' Gideon's voice growled from beneath his armour, which ran with blood and flesh. His horse the same, snorted and pawed the ground. 'Let the power leave, let his mind clear.'

'What in all that is in Heaven have we done. These were the Holy army....'

'As we were once. Their intent was clear. Your and all your kin's death.' Gideon removed his helm and faced Samuel. 'Your son has found his true spirit this morn...'

'Spirit, I saw him. I see him now. He...'

'I am a murderer father....'

'Thou are not, you protect. Your instinct was for your family. You read those that would hunt you and your family. They struck first. You protected all that you held dear. That is not murder, Brother.' Gideon looked into the bloodied face of James. This child had become man this morn. This man had become Forevermore.

'You realise that he will send an army to hunts us down.' Samuel was filled with rage at these Knights and hooded figures which still guarded his son. None of them seemed to see the carnage.

'The Church will never know of this. Nor will they ever know what happened here...'

'Are you mad. All these men, dead. Cut down...here.'

'Pa.'

'Son, we will be hunted to the ends of world for this.'

James looked up at Gideon, 'Is that our fate, Sir?'

'Can you trust me, Brother. Feel into my heart, can you trust all that I speak to you?'

James stared into Gideon's eyes and felt a shift. He felt deep within this Knight's soul and knew that this stranger would become more than friend. He was truth, just as he had spoken. 'Sir, that I do.'

'James, these are...' Samuel spluttered.

'They are Knights, they are truth. We must place ourselves in their care.'

'Mage's, do thy work. Cleanse this site.' Gideon commanded. 'Peter, David capture the horses and take them to the abbey.'

Samuel and James felt the air change. The sense of a summer storm surrounded them. The Mage's had begun to chant a strange but beautiful song. James knew the song, deep within him. They were asking the Earth to cleanse the death from the road. Samuel froze, 'Did his eyes deceive him, was madness taking his mind.' He thought as he watched the soil soak away the blood. Roots rose out of that soil, coiling like the snake. Each root choosing pieces gore, limbs and whole men. Entwining them like the spider winding its prey in a silken cocoon. Winding, twisting every piece of human flesh. He watched in horror as these, these bloody parts were dragged beneath the Earth. The Earth closing over them. Gone. Even the blood-soaked Knights and their horses were clean. Their armour gleaming. James clean. Samuel clean. Birds sang and the sun soaked through the foliage of the trees. The Mages stopped their haunting song. Gone.

Gideon's words rang in Samuel's mind. 'No one will ever know.'

For the first time, as Samuel viewed the beautiful hedgerows and trees, he knew magic and knew his son was part of magic. And he wept.

'Pa, mother wakes.' James placed a hand on his father's shoulder, 'Pa,'

'Yes son, she must not know of this.'

'It will not be spoken of Samuel. That I promise you.'

Samuel nodded at Gideon and climbed into the cart, where Martha now stirred.

'You must come with us.' Gideon's voice held command. 'This day you must also vanish and we will ensure that you do.'

'Aye. James, drive the cart. Follow them while I tend to your mother. Said a still shaken Samuel, who climbed into the back of his cart.

The Knights turned their horses and the Mage's climbed into the cart. James knew that they had expended much of themselves to ask the Earth for its help. He turned the horses and set off after the Knights. He asked the Earth to clear their tracks as they moved on to the abbey. The Earth was happy to do his bidding. He thanked the Earth and as the two old cart horses set off to the abbey, James thought of the new road they were taking and felt the Earth moving in him, as if his very soul had been opened to the heavens. He became a creature of instinct, as if all the Earth spoke to him. As the old cart horses moved at a steady trot, they seeming eager to get to the safety of the Abbey, he let the Earth bathe him. He felt the....Energy....yes that was what is was called, pass through him, around him. Everywhere and in every thing....Energy.

The abbey was bustling with activity. As the Knights raced into the courtyard, stewards rushed from the stables. Knights jumped from their mounts and the stewards grabbed their reins and led the battle-weary animals into the comfort of their stalls. Soon all the armour and livery were removed and sent for cleaning and repair. The horses soon groomed, cooled and fed. Gideon paused to see his faithful Hector. The horse steaming in his stall, snorted when Gideon approached.

'There now my old friend,' rubbing the horse's muscled neck and ears, 'aye my old boy, battle is becoming hard on us both. I will see honeyed oats are brought to you.' He smiled as Hector pushed his muzzle into his chest. 'Rest well friend.' With a last rub of the war horse's ears and nose he left him to his rest, ordering oats and honey for him. That would see him content. A well-earned meal for such a faithful friend. Hector had been a young three-year-old when Gideon had come across him. A Beautiful, powerful rich chestnut stallion. Snorting and stamping with arrogance in his field. A King of his domain. Throughout the years they had become almost brothers. Hector would move before even Gideon could give his command;

their instincts combined into one physical warrior. But Hector would take no fool. He made sure everyone knew he was a King of Stallions, in some-way, Gideon thought, Hector was very prideful and laughed as he thought of his old war horse. How he would snort, raise his huge head and strut if a young filly took his fancy. Once even unseating his master to then bound off after a rather beautiful black filly. The owner of the said filly in a fit of fury at the audacity of the stallion. It took a goodly sum of silver to overcome that indiscretion of his lustful stallion. He found himself smiling at the memory. The Duke's beet red face seeing his perfect Arab filly mounted by a common Warhorse. The Knights had drunk a toast to Hector that night and to his master's sore arse from being tossed from his mount.

The cart rumbled into the courtyard. He could see James and Samuel in the back, holding on tightly to his wife. The Mages sat along-side. He was still confounded by this young lad. In days so much had been turned on its head. The young child and her great aunt and uncle. The uncle an ancient bloodline, living in their mist. Their niece in the hands of the Cardinal de Gosse, and him a Fallen. And now James, a Forevermore, newly emerged, brimming with power, being hunted down. All under the gaze of the Abbey. And of course, Kydan. Calling as all this unfolded. The Fates were at work here. And it would seem his peaceful days were over once more. Once more the Knights would run. It was a saddened state they had become. So, few of them left, most now in the new lands. And so, it was their turn to take flight and head for lands far across the ocean, to join their Brothers in a far distant land. To perhaps forge a new Empire alongside the strange red skinned natives, who still held onto the old Gods. A land untainted, unaware of this land which was now filled with blood and a spiteful God and cruel Church.

'James, give the cart to the stewards they will tend to everything. Bring your family and follow.' Gideon ordered the young man. James jumped from the cart and helped his mother out the back, Samuel followed. The hooded Mages moved more slowly off the back and stewards rushed to help them into the peace of the Abbey. Rest and food would soon restore their magics. Gideon could see James struggling to contain his magics, the air around him filled with radiating power. Monks, stewards and Knights alike gazed warily at the young man. Only the Mages seemed uninterested, too exhausted to worry about this newly found Mage. Gideon knew that he was no Mage. The power this boy held was not just of the Earth but of the Forevermore. Was he the savoir of the young female Cardinal de Gosse held? But that female....

'By all in the heavens!' Gideon stopped in his tracks as he mounted the stone steps into the Abbey. 'The picture forms, Kydan!'

James almost barged into Gideon, 'Sir, are you well. Do you require your medics?'

'Nay, lad. It seems revelation has taken into my mind. Come, let us see you and your family settled. We will find you lodgings, though they be humble in this establishment and have food sent to you. The Stewards will bring your belongings and you all must take rest....'

'We are grateful, my Lord,' Samuel said, 'but there is much....'

'Aye Samuel, you mind is riddled with questions. Rest this afternoon and evening. Allow our Abbey to settle into the night and in the morrow we will meet with clear minds.' Gideon smiled and nodded at Samuel, thinking how it perplexed his mind. Samuel, Amy's torturer! Did Samuel's family know what he had done, his past? But of course, these are God-Fearing people, if they knew, then they would condone the barbaric practices the Church carried out. Samuel was carrying out God's will. And witches, warlocks and all manor of Satan's children deserved no less than the pain he inflicted and a death they so rightly deserved. How this Church has corrupted, how it had taken the Healers and Mages and formed them into something so fearful, creatures to be destroyed. The sorrow was immense in these lands.

'Aye, as you wish my Lord.'

'Pa...'

'James, our Lord and host is right. We need to rest. Your poor mother....'

'Yes, Pa.'

'Let the Lord be about his business and we will see what the new morning brings, eh lad? Impatient as always.' And he smiled at his son, but deep in his belly fear lied ill. All he had seen, the brutality of his son, his head ached with all the horror. These strange Knights, infamous now and at Roche Abbey. Not the goodly monks as all the folk thought. But brutal warriors it seemed, living under the very nose of our Church. God certainly did move in mysterious ways.

Two stewards appeared behind them carrying their meagre belongings. Gideon stood aside, seemingly lost in thought. 'They will guide you to your lodgings.'

Forevermore

'There seems a shift in our realm?' Raphael sat under his favourite tree. Michael wondered if he would ever tire of its fruit.

'It seems so. The Fates are about their games it would seem.'

'Did Kydan follow instruction and visit with Gideon?' Raphael asked.

'That he did. The child is within the walls of the Abbey. They will begin their plans to escape. And as predicted the new Forevermore has emerged'

'Do you believe that this Pope of Rome still manoeuvres this priest?'

'I believe there is far more in this matter than we see. This priest seems intent on Amy and The Nevermore, more likely he sees The Nevermore as Hell. Where the souls of dead reside in their so-called purgatory. But I soon think this Pope will have no control over this Mage, hiding in plain sight. This Mage works a cunning plan, that I cannot fathom, and I fear he will soon learn of Amy's child and her significance.'

'They play confusing games. They constantly move to outwit, gain power. And yet this priest, he changes with each age of man, once a living god in the land of the Pharoahs, a Roman warrior, and then a seer of the Norsemen, soldier of the Christian God and always a Mage that turns on his own. I am at such a loss of him.' Raphael muttered.

'It seems we are charged with watching over a realm of strange, selfish creatures. Even those that have all they ever could dream of; they continue in their games. And live a life that in the end is one of pain and sadness. Yet those born into servitude, those born in poverty have more honour, love and care in their souls for all their mortal sufferings.'

'Does it confound you as it does I?'

'My brother. These creatures confound, perplex and drive such rage into my soul. But our aim is to undo the work of our Brother Lucifer and find him, free The Father and then The Mother will rise to join her mate. What her rage will bring to these creatures I cannot guess.' Michael said.

The Watchers understood The Forevermore is creation and destruction. It binds the universe; it creates but it will also destroy. Out of Nothingness came an explosion of life and that life will once again return to its first state. No life can understand, though it may try. No life can see its soul. Life is a gift. The Fates may weave their cloth, but in life there is choice on how to use that gift, for Choas and Darkness will always conspire to corrupt the destinies that The Fates weave.

'Well Brother Michael, my head swims. Come I think we should go to the arena. It has been a while since we have had a good spar together, and sent your arse to the sand!'

Michael roared with laughter. 'Send my arse to the sand. Your belly full of the confounded fruits you have just eaten, it will be a wonder that you could pluck a feather from my wings before your fat gut is bent over in cramps.'

The Cardinal and Amy

After her mid-day meal and her strange conversation with him, she wandered the manor. The public rooms as she had seen we sparse, even austere. She had ventured into the domain of Judith, found Sally there. The kitchen was well stocked. Pheasant and rabbit hung. Large cheese wheels and all manor of vegetables, bottle fruits, bread, salted meat preserves and strange coloured powders filled the shelves. The large stone oven heated the room, but something lingered there. A faint odour, one she knew well. Her senses were drawn to the heavy iron bound door.

'There aint nowt down there but the cellars. We ave workmen down there.' Judith grumbled at her. Sally glanced up from her large mixing bowl.

'Apologies mistress, it must be fetid air that moves from there that draws my attention?'

'Fetid, aye and it does no service to my kitchen.' Judith scowled at the heavy door. 'Aye know not what he be up to down there, but seems to be a lot of trouble over a new wine cellar, umph, wine cellar! How much wine does the Cardinal intend to imbibe? He doesn't drink that much and he certainly is not generous in his sharing of it either. More to it, but best keep out noses out of the pot, lest they be burnt off.'

'Will you be staying a while then Miss?' Sally chirped, now red faced from mixing the ingredients in the large bowl.

'I think that will depend on the grace of our esteemed Cardinal.' She smiled at Sally, 'I will leave you in peace Mistress Judith. I may take a walk round the garden, it looks lovely.'

'Aye lass, best not let him find you down here, you being his guest an all.'

Amy left the warmth of the small kitchen, leaving the odour of death behind. She could not sense beyond the iron door but all her instincts led her to believe that it was the entrance to the crypt she had been held in. The manor house and church had truly been built over an ancient Pagan site, as he had said. It would be one door that his Wards would be most powerful.

The sun carried the warmth of the promise of summer. She walked along the neat gravel pathway and the neatly trimmed box wood hedges. The box wood hedges forming intricate patterns and filled with all manor of herbs. Some she found most intriguing, Valerian, Wolfs Bane, and even Mandrake, Tansy, Foxglove, and Belladonna. 'It seems our Judith likes her poisons too!' She thought, surprised at the wealth of herbs but more the poisons. Along with all the herbs for the kitchen, there were rows of seedlings, fruit trees and berry bushes. At the far end was a stone summer house, which looked like a temple of sorts. Two large doors, which glass had been set into the frames fronted the beautiful temple. She opened the large doors and stepped into the large room, carefully closing the doors. The room was humid and beautiful flowers she had never seen before were growing in huge pots. She realised that a large brazier glowed in one corner and the roof had been set with glass. His wealth was truly made plain here. To be able to afford glass in a room for growing. Truly a wonder and an extravagance. Only the very wealthy in the land could ever dream of glass windows and of course the Church. The Cardinal had paid for master craftsmen to make beautiful windows for the alter of their new church. Glass of all colours, depicting Jesus and the saints, truly beautiful and more so when the sun shone through the window.

There were lemon, limes and orange trees. In one corner a small ornate carved wooden bench. She sat and enjoyed the fragrances from the trees and flowers. It was a moment of peace and beauty. She allowed the Earth magic to flow into her. It was clearly a place he had not bound in iron and she sensed no Wards. It was almost as if she could sense him coming here to do as she now did. To sit and enjoy all that the Earth could give, but it would seem that the Earth would no longer answer his call. His call to the Darkness had barred him from Earth Magics.

'It is not so far from a likeness of my home, this place.'

Her heart pounded in her breast, she dared not open her eyes. He could not be here!

'My love, I risk all that I am to be here.'

Her eyes opened and he stood before her. 'And I would not wish you to risk all.'

'Just a few moments, just to see you, touch....'

She ran into his arms, which embraced her, crushed her to his chest. His soft white wings folding round her as he had when they first made love. Their powers ebbing and flowing between them. Their souls entwined. 'He will sense you here, he cannot know of us.'

'Ssh, be still. Only moments...'

'Only moments, but an eternity of love, I am forever yours, Kydan.'

He vanished, he should not be here but he had found a moment in time, and stole it. Anymore would be dangerous to them both. But a moment can change pathways, moments can change a life forever. She lowered herself back onto the bench. Tears gently slipped down her flushed cheeks. She would treasure the few moments of time they had just shared. And those moments in his arms fortified her, gave her courage and strength to carry on. Her teared eyes fell on a single pure white feather that lay on the warm stone floor. She walked over to it and picked it up. It glowed at her touch. Smiling she tucked it away to her breast. Its softness brushed against her skin, a reminder of him.

He stood, silently, watching. This beautiful woman intrigued him, confounded him and yet, yet there was a familiarity to this beautiful creature. He remembered her mother, Angelique. He was a soldier then and had played a wonderful game of cat and mouse with her family. Amy's grand-father so righteous, so morally pure. 'But you were so corrupt. All those repressed urges, crushed under the book of God. How I knew your grand-father sweet Amy and your mother. Such a powerful and wilful creature she was.' He whispered to know one but himself. His thoughts drifting to his days in Nottingham drawn to the power that was Angelique. Hiding as a lowly soldier. 'She gave herself up and I lost her but I will not lose you.' As soon as he had glimpsed her at mass, he knew who she was. His surprise was that he had not known of the child. Angelique must have cast a powerful Glamour over her to hide what she carried in her belly. 'Oh, beautiful Amy, how could you not be her child?'

'Lord Cardinal....' Sally choked from behind him.

'By Jesu, Sally girl. You half stopped my heart. You are as silent as a mouse.' He blurted out as he started.

'I....my apologies....you were talking quietly and seemed in deep thought.'

'Sweet girl, do not tremble. I meant no harm.' He smiled sweetly at the paled servant girl. 'I think I will have to purchase some hard leather boots for you and take away those silent soft slippers.'

'I will stamp around the house, my Lord Cardinal. Hard leather would cause such damage to the wood floors.' She stammered, and he thought this poor girl has no notion of his humour.

'It is fine Sally, what is it?'

'There is your afternoon visit from the council members. I have put them in the refectory with mead and cakes.'

'Oh, may the sweet Lord Jesus preserve us from those pompous men.' He groaned, how he hated the weekly council. Always grumbles, always protestations and of course the usual grovelling for funds. 'Come, let us greet the good fellows of Tickhill and see how much they wish to raid out of my purse this week.' And as he passed Sally, he saw her trying to hold her giggles at his comments of such prominent members of her town. He needed to get this over with as he required much thought-on Amy and why she was talking to herself in his summer house and why a deep fear rose up as she stood gazing up into the roof. It seemed to him that another presence was there, but shielded well from his sight.

'Lord Cardinal, we must lodge our deep concerns and protestations at all these, these so-called un-Godly creatures that seem to be in our midst. The townsfolk are becoming increasing suspicious and rebellious. It seems now that two prominent and well-respected families have vanished, leaving behind good business and good farm lands...' Thomas spoke loudly and pridefully. He was a notable land owner and over-thought his status within the council. And was known as a greedy man. The man who had so coveted the Widow Smythe's lands.

'Sir, whom ever these two families are, and their choice to leave is of no concern to me. The widow Smythe, inquisition was duly taken and she was found to be of Satan's spawn. Do you now take offence at the Holy Church of Rome's methods or its justice which was carried out in accordance with the express wishes of our Holy Father the Pope?'

'No of course not, but our townsfolk are simple, illiterate and Godly people who see your arrival and this sudden increase in demonic forces as an omen of ill fate...'

'My purpose here, is to eradicate your demonic forces and my arrival was of the most-grave importance. But if you wish I will write immediately to the Holy Father of the council's discontent at my methods....'

The other nine, over-fed and pompous men paled. Thomas had over stepped. All knew he had his axe to grind as the price the good Cardinal had extracted for the Widow Smythe's lands.

'Please, my Lord. Our good townsman Thomas means no disrespect. We are all most pleased that our most Holy Father of Rome deems us in such dire needs of your most holy works, Lord Cardinal….' Spluttered the Sheriff, who glared at Thomas.

And so; the good gentlemen of Tickhill grovelled at his feet once more. He would never in all his centuries of life would have believed that these stupid creatures would become the grovelling servants of this Church of their one God. It was power unproven, for who could dispute something that could not be seen, who could rise against a man who spoke the words of a God. A God that was vengeful and who would mete out his punishment at any slight of disobedience.

Soon the council men left and he sighed with relief. They would not dare to go against him again and leaving with a fine bag of gold to put to the furtherment of good works in their town. He had little doubt where the good works would go, mostly into their own fat coffers. He cared little. Once the portal was opened to The Nevermore, gold and good works would be of little use to the Godly townsfolk and as he bade farewell to the last man, slamming the great oak door loudly behind them he made his way to the kitchen.

'My good mistress Judith. Would you make supper for two this evening? I think a simple broth and some of your fine fruit loaf, cheeses and grapes would most greatly serve.'

'Yes, of course my Lord. Is young Amy to stay awhile then?'

'Oh, I believe my charge will be required to lodge for quite some time.'

'Then by you wishes, would you allow me to use the household account to purchase some clothing for the young one. One dress and no, err, beg pardon, no under clothing will cause inconvenience I would think.'

'Why mistress Judith, how would my home survive without you. I gave not thought to the child's needs. Please buy all you need for her stay with us. If your household account is diminished, I will ensure double is placed in your strong box by weeks end. Again, my gratitude to your great care of my household.' And as he turned to leave to go to his study, he saw the great pride swell up in his housekeeper's face. He could never fathom why the higher born would be-little those of lesser fortune. He enjoyed their adoration from his simple words, spoken to ensure their continued loyalty.

His study was his haven. And as he sat by the blazing fire, he contemplated all that was transpiring in this pathetic back water.

'It seems our Jed and Elizabeth have fled.' He thought. 'Where would they vanish to. Both had no kin and no word had been mentioned of the sale of their lands. So, where would they go to, who would harbour them? Why would they abandon their charge, Amy?' Puzzle after puzzle. 'Did they think her dead?' His mind could not figure this puzzle. But it was fortuitous, the townsfolk would believe that Amy was truly a witch, for even her only kin had fled from her sight? Elizabeth was of no loss, her magics were poor and her husband, well he was as weak too. It was Angelique and Amy that had carried the immense power of their bloodline. His dark warrior entered the dark, warm room.

'Have the contingent arrived back?' He spoke to this noble warrior. His respect for these noble men of war never left. Fearsome and as courageous as the beasts of their lands. The warrior spoke only in his native tongue.

'None have returned.'

'Strange, I would have thought I would have heard the raucous banter of those crude butchers by now. Perhaps they have happened upon a fair tavern?'

'Negenday and Senbal have not returned.'

'Now my good friend, now I do believe that is to be of concern.'

'Yes. I will travel their path and seek answers'

'Very well, be of good eye, this land is ancient and has many dark secrets.'

'Bandihi will take care. This is vile Earth. The Gods show no favour in this place.'

'Yes, my friend. This Earth is a dark, writhing filth. Take care.'

The warrior left to find Dubanihi, his brother. They would soon find their brothers trail and find their kin. He rose and walked over to the book. He felt its hum, a deep rhythmic thrum. He hovered his hand over it. But as soon as his flesh touched the tooled leather, pain ravaged his body.

'Dark creature, the Oblivion awaits your soul. We remember who you are. We know you, dark creature.'

'It will not allow you entry. You are not of the light anymore.'

'Amy, you are as silent as that waif Sally.' He looked over at the dark-haired beauty stood just outside the door. '

'Who are those men?'

'You mean my guardians?' He smiled at her. 'Please, come in. Be seated. There is some time before supper.'

Amy walked over to the book. The large claw clips sprang open and she placed her hand on the ornate binding. 'Sleep, for I need you not.' And the claws clicked back into place.

'It gives you pleasure to know that it will not reveal itself to me?'

'Of course, why would it give itself over to you. You would use it against the light. You would use it for power.'

'Come sit.' And he guided her to the soft fireside chair. 'Those men you asked of. Well they are known as Nubian. They are from the lands beyond Jerusalem. Lands of vast plains, huge mountain ranges and impenetrable forest. They are a noble and are from a warrior tribe. They live as all humankind should still live. Living alongside nature, hunters and gatherers. Not like these lands with their festering towns, filled with filth and pestilence. Their Gods are Gods of nature, not a vengeful God-man who seeks bended knee and unquestioning devotion.'

'You truly hate the faith, do you not?'

'No, no, I do not hate. I find it wonderful; it is humans that I find have become merely a pathetic shade of what they could be. Their knowledge of medicine and science grows but then this faith rises and crushes all knowledge down. Destroys the healers, those wise women who see the babes into the world. The Mages who bless the land and seek the love of nature to grow all the fruits of the land and see all the game to flourish, they are also destroyed.'

'But why then do you hide in their holy places and carry out their work?'

'To rule, to become their Father.' His eyes glowed and the shadows thickened. The Dark moved to him, fed his magics. 'For my child do you not see? They are lost, it seems these humans need to be led, just as sheep in the field. They only become discontent when their rulers flaunt the wealth, while they starve, when they see injustice and cruelty….'

'And you do not wish to rule as king or vengeful God?'

'No, no. When I rule, there will be no God, no King. I will return to the old way. The worship of the Earth, of nature. All will live as equal. All will work in a place they are able to labour. Those of intellect allowed to flourish, those who seek the beauty of art and music be able to create. The mighty farmer revered as any king. The women protected and worshiped as the bringers of life, the nurturers of life and the healers. For are they all not humankind?'

She was stunned to silence. There was no argument here for her. How could there be? But the way he referred to them and not as us. He spoke as if he was not of humankind make. 'But what of the Red Dragon?'

'Red dragon?' his face contorted, like he was trying to remember.

'The dragon you dream of.'

'I let my Wards down in those moments, so you can see my, erm, let's see – visions?'

'Is that how you see them, as visions? I sense more memory than vision.'

'A dragon is a mere fable, a childish monster to fill nights of dark tales.'

'I think you lie to yourself, my good Cardinal.'

'And I think, little child, it is you that now over-step. It is only by my grace that you are here and alive. Your family has fled so there are no kin to claim you or vouch for your good name.' He growled at her. Amy knew she had angered him. It would seem that this vision, this red dragon was more to him than he would let believe. As for having no kin, well that was her Earthly fate. 'I think it be time for us to sup and leave this conversation.'

The meal was simple but of good fare. Afterwards she asked the Cardinal for a book, which Judith gasped at, for she knew no woman that had been taught letters, as she had been by the previous cook. But the good Cardinal asked Judith to take her to the library and then Amy trotted off to her room, book in hand. Later Sally came with warmed milk and some sweet shortbreads. They talked a little and Sally left her to her reading and as she read propped up on her small cot, her eyes soon grew weary and she slipped into a deep slumber.

The raging storm tore at his flesh. And in that storm was carried the cries of millions of pitiful screams.

The Time of Destruction had come to these lands.

He could not do this, but he knew he had no choice. The Mother had passed her judgement. The Father had returned to the Final Rest. The realm was doomed to destruction.

He looked into her dark ruby eyes, saw red tears. She was strong and nodded to him. There was no need for words. But he would be quick, for that was the only blessing of his love that he could now give.

'My love, be done. Our Mother has judged. It is the will of The Fates. Be done. We will be joined again.'

The blade sliced through her scales, scales that protected her in the red land. A land of storm, of ice and fire. It soon met soft flesh and he drove the blade on to her two beating hearts. He turned the blade upwards as they had been taught. Severing her hearts from her soul. She made no cry, made no sound. She stared into his eyes and he saw them fade....

Amy jolted awake, sweat drenched her slight frame.

He had dreamed again, her Cardinal. These were no visions, they were memories.

The Beautiful Red Dragon – Love! She, this red dragon, in a red land was his love, his kindred spirit. She could only think that in his pain he had turned to The Darkness. Would she become as such if The Mother had willed her to kill Kydan? Could she even blame him for turning to such dark pathways? For the rest of the night her mind boiled with so many tumbling thoughts and questions.

The Cardinal slept peacefully. The Darkness creeping around him. Taking away the dreams. He would only have faint memory in the morning. Something on the edge of his memory, there but not there. The Darkness did not want him to remember. It wanted him only to feel the lingering sorrow and more so the hate of that memory.

James

When morning broke, the new summer sun promised warmth. The small band gathered outside their simple cells. Forlorn, lost and fearful of a future they could never comprehend.

'Good morrow, Samuel, Martha and to you James.' Jed whispered in the cool stone corridor. All was quiet on this morn of change. 'I trust you are well and had chance to catch some sleep?'

'Aye, Jed. Some sleep was granted.' Said Samuel, his deep rough voice loud and clear. 'Our James, mourns your Amy and paced the night away....'

'Samuel, Amy has not passed. She lives still.' Elizabeth spoke, shocked that they thought she had gone.

'Not....dead?' James stuttered

'Oh, sweet boy, no she lives still. Listen lad we have much to talk about do our two families, but my stomach aches for breaking fast and we must find out more about this strange place. For it is no Abbey that I am sure off.' Jed spoke and placed a large rough hand on the young boy's shoulder.

'Aye, son. Jed is right. I think my stomach is in the same mind too. We can find a place after breaking fast and hopefully meet with this Gideon and find truth from this place and what our future may hold.'

They quietly made their way to the refectory, only the tiny babe mewling in her downy shawl. 'I do hope I can find milk for the babe. It is not the best way to feed a young babe....' Elizabeth whispered to Jed

'I can soon make the milk good and there are enough Mages here that I am sure we can soon Cast to turn good goats' milk to be of sound nourishment for this tiny babe....'

'Aye, husband, my mind is so full of turmoil, I forget.'

'I think all our thoughts of all of us are a raging storm, but these are goodly folk and the Mages are here for good purpose too.' Jed said and Elizabeth relaxed and the rest of the small newly bound family visibly relaxed too. Jed's words soothed their tumbling, fearful minds.

As they reached the refectory, they could hear the chatter and the clatter of plates and knives. And all could smell fresh baked bread.

The great hall hushed and all turned to see the small group appear through the door.

David rushed over. 'Come, please come. You are most welcome here; all are friends at this table. There is food laid out at the side by the windows. Please take all you need. I would imagine you are quite starving?'

'Aye, good sir. That we are and any fare freely given is truly gratefully received.'

'No, sir. It is our humble honour to welcome you to our Brotherhood. And especially your son and this most precious babe. You are under our protection and all here will lay down their lives to protect you. So come, be welcome. Enjoy our table. Gideon will meet with you after and your confusion will be put aside.' With that David guided them to the food and soon all faces began to smile at the small family. Samuel loaded his wooden bowl with fresh, harsh bread, pork, cheese and a thick oatmeal which he lathered in honey. Jed and James were not far behind him. A slight, but beautiful female Mage came to Elizabeth and smiled

'I have rich milk for the babe. It will nourish her well, mistress.' And she handed Elizbeth a small jug which held rich milk and a carved-bone-boat-shaped infant's feeding bottle. The Mage had also fashioned a teat from soft vellum. Arabeth would not go hungry this morn. And as if knowing her milk was there, she began to cry out indignantly for the rich, foamy and magical milk. The rest of the Brotherhood began to laugh at the raucous cry of the babe.

'My blessing, mistress. I think this babe will be more than grateful.' And Elizabeth set about feeding the now wailing babe. The young Mage came back with a full platter for Elizabeth and smiled at the young babe. 'She is everything and our hope.'

Soon all were busy with the morning meal. The babe, Arabeth soon sated snuggled down into her cosy shawl and fell into deep slumber, as if all the world was at peace.

'Gideon will see you in the library as soon as you have finished. He has only this short time to spend with you this morning as duties press on him at the moment.' David quietly said to the small group as they finished their meal. 'I will take you. The Mages will also meet with you and your family. I am sure you would all like to meet with them to discuss all that is transpiring.'

'Aye, good sir. I think we all need help to remove confusion and fear....'

'Jed, sir. Please have no fear in this place. We are here at your service and most of all our service to the babe is without question.'

The library was quiet. Gideon had finished his morning meal and was now making plans for what was to be a most dangerous and troublesome journey. Messengers had been sent already. The Brotherhood's ships would gather at Whitby harbour, preparing to sail to Europe. This subterfuge would need to be executed without fail if they were to reach the Mi'kmaq peoples without detection. The Brothers on board would be waiting for the portals to be opened once they had reached Lachlan. 'We must be at Lachlan castle before Mabon.' He muttered. 'One month to train James, two months of travel. We must be at Lachlan by Mabon.' It was possible, but any delay would mean winter setting in. They could winter with the Mi'kmaq and travel to the summer lands the next year. It was the only plan he had. All the Mages were now at the abbey. He had the two families and all Brothers were preparing to leave. The Captains of the ships at Whitby would play their role. The Church would have spies there and they must report that these ships seemed to be preparing for a journey to Holland or the more Northern territories of Europe. Only a few would stay to watch over their houses. David had already made request to stay. He was a good choice, wise and young but would grow into a good master for the northern territories. He already had another nine brothers ready to commit to David as the new prior of Roche Abbey, where they would continue in goodly Christian works but protect the Labyrinth and their Brotherhood. York, London and Roselyn had sent word. They too would be at Lachlan by Mabon.

'We need to get message to Amy. Can she hold this Cardinal until they were safe at the castle?' Gideon's thoughts tumbled; how could they get message to her? How could they without his knowledge? He had seen first-hand this Mages power, for he was certain that is what he was. The mist that had made invisible those soldiers who came for James, they were bound in dark magics.

'Jed can solve your problem; he can reach her.' Kydan spoke.

'By all in heavens, do not approach in silence. Do you wish my heart to fail?'

'Your heart is as stubborn and strong as an ox.'

'Kydan, my heart is old and you peering into my thoughts. You know very well my opinion on that. I thought we had accord. Not...'

'Without permission. You act as old man today, grumbling and muttering.' Said Kydan as he stood in front of the huge fireplace, blocking all heat. He knew that Gideon would soon grumble at that too. How he loved his centuries with this Brother, on the battlefields of the Crusades and now in this final journey. The Mi'kmaq homeland would be Gideon's resting place. Gideon would be needed in future times and Michael had commanded that these Brothers, these warriors must take the Dark-Sleep until called upon. Michael had already caused great stir among the Mi'kmaq peoples on his visitation. The great tribe was already moving towards the coast in preparation for the ships of the Brotherhood arriving and their journey to the Great Cave.

'Jed can help to contact Amy?'

'That he can, his connection is powerful to her. Through their book can he make contact.'

'I understand not.'

'He can approach their book, ask of it to give council to Amy and I am most certain that it will gladly do so. She must hold fast while you leave. He will no doubt already know of your ships gathering at Whitby and be most puzzled by the gathering. I am sure his spies will be buzzing with many creative tales. He must be led to believe that her family is leaving for Europe.'

'Does he know of the babe yet?'

'Not yet, but she calls to his Darkness. The Darkness will feel her light, be drawn to it and soon enough he will realise that Amy is merely toying with him. Soon enough he will know that she is not the vessel that carries the prey of Lucifer, our Mother.'

'Jed, please, all of you enter and take a seat...' Gideon motioned to the doorway, where the two families stood, staring at the huge Watcher. 'Have no concern for Kydan, Samuel. I assure you he is more mouse than cat!'

'If only that were truth.' Spoke Jed with more than a little contempt. He still had no forgiveness in his heart for his transgressions with Amy, in all but name his daughter. What father would not be enraged by any man who had treated his daughter so?

Even more the birth of a child out of wedlock in these times of danger and moral judgement of love beyond the marriage bed.

'I believe it would be discourteous of me to stay, Gideon.' Kydan bowed his head towards Jed and took his leave. Samuel and his family simply stared as the Watcher vanished before their eyes.

'Please, come, sit. Time is short and you must now take on your new destiny.' Gideon commanded. He knew he must now show these families that they have a different path to follow and take away Samuel's family's beliefs of their world. Perhaps the long journey they must now undertake would give time to take all that he had to tell and show them into their minds. For the lands they would now end their days in were brutal, untouched by this society. The people that would be waiting to greet them, strange and primitive to their clouded minds of Church and God. Yet he hoped that they would soon see that the Mi'kmaq people were more, closer to their image of their God and Faith than of all their priests of the new faith they so worshiped now. His heart was heavy, but there was little choice for them. Jed and Elizabeth, were a far simpler task, Jed being Mage and Elizabeth, he sensed, carried some of her Mage bloodline. It puzzled him though of Jed's smouldering anger at Kydan. But, once again the same thought entered his mind. Had Kydan fathered Arabeth? Could it be possible? It was a thought that he must hold in his mind. It was best not to test those waters, for Jed, it seemed they were a storm that Gideon did not wish to enter at this time.

Soon all were seated, all were silent. The very air was thick with a thousand questions.

'Much of what I say and show you all this morn, I ask that you take as truth.' Gideon spoke plainly and clearly; he had no time to waste and these people had no choice in what path they now must tread upon. 'For I speak now of truth, truth of your reality, truth that will take away your very Faith. But be assured, I speak truth. Roche Abbey is merely a place where those you know as Knights Templar now hide, as do most of our Brothers who survived the great purge hide in the great abbeys of this kingdom. I am Gideon of Arcadia. I was born 223 years ago and have served the Brotherhood of The Watchers for 210 years...'

'What fantasy is this. What fairy-tales do you....'

'Samuel, sit.' Jed spoke harshly to his friend. 'Whether you choose to believe or not. You will hear Gideon and all he speaks. He speaks truth. You will hear him and you and your kin must obey him and follow this path...'

'You, so you are...'

'I am of the Mages, as is Elizabeth, Amy and Arabeth. And I know of your dark trade also! I will make pact with you. I will speak no more of those dark times in your life for I see your heart suffers under the weight of all that you have done. But my pact is that you now listen to Gideon and I am sure you will see there is no choice but to follow his instructions. Especially as your son's Quickening has passed, for he is now more powerful than any Earth Mage and is one and the same as Amy.'

Samuel froze, as the ice freezes the pond. He could not fathom what was happening. He nodded, for he knew not what else to do. He could not return home, for all the death he had seen in the woods, his son, a creature that he could not understand. So, he would listen.

'Be still Samuel. We have little ground left to us.' Martha's soft voice comforted him as she laid a soothing hand on his arm. James, sat motionless, staring at Gideon.

'He speaks truth, father.' Said James, his voice now deep and commanding. 'He knows, as I know that I would know a lie.'

'That you would, my Brother. That you would.'

What is truth but that what we see

The fire crackled and the heat radiated into the hushed library. All sat in silence. Jed and Elizabeth held their peace. Tiny Arabeth slumbered. Samuel and Martha sat, confusion and fear surrounding them. James seemed at peace. Jed felt the steady hum of his power, just the same as Kydan and his sweet child Amy. He knew they were all one and the same. They were born of the Forevermore. He often wondered where Angelique was now. Her soul would be bound to the Forevermore. She would not forget her lives as he and Elizabeth would, as all mortals did. But it seemed that she had left this realm. Who could fathom what The Fates conspired, what plans they wove for all creations?

The library door creaked and all started and turned. Two Mages entered, one the beautiful maiden that had so kindly brought Arabeth her milk. The babe stirred, sensing the Mages but soon settled back to her slumber.

'Please, enter.' Gideon spoke to the two Mages. 'These, our brothers and sisters must quickly learn of the truth of their lives.'

'What are these, these people doing here?' Asked Samuel. Taking no care to disguise his disgust and contempt for the Mages that had entered the room.

'Samuel, please husband. We have no place to go. The Cardinal, you so admired and respected now hunts us. Open your mind and at least hear what they have to say. After, if you wish to leave then we will. But a least hold your council for now.' Martha pleaded with her stubborn husband.

'Very well, woman.' He grunted at her.

'The Mages will take you to the Dream Realm. It would take many days to give council on our past and our beliefs. They can send you to a realm of dreams, there you will see all that I wish you to see of our Brotherhood, of the realms of mortals and immortals. Of all the ancient laws laid down by First Creation. Of course, it is by your choice.'

'What choice do we have?' Samuel spat at Gideon

'You have choice, we offer you shelter and a journey, one perilous, but one that will see you to safety. I offer you, life and a journey into the dream realm to see all that has gone before. Or you may leave us in peace. We will fill you cart with all your needs for your journey to York. I will even give two of my Brothers as escort. You can take your leave and go to your brother, but there you will be at the mercy of Cardinal Charles le Gosse and your Church. I cannot protect further than the road to York. I would ask that you stay and more so James. If the good Cardinal finds his true nature, he will ensnare him just as he has Amy. But Samuel, Amy knows of her nature, knows her power and I am sure she plays his games as well as him. James does not.'

'I stay, Sir.' James clear voice growled in the hushed room. 'Mother, Father. Do not take back to the roads. You saw the power of that man. You saw what I became. I could not control it. It still burns through me. We must stay, all my senses tell me so. So, I ask that you stay, at least until the journey to the new lands commences.'

Samuel looked to his son. 'Aye, so be it lad. It seems I am outnumbered in my family. I will stay and travel with them to York. There I will make my final decision. I saw that, that blue light glowing in you. I saw how you crushed those strange dark men. And I will not deny, you fair stirred terror in my very soul. Aye, so be it. You must know of what you have become. Jed, is it so with you?'

'Aye, Samuel. We are of the Mages. James is of the immortal realm. This Brotherhood has been a guide and protector throughout time....'

'And that Angel?'

'Come to the Dream Realm, see all and you will understand.'

Samuel took Martha's tiny hands in his and gently kissed them. She smiled at him and nodded. 'So be it, so be it.'

The two Mages formed a circle in the centre of the great library. Gideon stood watch and two others of the Brotherhood came to stand in watch too. Soon a great chalk circle was made and strange Runes were marked at the four cardinal points. They placed simple soft rugs inside the great circle and led each in turn to one of those rugs. Jed led the way, crossing into the circle. Laying himself down onto a rug and a Mage placed a soft pillow below his head. Jed crossed his arms on his chest. Elizabeth, handing the babe to Gideon who took her and placed her carefully into an open chest. Little Arabeth seem quite content to sleep away the morning, then followed Jed. Soon Samuel, Martha and James were laid into the circle.

Gideon picked up the chest with Arabeth slumbering inside, handed it gently to the two Brothers. They nodded and left. They would not make this journey, but guard the babe. Gideon stood at the North Cardinal point, outside the chalk circle. He would guide them in the dream realm and open their eyes to the truth.

A silver chain was first looped around Jed's wrist, then Elizabeth until all were bound as one and so would travel as one. The beautiful female Mage then took a leather pouch and a charred bowl from her bag. She carefully opened the pouch and place dried leaves into the bowl. The bowl was placed on a beautiful ornate brazier, covered in the same Runes. It was then placed in the very centre of the circle. The other Mage fetched burning embers from the library fire and set them in the brazier. Soon pungent smoke rose from the bowl. Quickly the Mages sealed the circle with salt and place iron at the four cardinal points. The circle was sealed and iron bound. None could enter, none could leave.

'Do not fear, many tribes and ancient ancestors have partaken of this. It will open your mind and we will guide you to the Dream Realm and to all answers.' Spoke Gideon.

'What is this Devils brew?' Samuel stuttered.

'No Devils brew, it is a rare herb from lands far across a great ocean, Salvia Divinorum. The Diviners Sage.' Jed spoke to Samuel. 'It opens your mind, allows your soul to Travel, to See.'

'We will guide you, listen to our voices only.' The Mages commanded. 'Listen for our song and we will show you all you need to have knowledge of and we will bring you home. Never follow anyone but our voices, never.'

THE DIVINERS SAGE BEGAN ITS WORK

ALL PASSED FROM EARTH REALM

ALL WALKED THE DREAM REALM

The Dream Realm

The bitter smoke, choked and burnt his throat. Samuel wanted to wretch and rise from his bed.

Euphoria, a peace washed over and over as if he were laid on the shores with warm ocean waves covering his body again and again. Her song was so beautiful, 'Hear me, never loose me, hear me.' Such a siren, pulling him back, but he sank beneath the soft golden sand, deeper, darker, cooler. He felt safe, cocooned in the soft sand far away from all his troubles, from all pain. Peace!

His body began to rise, faster and faster. He could see all the heavens.

'Hear me, never loose me, hear me.' The song continued.

He felt his arms pulled and remember the silver chain. He turned his head left and saw floating beside him. Who? Yes, yes, Martha. Love! He turned his head right, a man, but who. His name so close to his mind. Friend! Slowly his prone form righted itself and he saw another woman, she smiled at him. He saw him. Fear, power. Son. He was glowing blue, his eyes glowed red, he was without clothes. He was a giant, perfect. Warrior. 'True form' entered his mind, Forevermore. Son

'Hear me, never loose me, hear me.' The song continued

He stood in a vast hall, white towers, strange silver balls moved, no floated in their millions. He saw them! Michael, Raphael, Samael and Kydan. Angels, he understood now, Watchers! Huge they towered above him. Glowing as his son, one and the same. Red eyes as his son, one and the same. Forevermore.

A great vast garden. A tree filled with golden fruit.

A red world. A woman, strange red skin – dragon. A man, towering strength, great horns, cloven feet – devil. No, no – The Mother and The Father of Realms.

Planting the golden fruit. A red world. Dragons, but with human minds.

Destruction, pollution, war – The Father angry at his children. Judgement. The Watchers called. Death comes. A red world, now empty of life. A dead world. A world of storms and dust. Judgement!

'Hear me, never loose me, hear me.' The Song continued

Gideon, blood running down his armour. His massive war horse the same. Kydan there with him. Dessert lands at war, Crusades. All for God. ALL FOR POWER! Two faiths, one God. A God made in our own image! Gideon, Templars. Hoping for peace.

Strange chariots. Buildings covered in glyphs that made no sense. Rameses, god and man. His son beside him. No, not his son, but also his son. James, Anhur, God of War, both one and the same. Thousands walking into the burning desert. He knew this. Exodus. Moses. Not one God, no God only man, only creation.

'Do you see Samuel? See that God is a creation of man. God is not of creation. Your worship is false. Your worship is control. You become servants of God, servant of those that call themselves priest.' Kydan's voice growled at him.

Fear, so much fear. Judgement. Lies!

'Hear me, never loose me, hear me.' The Song continued.

A man, pitiful. Broken. Bleeding. A cross. His mind refused to witness.

'See. Open your eyes. See.' Again, Kydan stood at the foot of the cross. His wings now gleaming metal, sharp. His eyes glowing red. His fangs. His claws. His anger washed over Samuel again and again. 'Murderers. Killers of a Forevermore. One who brought you light. Murderers. Destroy all of humankind. Do you see Samuel, do you see?'

Another Angel, no Watcher. So much hatred, so much anger at man. His pleas to destroy us all for the murder of his Brother. A Brother that only wished to bring peace and love to humans.

A woman. Dark hair, no, golden, no, red. Beautiful ever-changing hair. A river of colours, a river of silk. Her skin, no not skin. Leaves, grass, flowers covering her, alive. No, a skin of nature. Eyes so blue, then green, then amber. Swirling. Haunting. Beauty beyond all measure. Our Mother Earth. Filled with sorrow at the loss of the man on the cross. But she would not pass judgement.

Anger, boiling, raging – Lucifer. Darkness. Dark power. Father Earth taken, hidden.

A huge horned man. Horns rimmed his face. His hair made of leaves. His, no cannot be. Legs of the goat. Devil. No, no devil. Devil does not exist. Cernunnos. Father Earth.

Lucifer, surrounding him. Dragged to a dark place. Chained. Forever dark. Father Earth imprisoned. Vanished from light.

A great tree. Leaves withering each season. Dying. Earth dying

BALANCE WILL BE LOST.

Lucifer. The blade cutting the wings, blue blood. Dark magic. Filling him. 'I will have my judgement, Mother. I will rule these creatures in fear and darkness.'

GONE. THE DARKNESS, THE OBLIVION HIDES HIM FROM VIEW. FROM THE FOREVERMORE. FROM THE FATES.

The woman weeping, Mother Earth. Dying. Retreating.

Sarah to Rachael

Rachael to Mary

Down the ages – mother to daughter.

Two hearts beat as one.

Carrying Mother Earth's heart.

Angelique to Amy.

Amy to Arabeth.

His child, Kydan, a child born of Forevermore's.

Until the return of Farther Earth.

Protect our Mother Earth's heart.

Protect Arabeth.

Until, The Time of Judgement. The Time of End of Days.

'Hear me, never loose me, hear me.' The Song continued.

A land so strange, red people. A land across the vast ocean. Mi'kmaq. Tribe.

An old man and woman by a river. Samuel and Martha? He saw himself, so many years down their path. He was Mi'kmaq. Home. Life. They were happy.

'It is time, come home. Hear me. Come home, Samuel.'

He did not want to.

Euphoria, peace, stay

'Hear me, Samuel. Come home.'

Smoke burned, he choked and gasped. Soft hands held his shoulders.

'Be still. Let the Dream Realm leave you. Slowly. Breathe deep.' The soothing female voice reaching into his mind. The peace left. He smelt the fire, the books. He opened his eyes. The dark-haired female Mage was leant over him. She smiled. 'Welcome back. You are safe. But lie still. We must break the circle and release the Dream Realm.'

He rested his head and did as she requested. Closing his eyes again. Wishing for the feelings he had let go to return. Strange words were spoken.

'Rise now and kneel.' Said that beautiful voice of the siren.

As he rose and knelt his eyes focused on all those that had journeyed with him. All kept their peace. The silver chain removed and place back into a carved box. The other Mage began to sweep the salt away and then tossed it into the fire. The iron weights were put away. Then he said strange words over water and washed away the chalk circle. That he poured into the flames, dousing the flames, but the fire relit. Samuel assumed by their magics.

'We have closed the circle. We will bring food and drink and leave you this afternoon to talk together. We will see you at evening meal. Gideon will meet with you this evening. Blessed be.' And the young dark-haired female Mage left with the other Mage. Samuel knew all had witnessed what he had been shown was truth. Samuel knew truth. All knew truth.

The Cardinal and Amy

She could not comprehend those memories. It seemed another world. A world where he had found love. A world filled with wonderous red dragons. But not those of the tales of humans. These were dragons who minds were enlightened. An intelligence far beyond those of humans. Their world filled with great cities. Not the brutish, fire breathing monsters spoke of in ancient tales. Then. So much pain as he slaughtered her. His kindred spirit. His duty overwhelming his love. And the simmering hatred.

Gone, those memories vanished from his troubled sleeping mind.

It seemed that the good Cardinal dreamed each night. She wondered, as she lay in the warm attic as morning light came, did he even remember those memories, or did they vanish as the sun rose. She felt a strange unease come upon her. It seemed their book was restless. As if in a strange battle with forces unseen. But she must be careful. The Darkness watched over his home. The book must be working to circumvent The Darkness. Fighting its power. She would not disturb its battle. It knew well what spell she needed and the Earth magic she would need to fulfil it.

'Not Earth magic, your magic, child. Magic of the Forevermore.'

The revelation was fearsome. Forevermore magic. Her soul, her essence. That was the price to trap this man. To bind him was to bind her as well. Two souls, one of dark and one of light, forever bound.

'Bound in stone. Until the Days of Judgement.'

It was a fate of darkness and cold. So, the ancestors spoke and so it would be. She rose from her bed and dressed. Judith had been generous. She had supplied all manner of ladies-wear and new calf skin boots, along with soft house slippers. Also, a harsh soap and sweet smelling rose water, comb and brush and an assortment of ribbon for her hair. Soon her toilet was complete and she proceeded to the downstairs refectory. There the fire blazed and there was oatmeal, honey and a pot of seeds and crushed nuts. The Cardinal swore by this meal for breaking fast, refraining from meat and cheeses. She found this dish quite delightful. The warm, oatmeal was made with rich cream and adding the honey and seeds made for a wonderful rich filling meal. As she sat to enjoy her food the Cardinal marched into the room. His eyes darkly ringed, as if plagued by little sleep.

'Good morning.' Amy politely spoke.

'It is a fair morning, but I fear my humours are quite sour this morn. It seems a night of disturbed sleep has caused this.'

'Perhaps dreams plague you, sir?'

'And perhaps it is those that intrude upon them that cause much disturbance?'

He also placed a bowl of the honeyed-oatmeal on the table. So, it was to be a game of cat and mouse. She was to be toyed with. The creature would use paw and claw and toss her around, helpless as any poor mouse that had met fate with a cruel cat.

'Apologies, my sour mood, sours my very words this morning.'

'I would prefer that.... Well, my Lord. Perhaps as we know of our true natures that we forgo our polite interactions. For I am under no misunderstanding of what you are, Mage. And that you quite well know of my ilk too? For are we not both Mage and we may have the pretence of goodly Christians, but both here know that it is only pretence. Yours for power and gain and mine for survival.'

The refectory door moved but by a fraction but he knew of the ears that were keenly listening to all said by those two who took breakfast together that morning. The Cardinal smiled. Those ears he would enjoy toying with and then removing. Making eyes blind and stilling the heart that was now greedily taking all their conversation to their bosom.

'So, young Amy. You admit that you are not of The Faith. That you are witch by birth and by ancestry?'

'I do not deem to answer a question that you already know. As you knew of my mother, Angelique and all those before us. Those that are of your own kind, those that you have mercilessly hunted and murdered.'

'My own kind. As you say, my own ilk. But my kind, no. I am Mage, but I do not grovel before these humans. Weak and feeble as they are. I choose to rule.' He spoke loudly

Amy thought the conversation strange. It was like he was no longer addressing her but some other being. Judith! Her blood ran cold. Was she at the door, was she about her snooping? And was this priest, this cardinal about his dark business. If so, then Judith had now sealed her fate.

'I have some duties this morning but we will meet this afternoon and perhaps discuss our ilk as you say in more detail. Please enjoy my library in my study if you so wish. I will advise our good house-keeper that you may spend your morning there if you so wish. I am sure there are many volumes of our ilk and ancestry that you will enjoy.' And with that he loudly scrapped his chair and started out the room. Amy was quite sure it was intentional to warn the silly, snooping Judith to quickly remove her ears from the door. She sensed the anticipation of the Cardinal; he would enjoy his new found mouse and toy with it mercilessly. Judith had no possible inkling of the darkness that had set its sight on her. And she prayed that she would hold her gossip from sweet Sally, for if she did not, she would also set the fate of her too.

A while later the Cardinal set about his games.

'Judith.' Charles called down the corridor. 'Good mistress, I have message for you, most urgent I believe.'

Judith came trotting up the corridor from the kitchens, wiping her hands on a damp cloth and looking quite pale. 'My Lord, a message?'

'Yes, your sister has taken on the vapours and could you call as soon as possible?'

'Oh, poor Maria. She is such a frail woman.'

'Good Judith, please take heed and go to your sister....'

'My Lord, what of supper?'

'I am sure if you leave some of your pie, bread and cheese, I am most certain that our small household can survive. Please take your leave with Sally this evening and visit your sister. And be sure to take a basket of your finest fare to her too and take a bottle of the honey mead. I am sure it will help restore her health.' The Priest smiled warmly.

'My Lord, my many thanks. I will leave out supper for you and then will leave this evening with Sally. I will return for breakfast….'

'Have no worry, I am sure Sally is quite capable of preparing our oatmeal for the morning. So, return for midday meal.'

'May the Lord bless you; your kindness is most welcome.' Said Judith, blushing from neck to brow at her master's kind words and deeds.

The Cardinal retired to his private library and made plans for the evening.

'Did that old hag spend time gossiping with our sweet Sally after our breakfast?' He spoke in the Nubian tongue and his faithful warrior spoke of Judith and her delight at discussing all she had heard. Poor Sally had begged Judith to speak no more and that it was of no woman's business to speak of the business of the Cardinal.

'Both know of our business. Well, then it seems that those two little chattering birds must not have chance to clack their gossiping tongues around the town. What of the men that were sent after the blacksmith family?'

'Silence, still no sign of them and no sign on the road to York.'

'Strange, I think there may be powers about this land. Messages come from the shores of Whitby. Great ships have arrived there, bearing men which my clever little spy says are not merchants as they perceive themselves to be. He assures me they are men of war, hardened and fierce. It seems the pot stirs, but to what end. Do the blacksmith family travel with Jed and Elizabeth? Were they ever on the York Road? It seems a game of deceit is upon me.' The Cardinal spoke more to himself, deep in his own thoughts.

'My little spy travels back tonight, travel with him. Watch the ships and all those who are aboard them.' He spoke to one of his warriors. It would leave him only one at his side while those two who set on the York Road returned. If they were able to return!

'Master.' The Nubian stated and left to carry out his duty.

He began to make preparations for this evening. His chattering little birds will soon be silenced. He then quickly left for his meeting with the masons at the church. The building works forever needed attention now that the final finishing touches were at hand. It was a simple structure that would endure time and the crypt would seal the ancient caves below. He had made sure that the only access was now through St Mary's Croft. He smiled as he walked the short distance to the church. His thoughts turning to all those who would pray and worship here, never knowing of the true power that lay just below their bent knees. The fracture between this mortal realm and the realm of the dead. The ancients had protected them, for many were found throughout these lands of the Northern tribes, for they believed that the two realms should only travel one way. The living realm to the dead realm. He had other plans. He sensed Amy had ventured into his library and he smiled as the Master Mason droned on about some delay to the marble stone slabs, he had requested be laid for the altar.

'Good sir, I quite understand the delay. Your men will not be laid off, for a delay not of your doing. It is entirely at my expense that I wished to bring the Altar stones from Italy. I am sure there are other jobs to carry on with at your convenience. Why do we not retire to the inn and I can provide us with a fine midday repast and we can discuss what other works that can be done in the mean-time.'

'That would be most obliging, my Lord Cardinal.'

Charles thought it would be a long bore to be at the inn with the Master Mason, but at least his intriguing guest would have time to explore his private study. And time with her own Book of Shadows. It was the first one he had found that was alive in its own sense of being alive. Many of the ancients had written of these books, books that become a being. He thought them mere fantasy, but it seems not. He had witnessed how it had opened and gave the words for Amy to heal her wounded body. He had seen the pages open, but to his eyes all was but blank plain parchment. If he gained her trust then he was hopeful that their book would place trust in him. In all his many lives he had not seen such a powerful line of Mages. And still living in the light. Most of those ancient of Mages he had tracked down and despatch had become weary of humans, tired of being exploited and used by them. Ever wanting more and more. Some had even seen their demise at his hands as a blessing. Finding peace in death.

The oak door creaked loudly, and she started. 'Foolish woman, he gave permission to be in here.' She thought to herself. The room was warm, another fire blazed but her nostrils took in the smell of old parchment and inks. She wandered around the shelves that a skilled carpenter had fitted to every available wall space. Only the paned-glass window over-looking the church let in the mid-morning sun. His desk was covered in all manor of strange objects, but she noticed that they were all of a Christian nature. It seemed to be a show of his Faith for those who had to endure the harsh wooden chair that sat before his desk. His chair was plump and covered in a rich red velvet. She smiled. He certainly had a way of being goodly but also of making it very clear of his position in this town. Sally had made her laugh when she had spoken of the good men of Tickhill all limping from his study and rubbing their usually large backsides, hoping to gain some semblance of feeling back.

'Welcome, I see you are in fine health.'

She turned from his desk and there in a dark corner was their Book of Shadows. She heard its kind words in her mind and trotted over to the book.

'Good morning, good Sir. I see he treats you kindly.' She thought to the book.

'That he does, but it will gain him no favour. We know his soul. Be careful of the game you play.'

'I need time.'

'That you do, you must play this game until the eve of Mabon. Then your babe will be carried away. Jed sent message to me. They move soon to begin journey away from you and the Cardinal. But as you play, he will soon begin to sense her as you need to become close to him. As you seek out his mind so will he gain access to your mind. Call upon me and I will give you concealment spells again to protect your mind if you wish to speak of your child and family.'

'I do not understand what he seeks.'

'He does not seek child. He knows his path. But all is bound in darkness to us and to the Forevermore. I see only darkness. But the ancestors speak of Lucifer, the fallen one. It is our belief that this Priest, our Godly Cardinal is Lucifer's puppet. Lucifer swore an oath that he would rule over humans in suffering and pain for the death of his brother on the cross. He has The Father, and The Great Tree bound from our sight and this Priest now seeks out our Mother for him. For he sees himself standing at the side of Lucifer, ruling all humankind. A Pope of Darkness.'

'But why would Lucifer allow him to rule. Why not rule instead?'

'Lucifer only wishes revenge, and to see humankind suffer. He believed truly that The Mother should have destroyed them when they took the life of his true Brother. A Brother of the Forevermore who died in a mortal body passed to The Nevermore and lost. That child is how a Forevermore can be destroyed. Many have journeyed to realms to guide the creatures that have grown there and many have perished in those mortal forms.'

Amy thoughts tumbled as the book spoke to her mind and terror seized her. 'But are not we Mages of the mortal realm, do I now see deceit? Are my ancestors not in the Forevermore?'

'Hush, child. You were born into the mortal realm by The Fates. You did not leave the Forevermore realm to choose a mortal form. Those that choose this path risk all. You and all your ancestors were born into this realm to be guides, healers and teachers. The Fates chose your destiny.'

'My head spins.'

'Of course, it does. You had no mother or grand-mother to guide you. I can only offer the simplest of truths to you. Your fate is set. Bone to stone, child, bone to stone.'

'So be it, rest well and gather all the magic you can. For I know I will need all to do this.'

The great book fell to quiet. She left his study and went to his formal library. Taking seat by the fire. She allowed her thoughts to wander as she gazed at the flames. Slowly her eyes weighed heavy and closed. Her preternatural senses working. Soon dreams came of Runes and the Cast she would need formed in her mind. The book was pleased. It was easier for him to enter her mind when she dreamed and form the Runes she would need.

'Hold him at bay until the eve of Mabon.'

Mabon, the Finishing Time. A good time to hold this Priest. Mabon, thought the book, yes, the Finishing Time. A time of reflection, at time to finish all things ready for the long winter. A winter that would not end for his sweet Amy. To hold him she must travel with him.

He left the Master Mason in good spirits after a large jug of ale and a hearty midday meal at the inn. The townsfolk greeted him as he made his way back to the Manor. He had expected to find Amy in his private study, but found her in his public library, tucked into a large fireside chair engrossed in one of his many books.

'Judith has prepared an evening meal for us and will be leaving in the early evening with Sally to go to her sister.' Amy said as the Cardinal walked over to her and sat in the other fireside chair.

'Her sister has taken ill and I relieved her of duties this evening so she may visit.'

'Most kind, but her sister is quite well known for her bouts of vapours. And poor Judith has to scamper over to attend her feeble sister.'

'I am sure Judith enjoys her fussing over her sister.' He laughed. 'I trust you ventured into my most private domain?'

'You know very well I did. Your Wards would have warned you of entry.'

'And did you find anything of interest?'

'Oh, my Lord Cardinal.' Amy smiled at the beautiful man lounging before her. 'You have many treasures, but none that would interest me. I do not wish to know anything of the Dark Arts. And you can be assured I will not meddle in there again.'

'And your own book, what of that?'

'He made polite conversation.' She smiled sweetly at him. Such games he liked to play. 'He will never allow you to read from him. Surely you must know this. He well knows your dark heart, good Sir.'

'He, so you know the first writer of your pages was a male Mage. But do you know his name. I think he has not given you that has he?'

'To know his true name is to hold dominion over him. I would never ask that of him, his spirit is bound to our book. He is its protection. I am not worthy of his name and even he deemed I was I still would not ask it.'

The cardinal slipped into silence; she had won her first battle. He now knew she did not know the spirits name who first wrote on the pages of their Book of Shadows. Jed had always warned her of never asking for his name. 'To know it would mean you could betray his name to another Mage, more powerful than you. To know it would mean dominion over him, he could no longer refuse you anything that was contained in the book. In your bloodline there have been Mages that have known his name and the power corrupted them.' Jed's words took on new meaning to her. Without his name their bloodline would always have to ask him for the Wards or Spells they needed. He had the choice to refuse if he saw a dark heart behind the request.

He sat in silence, gazing into the flames. He sensed she had thought she had a small victory. He was certain she did not know the first Mage's name. He was growing fond of this innocent child. Yes, she was powerful. He believed that even she had little knowledge of the power that emanated from her. Even his Darkness retreated from her. Her power was different, it was not the power of an Earth Mage, it was something far more. As for the first Mage's name. It would take time, but he knew that their book was bound by a spirit and was just as alive as they were, but she forgets how old I truly am. I will find the name somewhere amongst the archive he had gathered over the centuries. Somewhere his name would be found. The Ancient Mages were revered, not feared and cast out. But other matters needed tending to.

'Well good Amy. I will take my leave. I have much to do this late afternoon.'

'If I may, I would like to take my evening meal to my room and read...'

'I see you are reading our good Geoffrey of Monmouth, The history of the kings of Britain. A most studious friar.'

'It is the tales of this King Arthur that intrigue...'

'Oh, yes, Arthur. He was most intriguing as you say. He was not a creature of this realm, that I can assure you. And for all his good deeds, Godly chivalry, it counted for little in the end. Darkness still grows, does it not?'

'That is does my Lord, as you know only true well. But do you ask me to believe that you once stood side by side with this King Arthur?'

'Oh, my child. It has been so long since I have played such games with one with such a bright mind as yours. These weeks will cause for chess board of great whit and intellect. What joy you bring me. And with that he rose, laughing and left her in peace, but turned just before he walked through the doorway. 'Of course, I knew Arthur. A vain man, but he ruled well. I was known then as Merlin and he was one who I could not corrupt. As I say he was not of this realm. But Geoffrey makes for a good tale to be told of him. And I might add does tell a good tale of Merlin. Such a goodly Mage he was.' And he roared with laughter all the way to his private study. Amy quickly gathered herself. She made her way to the kitchen and made a tray for her evening meal. She also took a bottle of the sweet wine from the refectory cupboard, thinking it would steady her frayed nerves.

Her attic room was warm as usual. Sally had stacked the small fireplace and left her a stock of wood for the rest of the evening. She sat in her chair by the tall window which had been cleverly built into the roof and ran all down to the floor giving a view over the garden. It was a spot she loved. The small opener at the top brought in the scent of the herbs and flowers and the late evening sun warmed the room. She took her shawl and made herself comfortable in the chair and opened her book. She was now perplexed. Was she to believe that the Cardinal was once the great Mage Merlin in the tales of Geoffrey? She decided that he was. It would serve no purpose to lie, and he seemed a man that had little to gain by claiming to be the Mage that Geoffrey wrote about. Whether he was 1000 years old or 20 it served little purpose for her to brood over. There were far more pressing matters to deal with.

Movement caught her eye and she saw the Cardinal and the Nubian warrior walking to the centre of the garden. Both carried small chests.

'Now what are you about now?' she said to no one but herself.

He knew she was watching as he walked into the heavy scented garden, which buzzed with all manor of insect life. The late evening sun was still warm and offered light to their task. He placed the beautifully carved chest at the foot of a stone pond. His warrior did the same. The two chests were carved with the ancient language of the Egyptian peoples. Those carved glyphs denying leave for what was contained within. Rough gemstones set into the lids glinted in the last of the sun light.

'She watches master.' The deep voice of his warrior was disconcerting in the beauty of the warm, flower-filled garden.

'Yes, but I think our innocent child must be awakened to the true power and nature of the foe she now plays with.'

The warrior smiled.

'Have our two chattering birds left?'

'Yes, they had just turned down the Church lane when we came into the garden.'

'Good then all is set. We begin. Once all is set we must venture to the inn. It will be in our best interest to be with the good townsfolk. And I believe I will quite enjoy the Innkeepers evening fare and the turmoil that will follow.'

Amy sat still, watching the two converse or conspire. Sally and Judith must have left for the evening as he would not be about this business under the nose of Judith. A nose that tended to poke in all manner of people's business. She would sit, for it was quite clear to her that he knew she was at her seat at the window and could quite clearly see what he was about to set in motion. 'Then so be it, I will see all that you wish to show.'

The stone pond was a perfect circle and four decorative pillars were set in place. She soon realised the pillars were at the cardinal points. 'Ah, so clever. Earth, Air, Fire, Water. I see the carvings clearly now my eyes have been drawn to their attention. A perfect casting circle and the four elementals of the Watchtowers set in plain sight.' Her admiration for the audacity of this man grew. Who would suspect that this walled garden was a place of magic, and set above an ancient Pagan place?

He then waded to the large flat stone that had been set in the centre of the shallow reflecting pond. She laughed at his cunning. 'His Pagan altar.' She shuffled further forward now completely absorbed in his business and how he had deceived the townsfolk once again. This Cardinal, this Priest, with his wealth that he was so generous with. His beauty and Godliness. Who would ever challenge this garden? Who would ever understand its relevance? It was of no wonder that Lucifer had sought this Mage out. Cunning beyond measure.

His warrior lifted one of the chest's and carefully passed it to his master. Which he set on the smooth, polished stone in the centre of the water. The second was placed by its side.

'I call The Watchtowers, Earth, Air, Fire, Water. Come. Set this circle and bind in iron and salt.'

The warrior walked slowly around the stone pond. Pouring salt until the circle was sealed. He took another bag and placed iron pieces around the outer edges of the salt.

'The circle is bound, Master.'

The Darkness crept into the garden, slithering over the gravel pathways and settling in a seething dark mass around the bound stone circle. It was hungry.

He began the ancient chant, a slow murmur of words unspoken by any tribe that now lived. A language of the Pharaoh's, lost to time.

The Darkness grew and soon the whole garden was lost in its swirling mass.

The chest lids flew open as his chanting grew.

First a claw, then a paw. Bone, yellowed with age and tattered flesh and fur clinging here and there. Another followed. Then glowing black diamond eyes rose from the depths. A yellowed, snout. Huge jaws filled with long sharp teeth. Two heads now lifted from the chests. Rotting skin and fur still clinging to the huge skulls. Then haunches and ribs and backbone rose. Soon the back legs rose. Two great skeletal beasts rose. The bones fusing back together. Fetid skin growing and then dark black fur. Those black-diamond eyes glared at him.

The Cardinal watched as the great beast's took back their forms. The Darkness feeding them, causing their resurrection. Once their purpose served, he would return their bones to the chests to sleep in darkness.

The Cardinal reached out both his hands and rested them on the beast's heads. A touch so gentle, filled with kindness. He had love for these dead, foul beasts and they loved him.

He gave command.

They let out a great snarl. Then they leapt around him and bounded over the garden walls. A great feast awaited them. And they were hungry.

'Come my friend, let us go to the warmth and comfort of the Inn. I am sure they will be most pleased to see the good Cardinal taking repast.'

'Yes master. And all will see that the good Cardinal rests there that evening, so good alibi will be made.'

'My friend, of course. I will be in plain sight when all transpires. And I will, of course, be on hand to offer guidance when those beasts of Anubis have completed their work.'

With that the two conspirators left the garden. He gave a glance to her window. The darkness crept after him. The garden returned to its peaceful beauty. She remained still in her seat. Her blood ice, her mind filled with the horror of the beasts he had resurrected. She knew who those beasts would be hunting.

Death comes by tooth and claw

'My poor feet do ache. I spend so much time at the Manor that I always forget the hardship to my feet on this walk to my sister.' Said Judith, panting along the rough lane, carrying a large wicker basket filled with all manner of food and wine for her ailing sibling.

'Aye, your sister should be truly grateful for all your efforts to bring comfort to her. And that our kindly employer allows for such fare to be taken in kindness to her table.'

'Kindness indeed. We work our hands to the bone and a few meagre vitals from his cupboard to aid a weak and feeble sister, child it is his Christian duty, surely, to care for those who care for him so well.' Judith said indignantly.

Sally thought that she was being most unkind. She had seen her stuff her basket to bursting with the finest vitals from the store cupboard. And she had spent most of the morning making fine sweet cakes as well. The good cardinal never questioned Judith and her house-keeping. Sally knew too well, of her secret chest filled with the small coins that the suppliers donated to her for her loyalty and the securement of regular orders to the Manor. She had once seen Judith take a few pennies and then place them in this chest, unbeknown to Judith who had not seen Sally by the doorway. Sally decided to never mention this to anyone. Her job was easy and vital to her family. She kept her peace and her silence.

They heard the rumbling of a cart coming up behind them and stepped to the edge of the lane to allow it to pass by. The two ginger cart horses lumbered by and Sally soon saw that it was simple Edward driving the great beasts along. Edward may be of a simple mind, but his gift with all creatures was well known. He worked with Eric at the farm. Eric could only give the poor lad simple instructions, but Edward would see all tasks done, with no complaint. Eric said he had a kindred spirit to those simple farm creatures and left in his care the animals thrived.

'Good evening mistress Judith and miss Sally.' Edward said most formerly and removed his grubby cloth hat. Eric always made sure Edward was taught to be polite to all. His simple mind soon became filled with exuberance and could say the most inapt words.

'Good evening, Edward.' Said Sally, Judith remained silent and had the look that most carried when seeing Edward, contempt for the simpleton.

'Would thou like a ride, going right up lane. Going to take this grain to the mill.'

'I am fine Edward, I have only to go by the pond and then I am soon home. Judith would you like to ride with Edward? If he is going to the mill then he will pass by your sisters. It would save your poor feet.' Sally tried not to smile; she knew Judith would love to take up the offer but it would also irk her to have to ride with such a simpleton as Edward. She would get no good gossip from Edward.

'I think I would. My poor feet ache already. Thank you, Edward. It is most kind to stop and give kind offer.'

'Your company will be welcome, mistress.' Edward answered most politely and jumped from the cart. He clumsily helped Judith onto the cart's rough bench seat, but he grabbed a large, moth-eaten blanket and quickly formed a cushion for her. Sally thought Edward a kindly man, but he would always be a boy in his mind. He lived in the barn where her Eric laboured and was quite content, perhaps more so, dwelling with the farm beasts than any human. Eric had said how it was good for all. Edward has a warm, safe place and the farm had his protection for the animals. For Sally knew Edward would protect those creatures with his life. She watched as the two great horses plodded away towards the mill. She was glad to be on her own. The late evening was pleasant and she would enjoy the peace while walking home.

Two pairs of black diamond eyes watched the small gathering. Their prey so near. Thick drool darkened the earth as the beasts watched as the large woman climbed into the cart. Their attention turned to the young female. A mere scrap of a human. But enough flesh to satisfy their hunger. They crept in the lane's undergrowth. Paw by paw. Silent, the lush green hedgerow hiding them from view. If Sally had been a Mage, she would have sensed how the birds had become silent. How the very air seemed unmoving. But this young female was no Mage.

Her blood smelled so sweet and her heart beat strong. Her flesh would be tender and sweet. Paw by paw they crept. Silent. Death was coming to this young maiden. And her dreams would vanish in an instant of pain and terror.

Death was here in this small town on this beautiful summer's evening. It cared little of the suffering, the pain it would inflict.

She thought of her wedding day. On Sunday she would be wed to her beloved Eric. Her simple white linen dress was hung and waiting. Her grand-mother had made the lace collar, cuffs and simple veil. Her mother would make a garland of flowers that would sit upon her head. Amy had given her a pair of beautiful white slippers from the wardrobe that Judith have provided for her. They would be perfect for her day. After her wedding all the townsfolk would gather at her family's homestead. Her father would roast a great hog and the Cardinal had kindly offered many fine vitals for her guests.

The scream was never heard for it never formed in her throat. Her eyes saw the great black beast as it ripped her arm from the elbow from her body. Her eyes never saw the other beast that ripped her calf apart.

She saw the earth become red.

She saw black eyes, black fur.

She felt razor sharp teeth and huge yellowed claws tearing away her flesh. Her eyes beheld the huge black beast ripping open her belly and saw its huge jaws pulling her intestines from her wide-open stomach.

Blood, red thick blood, everywhere.

Her eyes saw all, but her mind could not reconcile that it was her blood, her limbs, her body that was being devoured by two black beasts from Hell's Pit.

Her last simple thought was the life she would never have.

The arm tore easily away. Her flesh was so tender, so sweet. The taste uncorrupted by time. Soon his prey was down. The sweet bloods flowing into the rich earth. He would forgo that blood. The earth could have its taste too. As his claws ripped open her soft belly flesh, he could smell the divine offal that they both loved. He and his brother tore with claw and fang, ripping the sweet liver, kidneys and intestines from the huge gaping wound. So sweet. Life. So long had they been bound and apart, soon they would return to their prison. But now, they could feast. The sweet hunger, sated by blood and flesh.

They cleaned their paws, licking every last flavoursome morsel of flesh. They would not feast on the rest. Their master had, forbade them all of her flesh and bone.

They heard another human coming along the lane.

They ran, as fast as the wind. Leaping over the wall and lying down before the pond. Sated. Content. Waiting.

Amy was still in her seat when the garden darkened. She thought the light was fading, but soon saw the creeping darkness once again move around the peaceful garden. They were back. Those huge dark creatures were now seated before the pond. Unmoving. They seemed like statues. She rose from her chair.

'Take heed, child.' The book spoke to her. 'These are the purest darkness you will ever encounter.'

She put on her boots and tied the shawl round her shoulders. She quietly padded down the stairs and into the kitchen. Her heart pounding in her ears she opened the door. It creaked loudly. The creatures did not move. The Darkness crawled around her feet. Then retreated. Her skin began to glow, a blue tinge, then brighter. Runes appeared on her arms.

'Feel the Forevermore, child.' The book spoke again. 'It comes to your aid. Your power rises, child of light.'

She stepped through the doorway. The darkness retreated, moving as if in fear of her. Her boots crunched on the gravel. The creatures did not move.

'Help us.'

'What have we done.'

'Help us. Free us. Forgive us.'

The creatures did not move.

As she walked slowly to those huge black beasts, she felt more power surge into her. Then, suddenly, she felt the souls. Two, trapped within those creatures. Their lifeforce feeding the beasts.

'See, child.' The book reached her mind. 'See why he traps the dead. They travel not to the Nevermore. He binds them in our sacred place.'

Her mind began the journey into the realm of The Darkness. 'He binds their spirit, their soul to the Earth Realm.' Full comprehension of this filled her.

She walked slowly to the beasts. Their fur was black as tar, and rippled in the evening breeze. They smelt of a rich dark musk, but also that fetid smell of death. 'Not alive, but not dead.' She spoke to the two enormous creatures.

They stood and turned to face her. Then slowly, paw by paw, moved towards her. *'Help us. Free us. Forgive us.'*

She stretched out her hands and lowered them to below the creature's muzzles. Their black eyes shone, but they barred no teeth. Slowly inch by inch they crept to her waiting hands. She felt the noses gently laid onto her palms. Her body glowed blue and the runes etched into her arms shone as bright as the full moon. She closed her eyes.

In a tongue she had never spoken, she gave release to the two souls trapped in these reanimated beasts. 'Blessed Fates, free these souls. Blessed souls travel now to your rest. All is forgiven. Rest now.' The garden stilled. The Darkness retreated. She felt two souls rip free from the beasts. In her minds-eye they became beautiful suns, bright and golden. She felt their peace as they passed through her own soul.

'Bless you, child of light.'

Then they were gone. When she opened her eyes, the garden was at peace again. The Darkness gone. As she looked down the great black beasts were now merely yellowed bones again. Some rotting flesh and fur still hung in places.

She knelt. She wept. Sally!

For as she released those two souls, she saw all they had done by his command. All the blood and flesh they had rendered to deaths embrace. Slowly she released the power of the light. Rising weakly and drained she made her way to her room. Her resolved stronger than ever. He must be stopped.

James

'You see now that there is truth and lies?' Jed spoke across to the other three figures seated now at the other side of the hearth. 'That there are always those that will corrupt great words and deeds to gain power and control. I do not ask you to believe in what you have seen, but I ask you to look into your heart. And by the time we reach York if you cannot find truth in our beliefs then stay with your brother. Live a good and full life. And let us leave, let us go and part as friends.'

Samuel was still reeling, and feeling light-headed from the smoke. Martha, sat motionless, tears fell freely. James sat ridged and smiled at him. James broke their family's silence. 'Aye, we all saw. It seems our simple minds have been cleverly used. We all seek answers to our lives. The Church has certainly given us one and bound us in fear....'

'And grown rich.' Growled Samuel, everyone could see his rising anger. 'Such deceit, such lies.'

'No, good friend. Not all lies. You see truth in Genesis. The Great Tree, the First Garden....'

'And our Lord Jesus?' he spat at Jed.

'A Forevermore who chose mortal life. His words were truth. He sought to help us find a better way. He sought to guide us back to The Balance. But those in power knew that he would lead them away from the God of Man. He would lead them to a simple life, and that any mortal could pray to the heavens....'

'And so, he was murdered. Just as I have condemned all your kind. Sent them to the flames....' Samuel placed his head in his hands and allowed tears to fall.

'You believed that this church was truth. How could you know that they had taken a Forevermore's words and corrupted them into a power beyond imagination? All mortals seek meaning. Once Mages gave some meaning, but there were also those that used their gifts to gain power and control. All mortals carry the weight of this truth. We have our own freewill, we choose Darkness or Light. Sometimes our pain and suffering causes change and we Fall, choosing Darkness. Finding balance in life is difficult, for life can be cruel, can tear our hearts to shreds. Life can make us bitter and curse our Gods, curse the heavens. It is not all so clear, not Darkness and Light, but Grey. Our lives are a fog of choices, of circumstance and most of all mystery.' Explained Gideon.

'And how do we stop the cruelty, the pain and suffering?' Pleaded Samuel.

'We cannot, as you saw our Father of Realms has been bound. The Great Tree of Life has been bound. Our Mother of Realms has retreated to a mere heart, beating in Arabeth. All we can do is protect this line of mother's and daughter's down through time. We will travel with the Brotherhood to the Mi'kmak tribe and far away from these Falling lands....'

'What if these new lands Fall, what if this Church follows?'

'The Fates decide. At this moment, this time of my existence, I can only take this child and hope...' Gideon said, see the confusion in Samuel.

'Hope, what good is that. I saw Lucifer. I saw his plan for all of us. Fear, control.'

'Lucifer is only one Forevermore. His anger, his hate is our anger our hate. He feeds off our Darkness, our need for power, our greed. Our good Cardinal is his puppet. One of many he toys with. Our Kings, Lords. All those that feed off our fear. That make us kneel to them. Our good King Edward, he has divine right given by God to rule as he sees fit. Ask this, have your eyes or ears ever beheld this God of Man, who grants divine power to our kings, our Popes? To say we must have Faith, to bow to this one book or fear that our souls will be sent to torment and purgatory. Fear, power and greed my friend. That is the gift of Faith, of the God of Man.' Jed Said.

'The blasphemy you now speak, Jed.' Martha said.

'Blasphemy....'

'No, Jed, please. You and Gideon have spoken. Please allow me to speak....'

'Forgive me, of course Martha.'

'I saw all that you saw. I saw the First Garden and that power. The Forevermore you call it. Could that not be God? Not the God that we now suffer unto but God of Creations?'

'Yes, that power could be our First Creator.'

'Mmm.' Martha pondered, then said. 'As I see. Our Church, our Faith may be false, but also truth. A few truths, tales of truth but tenants that have been forced upon us. To control us. To make us fear of our immortal deaths. But there is this, Light. If offers not guidance, it only creates and leaves us to The Fates whims. But in all that is that not God?'

'Aye, the Mother and Father are sent to seed a realm and guide us in Balance, in kindness and light.'

'But it is those creations, us, it is our own choice. Truth, kindness and love. Hate, anger, greed and power. All our choice?'

'Aye, I believe so.' Jed spoke softly to Martha, marvelling at her keen perceptive mind. How had man come to this, to allow the female to be so crushed when they offer a wealth of knowledge, insight and nurture? Once female and male were equal both offering light to this realm.

'Then we have chosen very badly. I will take the road you lay before me. And will hope to find a better way with these people you call Mi'kmak. I choose this road and I choose to learn. Teach us.'

'Our Mages, our Brotherhood will pass all knowledge to you, Martha.' Spoke Jed, who looked at Martha with renewed vision.

'Is this what you truly wish Martha?' Asked Samuel. 'I know we had agreed with our son's wishes, but is this truly your wish?'

'Aye, husband. You have seen the lies. You have played your part in the treachery of our Faith. Did not you speak, in the quiet of the night, of poor Mistress Smythe. How all your instincts led you to feel deep in your heart that it was Thomas who coveted her lands and cottage, that led to him to stoke the fires of lies of her being witch.'

'Aye lass, that I did.'

'Then let us leave this place. Let us forge new life in a place of new beliefs.'

'Father, it seems my mother has become a great Sage.'

All started to laugh and all in that small warm library made pact on that day. They would travel with the Brotherhood. They would become minds open to a new life.

'Now can we rest our minds. By Jesu I am starved. My stomach fair aches and growls like those great bears in the pits.' Said Samuel, his stomach adding chorus to his words.

'It is the Salvae. The herb creates fierce hunger after visiting the Dream Realms.' Said Elizabeth, who had remained deep in thought. 'I must retrieve out babe and find her milk. I am surprised her belly has not joined in the chorus from Samuel's belly!'

'I'll come with you. I wish to find Gideon.' Said James who stood and held his large hand out to Elizabeth.

'You not hungry lad? You are usually first at any table.' Asked Samuel, surprised that his son had not already made great haste to the food laid out on the far table. It seemed Gideon knew that they would be ravenous after their journey and prepared for it well.

'Nay Pa.' Said James. 'I need to speak with Gideon, but Ma, would you leave a plate for me?'

'Aye lad, go on. I'll make sure your Pa does not polish off every morsel on the table.' Martha said. She carefully watched Samuel. She saw turmoil in him. Her mind railed at all she had seen. Her Faith was now so much confusion but she knew they must run from the Cardinal. He had sent his soldiers to destroy them. Her Faith, well that could wait. She knew now that survival for her family was paramount, but Samuel? She knew his Faith would not be so easily put to one side. He was angry at his Cardinal sending his soldiers to kill them, but the Church, his Faith had always been steadfast. She thought that for all the visions, and the questions that they had brought, his Faith burned still. She could only hope that he would keep the pact made today.

Gideon was in the stables. Paying a visit to Hector, who was becoming unsettled at being stabled for so long. He set to work with brush and soon his beautiful war horse's coat shone. He oiled his great hooves. Pulled his mane and tail, removing tangles.

'Commander?' Asked James

'Aye lad, come on in. Now does not my beast look fine?' Gideon said and saw Hector lift his huge neck and prick his ears forward. 'He is a very vain creature is my Hector.' The huge horse snorted at him. James laughed at the pair, they seemed more brothers than man and horse.

James ran a hand over the smooth flank. 'He is truly a marvel.'

'Don't praise the bugger too much. He'll be prancing about like old Edward himself. Mind you this bugger here much prefers to be prancing in front of a fine filly. Think our great King would prefer to prance for those young lads, those fine French pansies that he adorns his court with. And I would think my fine horse here has more brains than that useless creature.'

James blushed and burst out laughing. There were many a joke in the Inn about their King's appetites, though none actually mentioned their King by name.

'Now my lad. Come.' And Gideon led him to the last stable. There stood a huge grey stallion. 'This is Laoch, it means Warrior in the old tongue of Ireland. He is my gift to you. He is young so you both can earn your place among the Brotherhood together. Watch him though, he has the temperament of the Irish blood himself.'

'Mine, but....'

'Listen well. Within this month you will train and travel the Labyrinth. Do not question, accept all that is given and give your very soul to this month. You may well be born of the Forevermore but the power you wield must be controlled. Kydan is watching over you. Do you understand?'

'Aye....'

'Aye, Lord Commander.'

'Aye, Lord Commander.'

'Very well, you have this afternoon and evening to eat and rest. Be in the refectory by dawns first light and make sure you are ready, bathed and have broken fast. Your days are now ours, and if you walk the Labyrinth, all the days of your future are ours too. Mark my words well, for once you have walked this path none can return to the mortal world. You are Brotherhood, being mortal or born of Forevermore matters not, you are Brotherhood.'

'My path is set, my Lord Commander. I have made my choice.'

'And I think you travelled a different path in the Dream Realm?'

'Aye, I saw a different road after our journey. One set for all...'

'Say no more, for that was a pathway shown by The Fates and for your dreams only.'

'Aye, my Lord Commander.'

'Right, young Laoch here needs a good grooming, and a good feed. You will find his saddle and all else in the next room. They need to be cleaned; you will find tallow as well. Laoch is to be treasured. He is a noble animal and will serve you well, but you will serve him well too.'

With that Gideon left James to his chores. The way the lad looked at Laoch, he knew he would care for him well. And the fact that Laoch had not lifted his hind quarters and booted James out of his stable, well that was a good sign too. Most of the stable-hands had left

Laoch's stable with a swift kick from him. Laoch was not a creature to entertain humans easily, but it seemed a Forevermore was more to his high-born tastes.

As he left, he patted Laoch's fine grey rump. The horse snorted and stamped his hooves. He walked away quickly; his standing of Lord Commander would not stop the great Irish stallion from landing two hooves on his arse.

The evening was drawing near. He saw the Mages standing, muttering and staring towards the town.

'What plagues thee?' Asked Gideon marching to the gathering.

'There is a shift. The Darkness rises.' Said the Elder.

'And?'

'Death will come this evening; it will bring turmoil to the town.'

'Can we intervene?'

'It would not be wise. It would bring our gathering to the notice of the Dark Mage that calls to this Darkness.'

'We must gather no attention. I have but one month to ensure all are ready to make the journey. Keep your presence here secret, at all costs. Do not make any move against him. This Cardinal must not know of our intentions.'

'Yes, my Lord Commander. We have only cast our Wards to hide our presence. All know of the peril of the man. No magic will be used. Our light will be hidden from his eyes.'

'Good. Stay within the Abbey. We do not know what prying eyes watch upon us.'

The Mages hastened into the safety of the Abbey. His thoughts strayed to Mabon. 'Will we be there in time?' he thought. More so would they survive and all reach Lachlan before the black eyes of the Cardinal found them. He prayed that Amy, be Forevermore or not, would be able to hold his attention and give them a good chance to travel the long roads ahead of them.

The Cardinal and Amy

The boy stood in the doorway of the Inn. His amber eyes wide and staring. His hands held in front of him. He said nothing. He screamed! The inn fell silent in an instant and all turned to the piercing scream. Ann, the inn-keepers wife rushed over to the young lad, Timothy. She stopped and stared. His hands dripped thick black blood onto the stone slabs that formed the floor of the inn. His shirt and breaches were smeared in blood. His eyes focused on hers.

'Timothy, by all in heavens.' She whispered, staring at the apparition in front of her. The rest of the inn's guests rushed over, tipping over stools and spilling their ale as beakers were cast down on the stained wooden benches. All stood and stared at the young lad.

Another voice, soft and gentle spoke. 'Timothy, that be thy name lad?' The Cardinal moved between the gathered crowd. All moved aside to allow him forward. 'Timothy, look at me.' The young lad's eyes moved to the sky-blue eyes of the Cardinal. 'Timothy, take long breath. Still you mind.' The Cardinal waited. 'Now young sir, please summon all courage. You are safe and protected here. Tell me why you are covered in what seems to mine eyes to be blood'

'Sss.hhh.ee.' He stammered, now shivering.

'She, who is she?' The cardinal spoke in the kindest of voice.

'The girl, the....' Timothy turned and sought out Eric. He had known he would be in the inn this evening, along with all the other young lads of the town. They were here to drink much ale. For poor Eric days as singleton would soon be over and he would be bound to be home in the evening with his new wife. The young lads would pour ale down his throat and carry him home this evening. It would be all done in jest, as all the young lads knew Eric had found a good wife. And his dowry of cottage and silver were a great boon to start his new life as husband and hopefully father. 'Sally, it be Sally. By the pond. Demons, I swear, demons got her....' He collapsed. He would say no more that night.

Eric paled and staggered. His young friends grabbed him and sat him on a stool. But the bridegroom launched himself up and ran, pushing all aside.

'Mistress Ann, kindly tend to Timothy. All of you, get torch and follow him. If the young lad speaks truth then Demons plague this town again!' The Cardinal boomed. Men rushed and gathered torches from the inn. The inn-keeper grabbed a huge meat cleaver and yelled at his fierce-some wife to bolt door and window. The townsmen rushed from the inn, piling into the narrow streets of the town. Soon householders came out of their homes, soon joining the melee. Men armed themselves with any weapon to hand. All headed to the pond which lay beside the castle. The women bolted door and window and herded their children and babes to the fireside to cower in fear.

The Darkness crept slyly around those filled with anger and terror. It fed those fears, and would fuel the anger once all was seen at the pond.

The Cardinal followed, his warrior by his side. Great yells of 'Demon' and 'Murder' sounded through the town. Suddenly the church bells rang. 'I must assume my good pastor has been roused from his bed!'

'It would seem so, master.'

'It would have been in joy they would have next tolled as young Sally walked up the aisle, but it now rings out the horror and sorrow that is to befall this town.'

'It concerns you?'

'Of course not. She was a pretty and innocent maid. A lamb. A lamb, as all lambs are. For slaughter and for sacrifice. Look at them, baying for blood. You can feel the hate and, more so, the fear. I shall have much amusement from this. Small-minded creatures.' The Cardinal laughed and they continued the march with the maddening crowd of men to the pond.

It was a howl of pain, of horror and of a heart broken into a thousand shards. Those shards tearing through his body, ripping him apart. His knees buckled and he dropped into the thick muddied blood that had pooled around his beautiful bride. The crowd stopped, silent and still. For who could comprehend all that their eyes beheld.

The pale white arm, ragged and torn, lying on the bank of the pond.

Pieces of flesh, now blackening, torn from limbs, scattered around the lifeless corpse.

Her eyes staring.

The stomach ripped apart, a ragged gash and the cavity empty of her organs.

Her long hair a halo around that pretty face, matted with her own blood.

All stared. Some turning away. Some retching.

Eric tried to lift her. The Cardinal, paying no heed to his fine cassock dragging in the blood and gore placed a soft hand on his shoulder. 'Eric, please. The Sherriff and Magistrate are being roused from their beds. They must see her.' Eric tried to fight him off, but the Cardinal held fast. 'Blessed son, please. This must be witnessed. Please. Eric's friends bent and lifted him away from his broken and torn bride. The Cardinal began final rites to the lifeless girl. The crowd bowed their heads in prayer.

Eric howled. The agony overwhelming him.

'Good men, take him to the house across the way. Ask the good mistress there to take him in. We cannot ask more of him. The Sherriff and Magistrate must be allowed to carry out their duty this night.' As the Cardinal spoke the gathered men nodded. All could see that Eric's mind was gone this night. It would be best Eric not witness all that had to be seen and done this night. Soon his friends had dragged the distraught man to the mill pond house. The mistress soon pulling the poor lad into her home and would care for him through the long hours of this night.

The Cardinal pulled his red cape from his shoulders and laid it over the poor girl. His creatures had inflicted much bloody destruction on this girl. It was now time to point the horror of this act to the good Mistress Judith. The Sherriff and Magistrate duly arrived and could utter no words at the sight of poor Sally.

'Sherriff, this is not the work of a man. Those bite marks and claw marks. All her innards are missing. It would seem....' The cardinal said.

'Witch, this desecration is the work of a witch.' The Sherriff interrupted. 'Have we not seen their kind in our good town. Was not the Widow Smythe, burned in our very square? Well it seems there is a Coven in our good town. And I vow that this poor, innocent maiden's death will be avenged. Search every home, we will drag these evil women from their Devil's bed.'

The menfolk roared and split into small groups. Conviction of their Godly intent put raging fires in their bellies. And with torches and weapons in hand they set off to every home in the town. They would this night find those brides of Satan. And they would burn.

'It seems that our good townsfolk needed little to stir up their cauldron of hate.' The Cardinal chuckled. 'They will soon reach the good home of Judith and her sister, who have no doubt enjoyed a fine meal and fine wine and will have gossiped the evening of tittle-tattle of mine and Amy's true nature.'

'And those items I secreted in her sister's home?' The Warrior spoke.

'Oh, my good friend. They will be easily found and both will be condemned by them.'

'Will the large women, with large ears deny all that is found, will she not point finger towards you and Amy?'

'Well, my good friend. Firstly, none will find my charge, for who knows that she is in my keep. Only a loyal soldier, now missing and that feeble-minded driver? He now lies in his grave. His heart gave out, with a little help from our good friend Foxglove. Secondly, who would believe two witches, caught with all tools of their trade, that me, the Godly, generous and benevolent Cardinal was in league with the Devil. Especially when I hand over her cache of coin and my own accounts, which will show how the good mistress has been overstating cost of my household to her own benefit and pocket.'

'It would seem that my master has mastered the true art of the sly fox.' And the warrior laughed.

The Sherriff and magistrate watched as the good Cardinal gave instruction to a small group of townsmen. They were instructed to bring a good long board that the poor child could be laid upon. The Cardinal then laid his red cape on the board. All watched in awe as the Cardinal lifted young Sally onto the board with such gentle kindness and carefully wrapped his cape around her. Again, he said prayers over her and placed his very own Rosery in her pale hand. Then instructed the men to carry her carefully to her family home. He followed.

The town soon heard of his great care of the murdered girl and how he had stayed vigil with her family. Until sun rose, he said prayers and stood as protector of her soul, so no Demon would claim her soul as his own.

Earlier that same evening.

Edward pulled up the great horses and leapt from the cart. He aided Judith from the cart as gently as his great strength would. Judith felt her being lifted by two great calloused hands and was most surprised how young Edward set her gently on the ground.

'Thank you, Edward, it was most kind of you to stop and bring me to my sister's home. I could have walked from the road, but I am grateful.' Judith smiled at the awkward young man. She had been surprised by his conversation. He spoke of the animals he treasured and how he was so excited that he had been invited to Eric and Sally's wedding and the feast afterwards. For all of his simple ways and slow mind, he was kindly and only saw good and kindness in all those people that he lived and worked with, especially Eric and Sally, who it seemed to care for him as a son. 'Here my boy, you take this for your trouble.' And she handed him a large meat pie, one of her fine honey cakes and a bottle of her finest apple cider.

'Good mistress, thank thee. I will be able to tell Eric that I have had the finest of food in the whole world.' Edward's voice filled with joy. 'Everyone talks of your vitals, mistress Judith. And I can now boast that I have tasted them.' With one glorious smile at her he took the food and jumped back onto the cart. 'I will save this feast until I get home and can sit by my brazier and stuff myself silly.'

'Go on, with your flattery. You are a good lad Edward. Go on now.' Judith laughed. Of all the praise she received it was this one simple young lads praise that had made her heart glad. She knew that he would sit in his warm, cosy loft in the barn this evening and would relish every morsel. She thought, as she walked up the path to her sister's humble cottage that she would make a little extra each week and send it to this man with a child's mind.

Later that evening.

'My, that has fair made my vapours better. You certainly have a gift with your cooking.' Maria sat back in her small cot by the fire. Her sister seemed less frail, her frame matching that of her own stout frame. Maria had become hip-heavy in her middle years and her long braided her fair glowed with health. Judith often had pangs of annoyance at her sister being so feeble, especially on evenings as this when it seemed her sister fair glowed in health, and then guilt washed over her. From birth she had laboured for her very breath, pulling in huge lung-fulls of air. Their mother had pummelled her back, hoping that her daughter would finally be able to breathe. Judith had soon learnt to accept that little attention came towards her with her sister ill most of the time. It also became clear to her and her Father that little Maria would use her illness to her advantage. Their father had soon found a place for Judith in service at the manor and told her to learn and find a life away from their home.

'Our Maria will be the death of your mother, for that child has my wife at her beck and call. Nowt I say can change that Judith, so get thee to the Manor and learn a good trade.' Her father had said as he dropped her off at St. Marys Croft when she was but ten years of age. She had never regretted her father's decision to put her into service. Her mother drove herself to an early grave just as her father had said. Little Maria soon learned that her father would take no tolerance of her tantrums and ailments. Maria had yelled that he must fetch back Judith to care for her. Their father paid no heed. He made quite clear that if Maria wished to eat, then she must cook. Her father had told her that if she wished for clean home and clean clothes then she must clean herself. Her father earned well as a Notary, but had no time for a child, who had ailments, but used them to her advantage. Maria's bouts of vapours became less frequent and she soon became mistress of their cottage. It was then that Judith realised that Maria was a spoilt child that her mother had pandered to. She could not blame Maria, but she held great resentment for her mother, who had had no qualms in disposing of her first daughter to service and cared little for their father. She had persuaded her father in his last years to leave the cottage to her, but allowing Maria to live out her life there. All his savings and other wealth was placed in trust with Judith who was bound by oath to provide a stipend for Maria so she could live comfortably. She had kept her word. When she retired from service, her dear father had insured that she would have a home to retire to. It was with that, that she had worked at the Manor and gained a fine reputation and a fine chest of coin for her own retirement. She would care for Maria but she would not become doting mother. Maria had proved in the past years she was able to care for her home and provide herself with meals. Judith had paid for a gardener to keep their homestead in good condition and grow a fine vegetable garden.

The loud banging at their front door woke Judith from her reverie.

'Open up mistress Maria, the Sherriff wishes to speak with you.'

'What in all of the heavens, Judith.'

'Be still, I will deal with this matter.' And she rose and walked to the door, pulling it open. 'What is this disturbance. My sister fairs not well this evening.'

The group of five townsmen barged into their cottage, the Sherriff followed.

'There has been dire murder in our town this evening. And a murder not by a man's hand. There are witches behind this horror.' The Sherriff boomed at the two women. 'We search all homes this night, for those vile creatures will be found....'

'And you think we are of that kind. You all know me and of my poor sister. Witches, perhaps you should seek one closer to the Manor.' Judith spat and then sealed her lips; she had spoken in anger and had pointed a finger at the Cardinal.

'Search the house, every corner and the garden too.'

The townsmen began to pull apart their cottage, finding a chest with fine silver and expensive linens. But the townsmen all knew that Maria and Judith were of good means. It was the next chest that caught all attention.

'That, that is not ours. I have never seen that before. Maria?'

Maria was labouring for her breath; and stuttered. 'No, that. I have never laid eyes on that.'

The chest was dragged to the table and forced open.

'Witches!' Yelled one of the townsmen. For the chest carried all things that witches need for their vile trade. Cauldron, black bible, a carved likeness of Baphomet himself with his horned head and goat's legs. Clay pots filled with strange and pungent powders. And laid at the bottom, a small besom broom and a black hooded robe.

'Take them. I think we have found our murderers.' The Sherriff gloated at finding these two creatures so quickly.

Maria and Judith were dragged by their hair, screaming in terror, to the jail. There was no need of trial, the chest condemned them. For does not evidence condemn? What was found in their possession that evening was enough? Even the good and Godly Cardinal had no need to produce Judith's hidden pension.

Amy, on that fateful evening had returned to her bed. She left the yellow bones where they fell. The power faded from her and as she undressed and laid down in her soft bed, she wept. She listened to the yells of the townsfolk. Stirred into frenzy, no doubt by the Cardinal.

'You can do nothing, child.' The book tried to soothe her pain.

'Tell me all that you know.' And with those last words her eyes closed and her treasured book entered her mind and showed all that had transpired that evening. And she wept.

As the early dawn's light crept over the now silent town, the Cardinal made his way home. Weary from saying prays over the dead girl. Weary of the stupid townsfolk. But they were happy, the gloating puffed-up Sherriff arriving at Sally's homestead and proudly announcing the capture of the witches. The family wailing in sorrow and then anger. The Cardinal feigning horror at who they had taken. The consoling words from all those present at how the poor Cardinal and those before him had been so deceived by the vile woman. As he entered his garden the Darkness embraced him. It soothed his soul.

'Master, look.'

And he saw. The yellowed bones of the beasts of Anubis. Gone the beasts he had resurrected to life. Just two piles of rotting flesh and fur and yellow bones remained.

'She is powerful, master.'

'Yes, my good friend. More powerful than I ever imagined. All pathways are now clear. Soon she will see my way is the only way for these cattle that believe themselves masters of this realm. Ignorant, savage creatures. Put the ring of Faith in their noses and they are led blindly into misery, servitude and suffering. All Lucifer needs is the Mother's heart, bound and then this realm is His and mine to rule in His glory.'

In shock and horror, he spent three days before the altar in prayer. The good townsfolk watched as their Cardinal prayed and they loved him more. For on the day that Sally should have wed, he held a great service and laid the poor girl to rest in his own crypt. He had handed over his own tomb to the family so the young innocent maid could be buried in the church grounds and her grieving family could also join their beloved daughter once God called them to Heaven's embrace. And so, they loved him more.

A month later Judith and Maria were carried from their cells. Their faces crushed by ropes tightened and twisted slowly. Their shoulders dislocated from being hung by their fingers. Battered and bruised they were dragged from the jail to the town square where braying, hungry townsfolk gathered to see the Devil's whores burn. Maria confessed quickly. Judith in a feat of strength denied all, even as the flames devoured her flesh, she cursed the Cardinal and said she would see Heaven's embrace and he would be dragged to Hells door to sit at the right hand of Satan himself.

'Oh, I do hope so.' The cardinal had thought as he stood with all the other townsfolk and watched the two sisters of Hell burn. 'Yes, dear Judith I do so hope.'

The townsfolk were satisfied. Justice had been served and the Devil's children had been routed from their Godly town. And they loved their Cardinal more.

The town would return to peace. The Godly and loved Cardinal would carry on his pretence. He and Amy now began their final battle.

BONE TO STONE!

A month of Spells and Plans

He stretched his aching neck, sweat poured down his huge muscled naked torso. His skin glowed blue and bright Runes glowed on his arms, face and head. His hair now shaved from both sides of his skull. In three weeks, his power had taken on all the Mages could teach him. He controlled the elements and animals. He could forge balls of burning fire and cast them to any foe that stood before him. Create storm and winds. Ask great trees to move and use root and branch to bind and tear a human apart if he so wished. Michael, Raphael and Kydan were astounded at this new born Forevermore. He had no ancestors and no previous lives. He was a first-born soul of the Forevermore. So, all thought!

'Again.' Growled Gideon. His voice echoed in the huge underground cavern that formed their training arena.

James wielded his sword. He stood at nearly seven feet tall now. He was eating more than six men. But he was still dwarfed by Kydan, who now stood before him. Both had naked torso's, James wore soft calf-skin pants and dark leather boots. Kydan favoured kilt, girdle and leggings. He had folded in his great wings tightly behind him. This was training so he barred no fangs or claws and kept his wings in feather form.

The blades clashed as each warrior weaved a beautiful but ferocious battle dance. James leapt and somersaulted over Kydan. It was one move that the Watcher could not do, his huge wings prohibiting it. And as he promised, he would not use the wings in this battle. If he had, the foolish James would have been sliced in two.

'James.' Roared Gideon. 'Foolish boy. Kydan shows restraint. If his wings had been prepared for battle, show him.'

Kydan spread his white wings, lowered his fangs and claws. The wings took on new form. Gleaming metal, each feather now a lethal blade. The Watchers skin began to glow and skin turned to blue-metal armour. Kydan flew into the air and brought his wings spinning down upon a stone. The feathered-blades slicing through the stone. The cut glowing blue and the iron held within the stone melting, then cooling and re-fusing to the stone, now in two pieces.

'Beware, foolish boy.' Gideon roared at James. 'Both the Watchers and many powerful Mages can turn flesh to armour and weapon. If you cross paths with a Dark Mage or The Fates send Watcher to seek your death, see well what foe you tangle with, boy!'

'Lord commander.' James bowed to both Gideon and Kydan.

'Fancy footwork and dazzling aerobatics with gain you no advantage. Use your magics, use the elements that call to you. Use storm, wind and tree to tangle and trip. Fire and flame to scorch. Your power controls the four elements. Use them. But remember a Mage has the same advantage.' Gideon lectured.

'No mercy, Forevermore.' Kydan boomed. 'Without fail, always strike the kill-blow and always make sure your foe is dead. A Mage, and a Forevermore can heal, as you know. If it is Mage or Forevermore you fight, always take the kill-blow and then remove the head. Mortals, well they stand little chance, but take the head so they cannot rise again by the Darkness.'

'My Lord, by your words I heed. No mercy. Take the kill-blow. Take the head always.'

'I think he understands, Gideon!' Kydan laughed and slapped the young James hard on the back. 'By the Eternal Garden, you fair run with sweat and fair stink. I think it be time I took my leave. You, my young lad, are in much need of the Roman bath house!'

Kydan vanished.

'Aye, lad.' Gideon laughed. 'I think my Lord Watcher is right. My boy, you wield power beyond all that I have seen in this mortal realm. You are young, and must now use the power wisely. Do not toy with a Dark Mage, for it is no game. Our Brothers have never shown mercy. Mercy is for the God of man but not for us. Mercy leaves you vulnerable. All knew on the battlefields that our Brothers fought to the death, we gave no mercy and expected none. You must be the same.'

'Aye, my Lord Commander.' James said, he knew well that he had to shed the words of God from his soul. He was Brotherhood and soon would walk the Labyrinth. Other Brothers came into the cavern, wanting to use the practice arena.

'Come, our Brothers need the arena. At end of week you take your walk.'

'So soon....'

'Aye, lad.' Gideon now solemn. 'All preparations are now done. We will hold our last mass on this Sunday and in early hours we leave for Lachlan Castle. And you must take the great steps before our journey begins.'

'By your command.'

'Come, the baths will be fair empty. Let this rabble be about their sports. And Kydan spoke good truth. I think even Laoch would not allow you on his back you stink like a midden in June!'

'And, my Lord Commander, if Laoch did not hold you in such high esteem I would fair ask him to put hooves to arse for such insult.'

Gideon roared with laughter at the young lad's humour. This new-born Forevermore was a complex creature. A human-kind with powers of the immortals. 'Aye.' Thought Gideon. 'The Fates do certainly love their games!'

The next few days the Abbey filled carts and one by one they left for the road. Most acted out the role of pilgrims bringing the word of God to the Northern clans. When reaching the far north the carts would be abandoned to move faster over the great Scottish Highlands. Working the same fast-moving tactics of the Highland Warrior clans. Carry only what you need and move with stealth and speed. None could match the Highland clans for their sheer will and tenacity. Lachlan Castle sat on the shores of the great sea Loch Fyne. They would leave these lands from these shores. Patrick MacLachlan had sent word that all was ready, but to travel by stealth. The lands were in much unrest, rumour spread of Isabella, Edward's wife seeking rebellion and invasion. This year of our Lord God, 1326 was filled with unrest and rumours of rebellion. Gideon would heed Patrick's warning! Gideon had decided to split the travellers into pilgrims and merchants. Feeling less eyes would be upon poor holy men and merchants seeking silver. They would regroup at the northern border lands where land was harsh and less populated. In all his concerns it was the eyes of the Dark Mage, the Cardinal that he needed to be out of view from. Hopefully the young maiden Amy would keep his eyes away.

Roche Abbey was quiet. Everyone left was about their final preparations. His family were in their small cells. They had each been handed a large sack with strange strappings. David had shown how they looped the straps around their shoulders so the pack sat snugly on their backs. The Brotherhood used these packs on long distance journeys. Each pack carried all a Brother would need. Thick blanket, bowl, hunting knife and fine thread to make bow or fishing rod. Flint and dry tinder to light fire. And a small wooden box which David had called a Medicinal box, having many small clay pots of aids to healing, fine bone needles and thread to sew wounds. Even milk of the poppy, turmeric and oil of clove for pain. Silver coins were sewn into the seams so none could find them. Hidden at the base where hands could reach behind them were two fearsome short blades secreted in sheaths sewn into the base of the pack. Each was astounded by the clever idea and grateful. David gave them hard dry biscuits, tough dried meat strips and dried lentils, peas, barley were handed in rough cloth bags and then a bag of dried apples and pears. Each traveller carried their own pack. Each evening all contributed a small portion to a pot. Hunters would be sent to find rabbit, rat, squirrel or any other fish or game that could be found. Others would forage for berries, mushrooms, anything that could be thrown in a potage to be shared. He even gave each a small cloth bag which had rolled parchment, which carried dried precious herbs. 'They at least add some flavour, but I am sure you can find wild garlic and such. The potage does tend to become tedious.' David had said. 'But beware the cumin seeds, I have marked the parchment, it is a strong herb from the eastern lands. Gideon swears by it.

Each carefully packed their pack, the lambskin had been carefully treated with dubbin to help keep the rain out. They placed them by the door in readiness for departure. James had packed his earlier and left. He walked his path to Brotherhood this evening so had bathed, and eaten early. The others made their way to the refectory and found themselves dining alone.

'They will be in the Labyrinth.' Jed had answered the silent questions. 'Do not have concern, there are only two outcomes. James will walk through the Labyrinth and pass into the Brotherhood's temple or it will refuse him entry. Whatever outcome, he still travels with us to the new lands. But I am most certain that the Labyrinth will welcome him.'

'I am sure that either outcome is a poison chalice!' Stated Martha.

'How so wife?'

'I would wish him with me as son in the new lands, but as Jed says, the Labyrinth will welcome him. You have seen the power he yields. It is hard to think that I carried him in my belly and brought him into this world. We will lose a son this night. If the Labyrinth refuses his entry to their temple, James will be distraught as his mind and very soul he has bound to these warriors. He is not even in fear of those Watcher creatures no longer but feels the bond between them...'

'Dearest Martha, I am afraid that James will become Brotherhood, both Jed and I are most certain. He is born of The Forevermore, he will live in this mortal body for hundreds of our years. Just as the Brotherhood are granted long life by the power of The Forevermore. James is first-born, he will never lose memory of all the lives he will live through time.' Elizabeth spoke and gently took hold of Martha's hand.

'Will it be so with your Amy?'

'Aye, if she survives the Cardinal.'

'Oh, Elizabeth. Where is my mind. I forget your own troubles...'

'Hush, all carry deep thoughts and torments of mind in these dark times. I focus on our babe, our journey ahead. It is all that we can do, none see what the future holds or what path The Fates are laying before us.'

'Come.' Samuel spoke. 'Let us take this fine mead and those strange almond cakes and retire to the library to await outcome.'

Anhur Reborn

The pure white robe did little to keep out the chill. His bare feet, he placed carefully on the worn stone steps. The tallow candles flickering dancing shadows in the narrow, steep tunnel he now walked down. As he took the final step into a large stone atrium, his eyes beheld the three stone archways Gideon had described. He stood centre of them and closed his eyes. He felt the power surge into his frame and he remembered instruction.

'The Labyrinth will only allow those worthy to pass. Only those of noble heart. Only those with honour and courage. You do not see your path. You walk in darkness towards the light of the temple. Choose a gateway, walk in darkness. You will find only two outcomes. You will return to the gateways, barred from entry. You will pass and find passage into the Great Temple and be reborn Brother. By many names have we been known; you will know us as Knights Templar. But we have travelled down time, always in the service of The Watchers and The Fates. Obedient, always in honour and courage do we serve. No mercy to our enemies.' So spoke Gideon in his mind. *'Do not walk this path lightly, for you surrender your very soul to the Brotherhood. Walk well my friend and I will call you Brother at the end of the Pathway.'*

Gideon had spoken those words at top of the stairway, told him to leave his mortal clothes behind and put on the simple robe. He was instructed at the entrance to the Labyrinth to discard the robe. To walk The Pathway in his own true skin. Then he had left him and walked down the stairs disappearing into the Labyrinth. Now it was his time. He removed the robe. Naked as a new born babe the seven-foot-tall, muscle bound warrior, bathed in bright blue runes took his first step. He chose the right-hand archway. Darkness enveloped him. Silence enveloped him. Even his glowing runes could not penetrate this black tomb.

He began the walk of The Pathway.

The Pathway to the Brotherhood

The Brotherhood of his destiny.

He closed his eyes and let his inner eye guide him. Ten paces and he turned left, he felt part of his humanity leave.

Welcome Brother, welcome Forevermore.

Twenty paces and he turned left again. Obedience washed through his soul.

Brother your soul belongs to the service of The Fates.

Five paces and he turned right. Courage, honour and strength poured into his soul.

Brother, feel the power of our kind, welcome.

Ten paces and he turned left.

Brother, we grant you the gift of Earthly immortality and grant your soul entry to The Forevermore, forever your soul will be immortal. Welcome Brother.

Light penetrated through his closed eyes. He opened them. He stood in the Great Temple. He saw all that Gideon had described. The towering cavern with starlit roof. The Great Dias and the four pillars of the Elementals. The sheer beauty of the carvings. The pentagram glowed blue, the four elementals hovered as blue globes over the four pillars. All the Brothers watched in silence.

Suddenly, his power increased. Every fibre of his being filled with the power of the elementals and the Forevermore. Pain tore through him as his skin began to change. Each skin cell becoming gleaming metal. Growing from feet, to leg, to torso and head. He drew every ounce of courage. The elemental of Earth gave him armour from the metals of the Earth. The power increased sending it out into the town of Tickhill and the surrounding farm lands. This explosion of power raced into the Earth, into the skies. The Earth shuddered. The skies darkened and soon a great storm grew over the Abbey and the town.

'Call upon the Earth and I will give you armour. Power over Nature.'

He lifted his now metal clad arms and opened his hands, palms towards the cavern roof. A glow, then more. Raging balls of flames formed in his palms.

'Call upon Fire and I will give you light, warmth and the weapon of fire.'

Wind swirled around him and within his mind he moved the storm.

'Call upon Air and control the winds, storm and thunder.'

Water slithered along the dais, crawling round his armoured feet.

'Call upon Water and create ice and wave, rain and storm'

'We the Elementals of the Realm of Earth serve you Brother and Forevermore, but only in The Light. For we serve no servant of The Darkness.'

On that evening was born a Brother of the Watchers. One born of the Forevermore. A Warrior of the Light. The Price he paid was his Earthly mortal soul. For one could not be Brotherhood and Warrior of The Fates and have free will. For he was now servant of The Light, Guardian of Earth Realm and the Mother and Father. He would never know wife, or call any place home. When his Earthly mortal physical form failed his soul would not be reborn in innocence as a mortal. For his soul would always be his, his memories always his, and he would always serve The Fates. His soul would pass into each creation at the command of The Fates.

Michael, Raphael, Samael and Kydan appeared on the dais. They took on their true warrior form and acknowledge the new warrior that stood before the Great Temple Dais. Gideon stared at the warrior before him. The boy, now man and Brother. His silver-blue armour covered his huge frame, Runes glowing with immense power. The helmet visor lifted showing glowing red eyes. He remembered the ancient tales of the Pharaohs, of Gods who lived among human-kind at the forging of civilisations. The stories that The Watchers told. Here, now before him stood a Warrior God, a God of War. Anhur, Odin, Lugh and so the names fed into his mind. 'Maybe those Gods were men such as the man that now stood before him.' He thought.

James closed his hands, the fire balls vanished. His mind filled with the knowledge of his power. He drew it from the Earth. Lightening fired from the cavern ceiling and powered into every one of his Brothers. He fed strength into them. The Mages power surged. His gift to those that now stood as Brother.

Gideon felt the searing pain as the bolt struck him. It raced around his body, renewing his aging body. He felt youth, vigour and strength return.

'Anhur, God of war.' Spoke Michael. 'Welcome my reborn Brother.'

'Anhur?' James questioned Michael, confused.

'So is your name, reborn Brother.' Raphael answered. 'You gave your immortal life to guide those of the desert lands when human-kind was but emerging into civilisations.'

'But I carry no memory of those lives?'

'You gave all to help human-kind, but it seems The Fates found you worthy of re-birth.' Michael continued. 'You have no more your memories, but we, Brother know you. I would know Anhur's soul.'

'Anhur.' James spoke, his true name, his name of The Forevermore and a name given by The Fates.

'It seems that The Fates give you second chance, Brother.' Gideon spoke and walked over to Anhur, God of Warriors and embraced him. 'Welcome.'

'Welcome.' So spoke all those in The Great Temple.

Anhur, Earth Realm God of Warriors and War.

Reborn.

Day of Storms

The sky darkened; a summer storm seemed imminent. Deep purple clouds formed blocking the earlier pale blue skies. Wind stirred. Cool on her bare arms. Birds became quiet, as if waiting for the first rumble of thunder. She had been gathering herbs for evening meal. With Judith and Sally gone, she had taken to making their meals. She had caused him much amusement when she had said how easy it would be to add a little Hemlock or Belladonna to his meals!

'You do have quite an evil mind.' He had laughed. 'Perhaps you are not the prim, innocent little maid? But I have not worry of your fare. You play as much a game as me, Mage!'

And he spoke truth.

This evening her sorrow was not soothed by the fragrant lavender and the pungent rosemary. Her heart filled with a deep unmoving anguish for Sally and Judith. She had been fortunate that she had been unable to witness the horrific deaths of Maria and Judith. She had hidden that day in her attic. Fearing to even venture out into the garden. Hearing the townsfolks yells and screams of anger at the two women. After the town had quietened into everyday matters. She had taken to preparing their meals and doing housekeeping. It passed time and she could avoid the Cardinal but not always!

Many days he had called her to his study. He would question and discuss all matters of magic. She became weary of his constant questions. Most he knew she could not know. Her little knowledge came from Jed, who had endeavoured to withhold as much of her heritage as possible. Then he would lecture on The Darkness and how human-kind should be ruled. Fore were they not sheep, to be tended? Had not their own Church decreed them lambs and their messiah their shepherd?

The garden became cold. She pushed her thoughts aside and hurried inside to the warm kitchen. She had not seen any further workmen entering the cellars. He had even left the iron door unlocked, but his Wards remained in place. She had so far feigned from entry. The souls of those trapped there by his magics caused her much pain. The book had warned her not to show the power she had wielded on those dark creatures he had resurrected.

'Still mind, child.' He spoke into her mind, the book always there, humming in her mind. 'His ears are always keen to you.'

'This power builds, it burns.'

'Not long child, hold fast.'

Thunder rumbled. She felt the tingle of the lightening, readying itself to strike. The Cardinal wandered into the kitchen, a place she now thought of as her domain. 'It seems a good storm rises from over the Abbey.' He sniffed the air. 'More than storm it seems, though.'

'What meaning, more than storm?'

'There is a power rising, one that seems familiar but yet, distant. Like a memory that is there but misted and just out of sight. Like you.'

'Like me?'

'Yes, Mage but something more. A power not of the Earth. These days have fair tormented my mind.'

'Perhaps the torment is well founded. Murder, deceit, these seeds you sow. This Darkness toys with you. It may have come to claim its price.'

'That it may have. I think not. It seeks what I seek. We both are servants of Lucifer.' Riddles, always he spoke in riddles!

Lightening breached the dark clouds. Brilliant white forks tore down to the earth. Great thunder shook the towns homes. Wind raged. But no rain came. As the evening drew in the maelstrom continued, gathering in strength. All ran to their homes for shelter. Whispers of retribution were made. For some of the townsfolk had come to doubt their judgement of the two sisters. Had the Lord God truly received the sisters into Heavens embrace, as Judith had screamed while the flames scorched her pale flesh? Was this the beginning of His retribution for their part in condemning them?

The storm gathered. Amy suddenly felt her whole being torn apart. Burning pain. Then power. She saw a Knight, full blue-silver armour adorned him. His eyes burned red, red as Kydan's did. Her knees gave way.

The Darkness gathered around the Cardinal. He watched in rapt fascination as Amy lifted off the kitchen tiles. Lightening feeding into her. The Darkness drawing more power to keep the light away from him. His mind connected to hers. A Knight, huge, powerful. His mind said 'Arthur, but not him.' His knees gave way.

Outside the storm raged. A tempest of thunder and ceaseless blinding light. The church tower attacked. Its bells split and melted by tens of strikes. Never to ring again.

The hail came, blood red. Soon the whole town's streets ran red with the melting ice. Trees uprooted by the violence of the wind. Many split to root, were left smouldering by lightening. Cattle, horse and sheep struck down, blackened carcasses. The grain fields washed away, polluted with the red hail.

'ANHUR, FOREVERMORE!' Screamed the Cardinal as every nerve in his body burned. The darkness fought to expelled the burning power.

'Fight him child.' The book screamed into her mind. 'You show him too much.'

'ARABETH!' Again, the Cardinal screamed, the power trying to rip his fetid soul from his body.

'NO!' Amy yelled, pushing with every ounce of her will to expel him from her mind.

The storm raged, tearing the town apart. The mill was struck and burned as the volatile flour exploded and burned the structure to the ground. Next struck the cottages of the Widow Smythe and the Sisters. Both were also burned to the ground. It set it's sight on the farm of Thomas, he that had accused the Widow. Soon his barns and homestead burned. It would be many days after that Edward would be found. Lying with his animals that he so dearly cherished, both burned to bone. Eric had run to the barn, trying to save his dear friend, Edward. As the barn exploded, the dry timbers exploded into his body. He joined his beloved in Heavens embrace. His body found torn and broken. Thrown yards from the barn.

As all storms do, they pass by. What they leave behind is for mortals to witness.

She stirred. Every portion of her body ached. She shivered. She still lay on the kitchen tiles. The kitchen door lay in shattered splinters across the floor. A deep groan caught her mind.

His head raged, boiling pain. He moved. He could not fathom which part of his battered body was causing most pain. He dragged himself to his feet. Seeing his kitchen broken and shattered. He saw Amy, lying on her back. Her eyes staring at him. Walking over, he offered her his hand. He was surprised when she took it. Pulling her to her feet, he saw the bruises on her face and arms that would soon turn livid. He thought that he also must look the same. She pulled her hand from his as soon as she was steady on her feet. Terror bloomed in her eyes. She turned and ran, staggered towards the hallway. He let her go.

'Anhur, Forevermore, Arabeth.' The names rang in his burning mind. 'Adam!'

'It will do you no good to know my name, Cardinal. I will not surrender to your Dark Will.'

'You deem to speak now, ADAM.' The cardinal thought to the book. 'First man, first to take the gift of knowledge. First Mage, first to corrupt the bloodline of man. Oh, what joy this brings. The corrupter of human-kind. You hide in the light, corruption of man.'

'Since the first man rose from our bloodline, I have offered redemption to the light. I will not bend to your will, Dark Mage.'

'We will see, we will see.'

She dropped on her bed. 'He spoke her name.' She was terrified. 'Kydan, hear me. You must run. She must go this night. He knows her name. He speaks of one called Anhur. One born this night. My power rages now. I must, I must take action now. For he speaks the word Forevermore. RUN. THE DARK MAGE IS COMING.'

Run

James stood, gazing at the iridescent blue-silver armour that covered him. He could move with agility, it neither impeded or restricted his movement. His world was tinged with red and he knew his eyes now were those of The Watchers. He could hear every sound, the very heartbeats of all those gathered in the Great Temple. Anhur! He searched his mind and found no memory of his past. Taken when he had chosen his mortal life in those Eons of time behind. And now The Fates had conspired to make him man and Forevermore again.

'WE MUST LEAVE, NOW!' Boomed Kydan, his face contorted in pain.

'Brother?' Michael questioned.

'Anhur has connection to Amy. This Dark Mage, the Cardinal you call him. He has connection to her. They are Trinity. Dark and Light...'

'I do not understand, what do you speak of?' Questioned Gideon.

'One born of Light, Anhur, reborn. Earth Realm God of War. One cast into the Darkness, feeding off its power. And one, in between, undecided. All connected, The Trinity!' Kydan gasped, his mind tortured.

'Then The Fates set the destiny of Earth Realm in motion?' Asked Gideon.

'No, they set time. Three destinies. I see three, trapped in time. I see Mother, sleeping. I see man, alone, setting foot on their own pathway. We must leave.' Kydan knew now what path he must take.

'Brothers, leave Temple, prepare to leave this very morn.' Gideon ordered and all Brothers and Mages left. Only Anhur, The Watchers and himself remained.

'We must retrieve Amy; her mind gives over to the Cardinal, this priest of Darkness...' Anhur spoke.

'No. She must choose her own pathway.' Kydan commanded, though all saw pain and bitterness in his eyes. 'Anhur your path is set as all is set. You must leave now. You must protect Arabeth at all cost.'

'Why is this child so important? And I am named James, Anhur is stranger to my mind. As James I was so named and James is so my mind.'

'Very well, Earth Realm God of War, so be it.' Gideon said.

'Arabeth is....'

'You cannot speak of this Kydan....' Michael growled.

'I will speak Michael, for she is my daughter and he is God of War and he will protect her with everything that he is, be he know as Anhur or James. He will protect her.' Kydan spoke with anger beyond measure, for his daughter may carry The Mother's heart but she was still his and if The Fates had chosen to bring Anhur, God of War back to the Earth Realm then he would protect her with his life!

'Are we not all Brother's here and let us not pretend for do we all not know of Kydan's love for Amy and their child. It did not take me long to fathom why Kydan was so filled with sorrow and his care of the babe, Arabeth. It is not for us to judge this. Only The Fates can give a child to two Forevermore's. They have granted that gift. I swear on my soul, Kydan. I and those that I command in this age of man will protect your child. We will leave this morn and travel in all haste to Patrick MacLachan and take her to safety. That I now swear oath to my Brother.' Gideon voice echoed in The Great Temple.

'I, David. Guardian of this The Great Temple and Labyrinth so do swear. I will hold this place and our Brothers that now stay behind will protect this place down through the age of man.' David stepped out of the gloom, for he had not left with the others. 'Kydan, I give oath. I will seal this place, so will all other Brothers do so in all the Temples throughout the Northern Lands. From Brother to Brother we will protect these ancient gateways. That I so do vow.'

'David, I hand this temple to your command and all temples. For Guardian and Grand Master, you now be.' Said Gideon. 'Once we leave for Lachlan, seal the temples and protect until the day we are called.'

James, stood. Confusion raged.

'Arabeth is my daughter. A child of the Forevermore, but a child that is in peril.' Kydan spoke to James. 'I was protector of Amy's bloodline. But from the first moment I knew only love for her. She also felt our souls merge in love. That a child was born of that love. I can neither comprehend or understand. But know this God of War. Arabeth carries a second heart within her. That of our Mother. Lucifer bound our Father and the Great First Tree from our eyes. Our Mother in fear bound her heart to Amy's bloodline....'

'Mother and Father?'

'Think of Adam and Eve, the Garden of Eden. Your great tomes tell these stories.' Michael said. 'All realms have a Mother and Father, an Adam and Eve. They are gifted with a seed from the First Creation Tree. They plant and nurture the gift of creation. So was Earth seeded. Your Adam and Eve, our Mother and Father one and the same. They keep Balance and guide the creatures that emerge from that first seed.'

'Not always do creations keep that balance....' Gideon spoke. 'We, humankind, are beginning to move away from that Balance.

With Lucifer binding the Father and the Great Tree from sight, man began The Fall from Balance. If Lucifer, with the help of this Dark Mage, the Cardinal, can bind our Mother's heart. Man will rule over this realm, they will open their hearts to the Darkness. A being that is patient, that has time. Our Mother and Father guide creations, keeping balance with life and light. Darkness corrupts one creation with the power of rule over all other creations in their realm. We will destroy our realm, taking more than our realm can replenish. Polluting our lands, turning them to desserts. War, power, greed will rule. Harmony, love and empathy will leave us.'

'In your age of man.' Michael spoke. 'War has begun. We The Watchers and you The brotherhood are all that stands between The Darkness. But mark these words. When your Mother returns, she will pass judgement and if she so chooses, she will ask The Fates for your destruction and we will carry out that destruction and you and your Brotherhood will war beside us.'

'Is this true Gideon?' James asked.

'Aye, Brother. I warned you when you took vow that your soul belonged to The Brotherhood and The Fates.'

James looked at the four Watchers, and Gideon. He knew his path. If his kind chose The Darkness and destroyed this Earth then what right had they not to be judged by the Universe? 'So be it.'

'Aye, so be it. If End of Days comes, then so have we been judged by First Creation and all the Universe.' Gideon nodded at James. 'Now time is over for discussion. I know, lad, you have so many questions. Ones we will have time for on our long nights on the road. And you my Lord Watchers?'

'We return to our Verse and wait command.' Said Michael

'Our fates are in our own hands now?' Said Gideon

'Yes, my Brother. This is the journey of the Age of Man. Travel well my friend. Travel well.' And with that the four Watchers left.

'Come lad. Let The Fates lead us to journey's end or a new age of man.'

When all is grey

'Wake child, he comes.' The book roused her mind.

She had run in terror from him. When he had spoken those names. When her mind had been at once connected to this Knight and him.

'You are now bound as Trinity.' The book spoke. 'He knows my name, child. You must join him, child. You must let the Darkness in. It is the only way.'

'Bone to stone, Bone to stone. We are here. Join him.' The souls echoed into her slumber.

Soon that slumber left. She woke, drenched in ice cold sweat and fever, her hair clung to her damp skin. 'Join him?'

'Join him in The Darkness, then we shall come. The Light and The Dark. All grey, all still. Bone to stone.' The souls and her book pleaded. For they knew the sacrifice she would have to make. Only The Mother and The Fates could undo what they would cast upon both her and the Cardinal.

She rose and dressed.

'I see you are awake. How do you fair this early morn?' He said, he looked pale, the bruises livid purple on his face. She must look no better.

'It seems as if my very soul was battered by that storm.'

'It was no storm; did you not see The Knight. The God of War has returned.'

'God of war, you mean Woden?'

'They have been known by man by many names, Lugh, Woden and Odin. They have all been prophet and warrior. Many immortals have given all to lead, all have failed. I knew this immortal as Anhur. He gave up immortality to lead man, to bring harmony to humankind. He failed. But it seems he has now a second chance.'

'Chance of what?'

'He will bring judgement to humankind. He will bring End of Days to all if The Fates decide. He will bring war and annihilation to us.'

'You speak in riddles again. You say the Bible is mere fantasy of man, yet you speak of The Day of Judgement....'

'I did not say the Bible, Torah or the new faith, the Koran were untruths. They speak of many truths. The Creation, the rise of their prophets and their destruction. Do not also the pagan faiths speak of Ragnorok. The Mahabharata also tell of Gods and creation.

It is this Faith of Rome that now takes these ancient texts and uses them for power. Time has taken truth and turned it to myth and fairy tales. Man requires dominion of Earth. Man has no intention of living in The Balance. And Lucifer will give them control....'

'At what price?'

'Their souls to The Darkness. A realm ruled by one....'

'You, that is what you wish. To hold dominion over all humankind, to send this realm to eternal Darkness?'

He laughed, mocked her. 'Lucifer will rule, I will simply be at his right hand. To bathe in his Darkness, to feel true immortality and the power of the Darkness.'

'Does not humankind seek this fate? Do they not take pleasure in war, death and greed?' Her book, Adam spoke into both their minds. 'And with their souls given over to the Great Beast of Darkness, does not Lucifer return to the Light of The Forevermore?'

She froze. Why would her book speak so?

'I have kindly shown our good Cardinal the Light. For only from Darkness, only from complete corruption and destruction can Lucifer return. Our good Cardinal here. Well he will hold dominion over all those souls and he will be master of all of Earth Realm. The Realm of the Dead.'

'Come with me Amy. Humankind are a creature doomed. Join us. See these creatures of flesh and bone gone. Their putrid, pitiful souls ours to rule. We will prise the Mother from her grave and bind her forever.'

'And the child.' She could barely speak of her child, her babe Arabeth.

'She will die, either by The Mother's hand or mine....'

'Die, the Mother would not kill my child...'

'The one who holds the heart of our Mother will perish once our Mother is reborn. He speaks no lies.' The book whispered into her mind. 'Your bloodline was chosen, for your power as Mages. For sacrifice.'

Amy dropped. The Cardinal barely catching her before she would have tumbled in dead faint to the floor. This poor maid. Jed had not told her the fate of her bloodline. To carry the heart to the next generation until the Mother so returned to the realm and so sacrificing the one who carried her heart. If he had not intervened and taken her mother, Angelique, she would have been taught of their power and their curse. A curse she has passed to her very own daughter. A curse that could not be broken.

He knew that she would come to him now. To know what it meant to be of her bloodline. She would lead him to Arabeth. She was his. As was Adam, for it seemed he had little kindness for humankind. He may be a tool for Lucifer's will, but this realm would be his and Lucifer will have his destruction and revenge for his lost Brother. A Brother of Light, tortured and murdered for merely seeking the light for all mankind. To guide them away from greed and war. To seek kindness, love and care for all of creation.

'Does he speak to you?' Adam spoke into his thoughts.

'Who?' The Cardinal answered in his mind.

'Play your games, if you so wish....'

'I was there, I watched as his Brother perished on that cross. I saw the storm that raged after his Brother let go and passed into The Nevermore.'

'Did you see Lucifer, on that day?'

'I did, for I am Mage. I watched as the storm came, brought by his rage at what man had done. I watched as he raged at our Mother Earth for justice. As he ripped his wings from his body, as he chose The Darkness, I watched and saw the injustice, saw what evil man had become.'

'And you joined him?'

'He saw me that day, as the storm raged as I watched his anger and torment. I found him on the third day at his brother's tomb. I stood witness to him taking his brother's mortal remains....'

'Where did he take him?'

'Michael came, wishing only to ease his pain. To beg him to come back to the light. Lucifer asked only that his Forevermore brothers forget him, and to take his fallen brother's now mortal body to the Garden of the First Creation. Michael complied and his Forevermore brothers forsook Lucifer. I made pact that day. I would aid Lucifer and rule in his name. I joined him in The Darkness.'

'And now, where is Lucifer?'

'That I do not know, and I speak in truth to you Adam. Sometimes I feel his presence in my thoughts, his guidance.'

'He hides from all then?'

'Once I bind our Mother Earth as I did with The Father and our First Tree of Life, he will return and End of Days will rise and man will Fall.'

'Then I call you now Brother, for all I have seen as First Man, First Mage of Earth, I see only the dark hearts of this creation called Humankind. So be it Mage, so be it.'

'And your bloodline, Amy?'

'She will not sacrifice her daughter. That is all I can see in her mind.'

'Then the hunt begins and The Fall of Man.'

'So be it.'

Run Now

'Jed, wake. We must leave!' Gideon's voice echoed into their chamber as he threw open the door to their cell. 'Wake now, pick up your pack. Elizabeth, the Mage has your babe's milk ready. Go now!'

Jed shook his sleep filled mind. Arabeth began her morning yell, for both her milk and for her soiled diaper to be changed. The young miss would book no stalling from her keepers! Elizabeth startled awake. Her mind ached from the sudden rouse to wakefulness. 'By The Mother, his voice is fair like needles in my head.'

'Come, Elizabeth, we must hurry....'

'Why?'

'There seems a shift in the Magics of this land. Something. I cannot sense it. Light and Dark seem at one together. Like they have formed alliance....' Jed stammered, pulling on his clothes in much haste, like his mind was filled with ale and in fumble.

'Light and Dark in alliance, is that possible?'

'If our Realm is in peril and we begin The Fall, then both Magics in alliance will come to rid those creatures that Fall from The Balance in our realm.'

'Move, now?' Gideon's voice bellowed in the corridors. They could hear the clatter of many feet as those sleeping now roused themselves. 'The horses have been made ready. James waits in the yard. Consider your backsides well kicked this morn.'

'What in God's name is going on?' Samuel staggered out of his cell.

'It seems we must leave.'

'By Jesu, when did life become one stumble to the next. Martha, rise and make ready. I have no liking for this, Jed. It seems our lives are much in peril while we make pact with these Brothers….'

'Then take your leave, Samuel. This is your choice.'

'And let my son take up this, this. By Heaven I do not even have the words anymore.'

'Stop thy dithering, husband. Trust what you have seen, trust your son.' Martha growled at her petulant husband as she came rushing out of their quarters, throwing a pack at him.

'Wife, mind thy tongue.' Samuel grumbled but staggered back as the heavy pack smacked into his chest. 'And where do you find strength of two men to throw this so?'

'You are a bear with a thorn well stuck in his arse in the mornings.' Said Martha, ignoring his threats. 'Jed, ignore the bugger. Every morn does he not groan and grumble. I would think if I did not know better, he was husband that spent his evenings in his cups and wakes with stale Ale in his head.'

'Woman, thy tread on thin ice.'

'Shut up and make your way to the yard.' Martha pushed her growling husband along the corridor.

Jed and Elizabeth stood open mouthed. Even Arabeth had ceased her wailing. 'Well,' said Elizabeth, 'it seems our mild-mannered Martha has claw of bear and teeth of cat.'

'Aye, remind me not to stand in her pathway.' Said Jed laughing at the huge blacksmith being pushed along and receiving much tongue lashing from his timid wife. 'I would say more dragon than bear or cat. Come let us be gone and go find our babe's milk. I don't think I could stand another female in foul mood this morn.'

The yard was frantic. Grand Master David was bellowing orders. Horses were tethered waiting for their mounts. Laoch was pawing his great hooves on the cobbles. Hector, stood peaceful and showed total indifference to the melee around him, his many years with his master, Gideon had given him a distain to any human rabble.

Soon the yard was crammed with travellers. All Brothers were in full armour and Mages stood quietly in one far corner. Samuel stared at his travel companions. He would have to make decision in York.

'Your mind tumbles, Father.'

Samuel started as the deep voice spoke behind him. He turned and sucked in his breath. Red eyes glowed and stared into his. His son towered above him. His hair shaved on both sides now, glowed with blue symbols. Runes he had been told. His face carried the same markings. His whole body was covered, it was not mail and armour. It seemed part of him, like. He dared not think it. Like scales of the dragon, glowing blue. He reached out and was about to place hand on his son's chest.

'That would not be wise, Father.' James spoke, but it seemed as 'Father' was spoken with venom. And James picked up a fallen leaf and ran it down his ethereal chest. The, scales, armour shredded the leaf.

'Son, what, what have you become?'

'I have become what I was born to be. I am Trinity. I am God of War.'

'Son....'

'It seems Father that you still dwell with the God of Man. You must choose your path, Father....' James spoke in hushed but angered tone and was silenced by a scream.

'What are you, what have they done to you?' Martha screamed.

'They have done nothing but what I chose to be, Mother.' James voice never wavered and carried the same menace.

In that moment Samuel chose his path. He saw not God of War; he saw not Son. He saw monster, a demon of Lucifer.

'So be it, Father!' And James walked past them towards Laoch, who snorted at his master.

'What did he mean, Samuel?'

'It seems even thought cannot be concealed from our Son now.'

James strode into the centre of the yard. Silence followed. He thought of his Father's choice and thought that he must let Samuel find his own path. His was set. If Samuel was the one to set war on them, then that was their Fate. He closed his eyes and sought the Elementals. They came quickly to his aid. He drew the power from them. The others stood in silence. As he drew the elemental power, he pushed it into those of his Brothers, those of Mage and those that carried them to War. He pushed the power into every cell of their being. Each felt the shove into their body. The energy fed every cell. Brothers becoming stronger. The magics of the Mages increasing ten-fold. Their horses gaining strength and stamina for their journey ahead. Laoch found connection to his master, feeling his power. Bound as brothers.

Samuel watched, but James did not push to his Father. He had made his choice. He was no longer Father; he was no Brother or Mage. His path was his own.

Samuel watched, saw the blue light creep around everyone but him. He saw as it crawled into them. He saw only Evil at work. As James lifted his head, he saw his son's glowing red eyes stare into him. 'So, we know each other now, not son but Demon.' Samuel whispered.

The York Road was busy. Many travelled this road. Merchants, pilgrims and all those seeking new lives, work and those seeking to visit families, travelled along. Those that met this group of travellers saw the Kings guard on the road with pilgrims. The Mages casting illusion over all of them. James kept journey with Gideon. He had no time for his Father now, knowing his intentions. In that time on the road way he held his council as his father's mind and soul fought this battle of Faith. As they reached the city wall, they split into smaller groups. Each group entered through a different gatehouse. They each took residence at a safe house within the city walls. Samuel and Martha making their way to his brother's home and smithy.

'It seems your brother is doing very well.' Martha said. She had said little on their journey. Still puzzled at the rift that grew each day between her husband and son. James had not entered the city with them and rode with Gideon to another safe house. She dismounted and looked at the fine but small home. It was well maintained, being only one road back off the main street of Haymongergate. His smithy was also well appointed in a yard at the back.

'Brother, by Jesu, it is good to see you.' Samuel's brother came bouncing out into the rear yard where they had led their horses. His brother was round, thick necked and his cheeks red. Maybe too much Ale passed through his broad, red lips and by looks of his round stomach, too much good vitals. Geoffrey beamed at them. 'Brother, come inside. Matthew!' he yelled. 'God's where is that daft lad.' A young well fed and clean boy came rushing from the stables.

'Sorry, sir.' The fair-haired boy stammered. His poor face ravaged by the Pox.

'See to their horses and make sure they have good feed. They have long journey ahead. Then get that skinny arse into the house for supper.' Geoffrey beamed at the boy and scuffed the back of his head. The boy took their horses into the stables. 'Aye, he's a good boy. Orphan you know. Pox took the whole family. That skinny little runt survived. I thought that he must be a tough bugger so took him on as apprentice. Trouble is, he is scared to Hell's teeth of my daughters, apart from my youngest, April. Afraid she got the looks of her poor dad so they might be a good match. A skinny-arsed boy and a big-boned lass. He'll be looking after the babes and she'll be in the smithy.' With that he roared with laughter and grabbed his baby brother in a huge bear hug.

'Well Geoffrey, you certainly have not lost that bad humour. Poor April.' Martha scolded, but her bright smiling eyes spoke of her affection of this bear of a man. His daughters ran rings around him. No matter how much his poor wife, Mary scolded him about his big soft heart when it came to those seven maids, he gave in to their every wish he could accommodate.

Their house was warm with three large rooms downstairs, all well-appointed with good sturdy and well cared for furnishings. They even had wood panelling and a fine, well-appointed kitchen. Geoffrey's daughters came bounding down the stairs, all long brown hair and hazel eyes. Four were formed into the prettiness and small frame of their mother Mary. The other three, including poor April, were rounded, red cheeked and seemed as strong as their father. Geoffrey had said that the four prettiest were becoming quite the talk of the town. The other two, other than April, were already betrothed, which she was quite shocked to find out. 'Well, you see Martha. Those two buxom lasses, well they found good fine men, who saw their worth on their farms. They wanted no prickly, prissy maids. What good are they at the plough or slaughtering their pigs and such.' He had boomed at her. She knew Geoffrey would tell it straight. He held nothing with manners that befit the gentry. He was a freeman and commoner. Every penny he earned was hard earnt in sweat and labour and so his daughters had been brought up in same manner. But, she thought, those pretty maids would soon be snapped up by some shop-keeper or book-keeper.

'And where is James?' Asked the tiny, but pretty Mary. She barely reached the shoulders of Geoffrey. How she had managed to birth seven children was beyond Martha's comprehension. Geoffrey smiled down at his wife. Martha saw so much love in the bear of a man. Mary was loved and would be loved all of her days by him. Samuel had grumbled at how Geoffrey handed over every penny he earned to his wife, saying that he had no mind for numbers and would spend every penny in the The Starre Inn if he had chance and coin. But Martha had scolded Samuel. 'Mary, she has kept her home in good order, saving and making Geoffrey a man of good means and good stature in the town. His bills settled on time. His prices of good merit and his work the finest in York.' And she had also pointed out that Geoffrey never went short of his share of Ale in his favourite ale house. Samuel had stilled grumbled on about him being soft in head for no man handed his hard-earned money to a woman. Martha chose to ignore him. For was it not the women that made the hearth, scrimped away the pennies? Mended and made do? 'He is a soldier now, and has taken bed with his men.'

'Well, that is a tale I must know.' Said Mary, looking forward to hearing the tale. Not asking further, for she saw the discomfort on Martha's face.

That evening Mary had made a great fuss of them. Their supper was of a fine roast beef. Her bread was light. She had even made a fine pie filled with apples which had a strange spice baked with them, cinnamon it was called. Martha had never tasted anything like it. Mary had saved the best cream to go with the baked pie. Samuel and Geoffrey had gone out then to The Starre. She and Mary and her happy brood of girls had spent the evening by a blazing fire and gossiped away the evening. Soon Martha was shown to a warm room, normally three of the girls shared this room, but they had happily moved into the other girl's rooms to share a bed with their sisters. Martha had crawled into a soft feather down bed. Such comfort. Soft snores soon filled the warm, snug room.

'Aye, Samuel. I can only say, that what you have told me this evening. Well it's fair too much to believe.' Said Geoffrey after Samuel had told all of his dark trade of Death Master and all that had befallen him. 'Hold tongue. Let me finish. I call you no liar, brother. I know you speak truth this night. It is hard for a God-fearing man to even think of such things, such blasphemy.'

'I know not what to do. What do I do, brother?'

'Thy knows well what thy should do. You are as God-fearing man as I. You live by the Good-book. Those, men, Templars. You know of what our Holy Father says of them. Those Templars are Devil worshipers. Fore have we not all heard of the trials in France?'

'Aye, brother....'

'And if you son has taken their vows and passed over to the Evil One...'

'I cannot betray him....'

'Betray him or betray our God and our Holy Father. Choice is yours to make, brother. Listen....' Geoffrey spoke, words now slurring from the fine strong Ale. 'You must continue your journey. I will see to matters of Faith and loyalty to our God and Holy Father. Witness and mark all well, brother and send message back when you can of the road you take. Keep thy Faith and keep your eyes and ears keen.'

'Aye, you speak wise words....' Samuel spoke. His brother was right. His brother would deal with the matter of this to the Cardinal in his hometown. He would continue his journey, if only for his Son's sake and the saving and rescue of his soul.

Both brothers staggered home that evening. Assured of their righteousness. Geoffrey, who was never one to turn away from opportunity thought of the price he could extract for such information. This Godly Cardinal, Charles de Gosse would perhaps see fitting reward of this news of these demons. It could make good for dowry for all his brood of six, and then his April could make betrothal to his young apprentice. And continue his family business when age took away his working days. Aye, fortune knocked on his door this night.

'You speak little this evening?' Gideon sat his sore arse into the soft fireside chair and groaned.

'Aye, Lord Commander. I have many troubling thoughts this evening.' James spoke into the burning embers.

'See them shared, Brother.'

James sighed; it would do no good to keep these thoughts to himself. 'My father, he has thoughts of betrayal. For all you have shown him, his Faith still remains in his soul.'

'I never thought it would have left. Brother, your Father has had a lifetime drawing breath in this world of the One True God. You cannot expect to turn his world upside-down in one moment. Much of his Faith is pure and good. The words of his Book carry much truth and a message of hope and love. Is it not man that corrupts those truths and that message?'

'Man corrupts all.' James whispered. Gideon noted how he now spoke of man as other than he was. He saw James now as he would see a Watcher. Not humankind, but Forevermore in human form. He saw before him The God of War, the bringer of The Mother's judgement on Earth. 'What should I do?'

'Let your Father be. This journey will test all, including you....'

'And if he betrays us?'

'We will deal with him and its outcome.'

'If he betrays us, I will ensure he is sent to The Oblivion minus his head. One does not make pact then change tune. Oath is oath. Pact is pact. Break and death come's by my hand.'

'Aye, so let thy Father be. Go rest for tomorrow we leave for the Highlands of the North. We have but little time now before Mabon is upon us.' With that he rose and left James to his thoughts. He had been finding it more difficult to see him as humankind with each passing hour. But now he saw only The God of War, for the creature he shared this journey with was no longer humankind. He may be named James in this life, but his true name was Anhur.

The next morning all rose early in their safehouses. Packed and mounted they left in their small groups from different gatehouses once more. The road before them was long. All faced their uncertain future.

Betrayal

'You do this Geoffrey and you shall see not forgiveness from me. Mark my words you meddle. And it is fair not wise to meddle in matters of God and The Pope....'

'For once wife, I will do our Lord's work...'

'And how do you call this, this betrayal our Lord's work. You know of His plans now do you husband?'

The argument had raged all the morning after Samuel and Martha had left. James had called, but stayed only a short while to pass time and give greetings. Mary had been rendered silent, which for her was no mean feat, at the sight of her brother-in-law's son. But neither Samuel or Martha gave any council to their son's red eyes or huge frame. Mary decided that as they were leaving in the break of day, that some business was not her business. Whatever was about her husband's family was their business alone. In the early hours as Samuel and Martha left, Geoffrey had spilled the tale that Samuel had spoken of that evening. And what her husband now planned. She had raged at him all morning as he prepared for his journey.

'You will drag all our family into this mire if you do this.'

'Woman, for once cease your nagging. Samuel was right, your tongue has too much freedom for wife.'

'And you have too much store in tales which grow more fanciful with each jug of Ale you sup. So, go husband, and seal all our fates. The Church will show no mercy to any of us if your fancies are true. Mark my words, husband.' And with her final words she walked into their fine home and fair bounced the door off its hinges as she slammed it shut. The girls were cowering in the kitchen. Never had they seen such a fierce fight between their ma and pa.

'Girls, go pack everything you can into our trunks...'

'Ma....' Said April

'I seek no council from any of you. You will obey me.' Mary snarled at her brood, who rushed upstairs. She went to the drawing room and found and pushed open the secret panel. There she took out a strong box. It was all they had. And it was a fair sum. She had kept this from Geoffrey, for his spendthrift ways would have soon seen her years of saving gone in blink of an eye and many a jug of ale. For all her love of her husband, coin ran through his fingers as water ran down the streets.

'He brings destruction to this family.' She thought as she tucked the box in her trunk. She would not be party to his schemes. She had a sister in France. She was widowed and she would welcome them. 'You stupid fool, Geoffrey. To meddle in matters of the Church will bring them to your door.' And with that final thought she waited for her fool of a man to leave with April's sweetheart. 'They will all find others to give their hearts to.' She muttered, as she thought of April's sorrow at losing her Matthew.

She heard the horses clatter out of their yard. She gathered her brood. She would send the two daughters who were betrothed to their future husband's family's with good dowry and with tale of loss and sorrow to cover Geoffrey's madness. The others she would take with her to her sister's farm in Normandy. She hoped that the eyes of the Church would not find them there once Geoffrey had reached this Cardinal.

Amy walked in the quiet garden. Light moved around her, but always now the Dark mingled with the light. She had become Grey. Her power now transcended both realms. Both realms of Light and Dark fought for her attention. She allowed both into her soul. Adam, First Man, the spirit trapped in their book guided her. They had to work carefully now. Both The Knight and The Cardinal were intertwined with her soul. They were Trinity. Three souls merging into one powerful force. The Knight had faded though, as if moving away as each day passed. The Cardinal's soul was always near, but Adam had taught her shielding spells.

'Pull the Darkness in, slowly.' Adam spoke into her mind.

As she stood in the cool autumn sun she slowly drew in the intoxicating power of the Darkness. Her whole being tingled with power. It offered so much in this mortal life.

'Careful Mage. Keep the Light. Do not let the Light go.'

She pushed against the Dark and the Light grew. Pull and push. Control. She would have to surrender soon, but control was all now.

'My, my, child.' The Cardinal's heavy riding boots crunched on the gravel. He had taken to wearing the clothes of a Lord of late. Apart from Mass he now wore clothes of the gentry. After the horror of the death of Sally, the burning of the sisters and the great storm he had taken informal clothes. He stated that he needed to be ready to mount horse and ride to any part of the parish to chase down the demons that plagued this land. 'Your control grows. Does it not feel good? To be your true-self. To be the Mage you were always born to be?'

'Aye, my Lord Cardinal. I have no fear now. Do you still feel The Knight?'

'Nay, he moves far from us, but he cannot outrun his destiny. We are the Trinity and we are bound together.'

'My Lord Cardinal, messenger has come...' His Nubian friend boomed from the kitchen doorway.

'Well it seems more townsfolk need attention. What witch or demon do they now find I wonder?' he laughed and marched into the manor. The Nubian glared at her. He had no trust for her. Perhaps the Cardinal should have paid more heed to his warrior's thoughts.

A huge bear of a man was sat in his study. Huge hands with blackened finger nails wrung a grubby cap. His red veined cheeks spoke of much ale. The cardinal glided to his chair, sat and smiled at his visitor.

'To what do I owe your visit, good Sir?' He smiled angelically at the huge, but quivering man.

'Good Cardinal, I come in Godly spirit to you. For I bring news that has cost me much to bring for I have travelled many days and travelled many miles…'

'Good Sir. If you bring news that our good Church is in much need of, I will ensure that your pockets are not left empty for your trouble. These times are hard and our lands filled with the vile creatures of Lucifer.' Smiled the Cardinal, thinking that another Godly man, who came with gossip in the hope of pockets full of silver as reward. Did they not listen to their priests? Did not Judas' silver be warning enough. Did not their Good Book teach of ruination by profit and greed? He would never understand this Faith. 'Please, be not afraid. If you bring news of these vile goings on, then be assured I will recompense you in this Earthly life and bless your soul for your Eternal life.'

'It is true what they say of thee, my Lord Cardinal. That you are of such Godly ways, that you be a blessing in these lands.'

On that day Samuel betrayed his son, though he thought that he had not. And condemned his brother. Geoffrey told the good and kind Cardinal all of what Samuel had told him. Just as they had agreed on that ale-filled night in York. He had not the wisdom to understand that this was betrayal. He could not see what Mary had warned him off. He condemned Samuel and his own family. It was only by the swift wisdom of his wife that is own family would escape. For once the eye of the Church was upon its prey, it took to the hunt.

'Well good Geoffrey. That is a tale you tell, and fair disturbs my soul. But it seems clear to me that you had chance to go to our Archbishop William of Melton. For I am sure he would have been keen to arrest these travellers you speak of and hear of the heresy and blasphemy you have also spoken of today. Our Archbishop would have been most keen to be informed of this matter. Perhaps you had loyalty to Samuel? Perhaps you plotted with your brother and these travellers to come here to me with message because you wished to give them time to escape? And gather good silver for your pockets?'

Geoffrey began to sweat, his face burned. He knew he had made fatal mistake. Mary had warned of meddling in Church matters. 'No, please my Lord. Samuel said I must come to your good self. He said that you would be the one to believe such, such, err, creatures, demons could walk in these lands. I swear by all that is Holy, has not Samuel given up his own son? Did he not tell me of how his own blood has been taken by a demon of Lucifer?'

The Cardinal smiled at the stuttering, sweating, red-faced imbecile. 'Please wait here. And please do not think to leave.' With that the Cardinal marched out of the study leaving the poor Geoffrey to his thoughts.

When Geoffrey climbed the scaffold, with a broken Matthew dragged behind him, the following month, to the waiting noose, he thought only of his Mary and his daughters. His meddling had cost him all and he cursed Samuel for all that had befallen him. For in his final heartbeat he would never know of the fate of his family.

As the Brothers travelled North, the Cardinal set his sights on his prey. He knew not of their final destination only that Samuel had heard talk of the high lands in the North. It would take many nights for his creatures to be raised from their graves and hunt them down. His connection to Amy was strong, but this James, the son of Samuel and by all accounts, the demon that Geoffrey had told of was The

Knight. He was certain of it. But his connection was faint. He was sure this Knight was shielding his presence from him and it seemed Amy too. But he would hunt them down. He would find the child of Amy and rip the Mother's beating heart from her infant's breast.

Moving North, The Dead do Hunt.

Summer moved to autumn. Leaves turning golden. As they moved ever north, the days shortened, the land cooled and all felt the land settle into the Finishing Time. Each evening as light faded the travellers settled into a close camp. Their mounts would be tended to and well fed. James would talk with Gideon while they groomed their two great war horses. Laoch settled and his headstrong ways left him.

'It seems Hector has been good mentor for Laoch?' James said as he carefully brushed his beautiful and strong stallion.

'Aye, he seems less inclined to put hoof to arse these past days.' Laughed Gideon. 'It seems old Hector here has shown the young buck some kindly manners for his fellow human companions.'

'Aye.' James said. 'What you say, Laoch. Do you become mild mellow fellow?' Laoch snuffled into James hand and gave him a gentle shove. 'Aye, lad. I will get you your food. Perhaps not all impatience has gone, not when his belly is involved.'

'Aye, and my fair belly does grumble.' Laughed Gideon, patting Hector and finishing his grooming. Soon the horses were quietly chewing their way through their evening meal. A fair bounty of wild oats and apples were served to them that evening.

Each morning James would rise just as light broke forth. He would reach out to the Earth realm magics and ask for their bounty. As they travelled, much to the amazement of his companions, nature seemed bring them to all that the season of harvest could bring. Wild mushrooms, berries of all kinds. Always a tree laden with ripe, sweet apples. Always they found a camp site by a river filled with fat, rich trout. The hunters would return with rabbit, pheasant and deer. Never did they have to resort to poaching on some Lord's land. It was as if all of nature had grown on the free-road hedgerows just as they passed by. Each evening James would gather an offering and find an ancient tree. There he would give thanks to The Mother and Father and the Earth for providing for his Brothers and Sisters on their journey. As they passed through small impoverished hamlets the Brothers would seek out cheese, bread and Ale and pay a good high price to the folk. And so, the band moved ever North and the season moved ever closer to Mabon. The land soon became barren, covered with gorse and heather. They climbed higher. Soon snow could be found. But always nature gave up her bounty.

The days passed by; each traveller quietly lost in their own thoughts. Biting winds chilling bones. As they took to the north-western coastal road, they began to see the beauty of the harsh and bitter landscape. Towns were left behind. Small crofters were wary of the large group, but offered shelter and a warm hearth or barn. The strange travellers would leave by dawns light and the crofter would find a purse of silver coins left behind. For those travellers knew that the hardened highland folk would take no coin for their hospitality, so it was left to be found long after they had set on the road again. There were many tales told in the dark winters nights that year of many bands of travellers on the Highland paths. All travelling North and to the Western Shores. Some said it was the Fairy Folk, leaving the lands as the Church grew more powerful. Some said it was folk who saw war coming and were moving to the Isles to seek refuge from the coming bloodshed and civil war as Queen Isabella made play for her husband, Edward's throne. But all tales spoke of silver left behind from these travellers. Soon as all tales do, the tales became fireside tall-tales of mysterious Fairy-folk and strange warriors. Where tales once of truth become lost in legend and mystery.

'You be Gideon?' The red-bearded man stood in the highway. His hair just as red and long and in places braided. His rich red and blue hues of his tartan gave his clan. His legs bound in leggings and a thick over shirt. A Maclachan.

'Aye, I am, Sir.'

'I be Angus, here to guide you to Castle Maclachlan, my Laird awaits you.'

'I give thanks to your welcome. Have others reached your sanctuary?'

'Aye, there are nearly fifty now. Most making camp on the shores.'

'Aye, well we must be the last.' Said Gideon. 'I reckoned on seventy making passage this Mabon.'

'If my Lord would follow. I will show you way to the camp. My Laird awaits your arrival and has news that is most urgent.'

'Then show the way good sir.'

The travellers followed the red-bearded Angus along a narrow path that weaved its way along the shores of Loch Fyne. Soon they came upon a wooded area. Smoke weaved its way to the heavens. Horses whined. Voices could be heard. The woods opened onto a clearing which was crammed with the other travellers. The last of the Brotherhood and the last of the Mages of Albion still alive on this island. All stopped what they were about. Watching the new band of travellers arriving. James became wary and called his armour. He armoured Loach in the same fashion as his armour.

'Lad, these are Brothers here this day.' Warned Gideon.

'Aye, but is pays to take caution.' James spoke, watching all the camp.

'We have no enemies here lad.'

The Brothers and Mages all stared at James. Whispers had gone around the camp of this Forevermore humankind. They now knew those whispers were truth.

Another red-beard came striding forward from the direction of the castle Lachlan, whose tower could be seen above the treeline. The Laird, Patrick Machlachan. A descendant of the first Scots of the clans of Scotti. Tall and well built. Thick braided red beard and hair and eyes that shone a deep ocean blue. For all his status this man dressed in fine wool tartan, showed little else of wealth and power. Gideon knew of this man. A man born of harsh lands and constant clan wars. He was a man of word and followed the old ways but hid them well from the eyes of the Church.

'Brother Gideon. You are welcome, though you may find it hard pressed to find space to lay your head.' The great Laird roared and stared at James. 'So, it is true. My Lord of The Forevermore you are welcome in my lands. Peace be with us.'

'Laird Maclachlan, thank you for your welcome. My unease is born from the Darkness that seeks us. My apologies.' Said James and bowed his head to the Laird. His armour disappearing.

'My Lord, you be of wise council. For there are dark tales reaching these lands. Not only of Isabella but tales of all dead things rising, of demons and dark creatures roaming all through the North lands. For I believe you are being hunted...'

'My Laird, my Laird….' Yelled a young waif of a lad, fair wheezing his lungs, came bounding through the camp towards Patrick. 'Demons have been seen these past three nights in our lands. The Laird of Lennox sent out messengers to warn all the Highlands. He says the dead are rising at Balloch. For many nights now, the dead things rise and search for the Brother's. By dawn many of our folk have been found dead, as if….sorry my Laird….devoured, good folk ripped open and… The demons gone by mornings light, no sight or sound of them.' The poor boy collapsed to his knees.

'Aye lad, now message has been given. Take rest and food and then get back to your Laird. Tell him Patrick Maclachan gives thanks. My prayers are with him and his kin. Now find strength and go lad. Waste no time. And take good care on the road home.' Patrick spoke calmly to ease the young lad's terror and also not strike panic into the camp.

'Aye, Laird.' The waif heaved, his breath yet to return and so his colour, for his complexion was as pale as the rising dead themselves.

'We have little time.' Said James. 'It would seem that the Cardinal knows our heading and hunts us down. I have sensed his Darkness moving ever closer.'

'How would he know our path?' Asked Gideon.

'I know not, but I have some inclination.' James said and glanced towards his father and mother.

'Balloch is a fair distance from us. We will be ready to leave before they come.' Patrick Maclachan spoke, his heart heavy for he knew his days here on these shores would soon be over. Most of his clansmen had voted to travel with their Brothers to the new lands. He had sent word to Rosslyn that his cousin would become Laird. Rosslyn was now sealing the caverns beneath the keep. Their labyrinth would be sealed as all would be. Patrick knew this day would come in his lifetime. A great Seer had foretold of his Great Sleep and future in times far beyond his natural grave. 'I will return to the Castle and make ready. The evening will soon be upon us.' And he strode away to make ready for the coming battle.

Patrick was wrong that they had time.

The Hunt

'Wake now! Hurry, wake. He is hunting!' The book screamed into her mind. She bolted awake.

'You are betrayed!'

'I do not understand, how can we have been betrayed?' Amy thought as she fumbled for her clothes.

'A brother has betrayed us all this day.'

'That messenger…'

'Geoffrey, the brother of Samuel, who travels with your babe and The Knight. Child be warned that Knight is James, and Anhur reborn, God of War. He will kill all that try to take your babe. James, son of Samuel, born of the Forevermore will show no mercy to any creature that comes between him and your babe.'

'James, James is The Knight I feel in my soul, The Trinity. He and his family travel with my family?'

'Yes, but heed child, James will destroy both you and the Cardinal to protect Arabeth. The Watchers can no longer aid in this,

so The Fates have spoken. It falls to the Earth realm to protect the Mother's heart.'

'The Fates leave us to stand or fall. Then it is time?'

'It is my child. Bone to stone. You must sacrifice all now. For the Cardinal is the Dark, James is the Light and you stand between the two. Mage of the Grey.'

She raced down the stairs. Her heart pounding, her heart breaking. Only time and The Darkness stood before her. For her Arabeth she would do this, she would not allow The Dark Mage, the Cardinal to take the Mother's heart and in turn murder her child. Nor would she allow The Light, Anhur to slaughter her family and no doubt her daughter if the Cardinal came to take her. For The Light would never surrender the Mother to the Dark. For if the Cardinal ripped the Mother's heart from her child and destroyed her heart, he would grant passage to the Darkness to open The Nevermore. He would control the realm of the dead. Their souls at his mercy, never to be reborn. The Father would be lost forever. Earth realm would Fall. He would become King of Darkness and Death.

She raced around the manor. She could find him nowhere. The garden was also quiet. The cellars!

She raced back into the kitchen. The iron bound door to the cellars and to the ancient crypt was open. No Wards blocked her entry.

We are here. Do not fear us. We are here. Bone to stone.' All those soul's he had chained to this place answered to her fear. 'Draw the Darkness to your soul, surrender to it.'

'They speak truth.' Adam reached into her mind as the souls had done. 'We are all ready. We all know the sacrifice you make. We choose to make it with you, Mage of the Grey. Save the Mother's heart, save your babe. Anhur will carry her away.'

Amy stared at the great iron door. She closed her eyes and stilled her pounding heart. 'For you Arabeth. For you James, Anhur, God of War and protector of the Mother's heart. For you.'

She reached into her Forevermore Soul and pushed out its Light.

A great shift moved through the Verse.

The Darkness smiled, soon the Realm of Earth would belong to it.

The Watchers grew uneasy. They felt the Shift. Their souls stirred to Anhur. They felt the Darkness rise. Man had cast the dice of their fate.

It crept into her soul. Carefully. Creeping. A deep cold ran through her blood. It came. She welcomed its embrace. Its power surged in to her.

'My Lady Grey Mage. Two of the Trinity welcome me. The third will soon be gone from this realm. I destroyed Anhur once before. For I am the Darkness, I am Oblivion, I am Lucifer.'

'My Lord, welcome.' Amy spoke to the black and cold, the nothing that was un-creation.

'Go to my Dark Lord. Help him hunt this night. For your sacrifice of our Mother's heart and your daughter, you will be at my side, always. You shall rule with my Dark Mage. For he will rule in my stead and you shall become Death, the eternal corruption.'

She pulled the iron-bound door open. She stepped through, down into the depths. Remembering when she had first been dragged down the worn steps. Remembering the stench of decay. The sorrow of the souls. Their pleading. She walked through the wine cellar that those pitiful men had dug out. There at the far end steps led down. Once more she followed the path down into that ancient crypt, a path she knew from memory. A memory of a man she had cared for, a Death Master. Samuel. Betrayer! Memory of such pain. Now she walked as the Grey Mage. Now she walked not in fear, but in anger. An anger that raged through her. The Darkness revelled in her soul as her anger grew.

So intent was the Darkness on the Grey Mage's anger that it did not see the Light, waiting.

'Call the ships, all Mages rise and call the ships!' James roared into the dark camp site. 'Rise now, the dead come. Rise and call the ships.'

Gideon rushed his tired body awake, Patrick and his clansmen came racing from Lachlan Castle. 'James has called the ships. The dead come, my Laird.'

'Then it begins. Will the Mages get the ships here in time?'

'Aye, I believe they will. But we must fight until they arrive.'

Rise, my children. Rise my dead ones. See my prey. Hunt, for their blood, flesh and bone is yours.' The Cardinal spoke as he knelt on the very tomb that Amy had been chained to. 'Come, rise from your slumber.'

He had finally tracked them down. Each night he had come to this place. The workmen had finally found the second cave. The portal remained intact. The crypt where he had first met Amy, was the resting place of a Guardian. But her power could not stop him. He had broken her Wards and his workmen had found the entrance below this chamber. There below this place he found the portal. It would allow The Darkness to connect to The Nevermore. A portal that would see all the un-reborn souls dragged back to Earth Realm. Just as the souls he now used to enter into those mouldering corpses, so he would raise an army of the dead. All he needed was to destroy the Mother's heart.

Amy stood and stared at the Cardinal. Kneeling. He drew all the power his soul could receive from The Darkness. She stepped into the chamber. She saw the new entrance. He had found the passage to The Nevermore. She saw the bodies of the workmen. Decayed and rotting, she could see that their throats had been sliced open.

'Adam, bind the door in salt and iron, forever!' She whispered in her mind, placing a concealing spell over her thoughts.

'So be it Grey Mage, travel well. We will meet again!'

The door closed. The door sealed. Salt and Iron formed and sealed the door. A seal of The Forevermore. A seal that could not be broken.

The Earth shuddered. The ground pitched and mounds grew. Kilmorie Chapel's dead began to rise. The dead rose. Rotting corpses given life. Angry and born of death. They rose at the command of the Cardinal. Clawing their way into the moonlight. Soon other dead creatures began to stir. The wolf, the wildcat, dog and deer all rose from their Earthly slumber. Black-eyed, yellow claw and tooth. Mouldering and rotting flesh and fur. The hunt began.

The quiet town of Whitby awoke to a full moon and a storm of Hell. The Mages on the shores of Loch Fyne called to the ships of the Brotherhood that were harboured that night in Whitby. Those that captained those ships soon rose to the call and prepared. For this storm was born of magic. The townsfolk spilled onto the docks. Lightening that had never been witnessed filled the air. Winds blew more ferocious than any old seadog had ever seen. Huge waves poured onto the shores, but left the harbour untouched. A strange blue light glowed in the sea in the harbour. Surrounding the ten ships that had been docked there. Mysterious and silent. Many ran back to their homes, locking doors and sealing windows. For the Devil had come to Whitby. All prayed. One dark warrior watched as the maelstrom increased. 'No Devil played here this night.' He thought. 'Earth magic!'

The ships vanished.

The great Nubian Warrior knew a great hunt had begun.

Amy silently crept into her previous tomb. The Runes glowed red. A black tar seeped into the chamber, moving as if alive. The Darkness had form. Darkness was un-creation. Consuming all. Feeding off all that First Creation had born. It would not cease until all realms had Fallen, then it would consume The Nevermore. There would be no rebirth. There would only be The Forevermore and The Darkness. Her veins became black, her eyes turned in black oceans of power. Her dark raven hair shone. Nails turned to long black talons. Power. Such power. She took all The Darkness could give her soul.

'Is it not beautiful. Do you see now child, Mage of the Grey? Do you not see how Creation is only corruption? Once we have destroyed the Mother's heart the gateway to the Nevermore will open. Death will be our army. No more Creation. Only Death. You Grey Mage, you will be that Death.' The Cardinal smiled at the Grey Mage.

Those on the shores of Loch Fyne waited. Jed and Elizabeth were mounted. Samuel sat silently on his mount; Martha mounted beside him. He knew his brother had sent word.

'What did you do Samuel?' Martha asked.

'These are the Devil's children. They corrupted our son. Geoffrey sent word to our Cardinal.' He lifted his chin, indignant to the pitiful stare of his wife. He believed in his Church; he should never have doubted their word. His Pope, his Cardinal, they were the truth. Not these, these men that had become creatures of Lucifer.

'Oh, husband. It is by your hand that we die this night.' Martha said and wept. She looked across the still Loch and up to the bright full moon. 'I hope your God will forgive you this night, husband. For I cannot.'

'Mother, join Jed and Elizabeth. When order is given do as commanded. We have but one chance.' Said James, his armour glowed. Loach glowed, his horse hair now fine needles that would slice skin. His eyes glowed red as his masters. 'Father made his choice. Go mother.'

Martha turned her horse and took one last look at Samuel's defiant gaze.

'So, my son....' Whispered Samuel into the dark night.

'Not son!' And with those words Anhur drew his sword and cleaved Samuel's head from his body. 'Not son, betrayer I send you to The Obivion.'

Gideon and Patrick watched as Samuel's body slipped from his mount. Blood glowing on his steed's hair.

'That be a Forevermore.' Said Patrick and moved to the side of Loach, who snorted and pawed the ground. He paid no heed to the headless corpse. He knew a Forevermore would never forgive those who broke oath.

'They come!' A voice rose from the dark. 'There on the hill.'

'Mages, cast now.' James roared. The steady chant began. Martha stared at Jed and Elizabeth who she had joined on the sandy shore. Martha did not witness her son taking her husband's head. She watched the still water, as Jed and Elizabeth's voices joined with the other Mages. All mounts faced the sea and the moon. She felt nothing, her soul empty. Her husband had betrayed her and her son was lost to this strange world she had been plunged into. The Loch moved. It was strange at first, but it was moving. No wind stirred, but the water seemed alive.

'Hunt, my children. Kill all. Kill the babe and rip out the heart of the Mother.' The Cardinal hysterical laugh bounced around the small chamber. He could see through those rotting dead eyes. He could see the great Loch and the Lord of Light. He could see her. Jed had the babe wrapped tightly to his chest. But her heart glowed in the dark night. Mabon had begun. The Finishing Time!

'Here they come.' Patrick yelled to the Brothers and his clansmen.

The thunder of many feet, hoof and paw echoed down the hill. Human, wolf, wildcat, dog and deer bounded down towards its prey. They smelled fresh meat. They smelled the blood, the flesh and bone. They would feast this night.

Life fought death. Sword and axe fought claw and teeth. James and Loach charged into the fray. No teeth, no claw could rip through Laoch's armour. The horse ripped at the creatures of death. Pounded them with hoof. James sliced the creatures. Gideon did same. The Clansmen fought without steed. They fought with a ferocity born of hard lands and harder life.

Lightening filled the sky. The wind grew at the Loch shore.

'Ready yourselves.' Shouted a Mage. 'They come!'

'Jed, I do not understand.' Screamed Martha

'When given command, you kick your mount and run to the water. Do not stop...'

'We will drown!' Screamed the terror filled Martha.

'Do you trust me, Martha?'

'Aye.'

'Then charge your mount, and do not stop. Run to the water!'

'They are here.' A voice bellowed in the maelstrom.

'By all in the heavens. Are those Ships?' Martha yelled.

'Remember do not hesitate. If you do you die.' Jed yelled at her.

She walked to the other end of the tomb. Her raven hair streaming as if carried by the wind. Sparks of dark red lightening bounced around the crypt. The cardinal's black diamond eyes glowed back at her. He smiled. His mind gone completely to The Darkness. She climbed onto the tomb. He did the same. Two creatures of the Dark. His scent overwhelmed her. Her body ached for him.

'Stay strong, we are here.' The voices of the souls spoke.

They were two predators. Both stared at each other. Black diamond eyes. The Darkness circled them. Feeding off them.

He looked beautiful, powerful. Her body yearned for his touch. She kneeled on the stone slab that she had once been chained to. Her hand reached to him.

James felt the shift. He felt his Light being drawn away. 'Amy, The Grey Mage falls.' His terror grew. Still the fetid creatures came. One of the clansmen fell. Wolf and human corpse tore at his flesh. Ripping chunks of bloodied flesh from his bones. His screams filled the moonlit night. Others also fell and were ripped apart. James watched as flesh was devoured. Soon the creatures that had fed began to take more form. Death feeds on death. Death consumes all. Un-creation.

'The ships are here!' James heard a voice from the shore.

Her hand touched his face. She smiled. Her black nail ran down his cheek. Followed by his black blood. He watched as she took that nail into her mouth, tasting his fresh blood. His manhood swelled. His love overwhelmed him.

'My Lady Grey Mage.' His voice now dark and cold. 'Be mine. Let us rule together....'

She plunged her nails into his chest. He roared.

'Ride to the ships, ride with all thy strength.' James bellowed into the night. Each horse turned and galloped to the shore. Each clansman turned and ran. Many were pulled onto a horse and told to hold fast. The horses ran. As their hooves hit the water no splash came. The water became as solid as the very Earth itself. The Elemental, Water, gave hope and passage to the ships. The hum from the Mages continued. James drew all the power the Earth Elementals could give him.

'Do not falter, do not stop. Run to the ships. Death follows on swift feet behind.' Gideon boomed at them.

'We will drown!' Screamed Martha but pushed her horse on. She would rather drown than be at the mercy of those creatures.

He could not speak. Her eyes turned from black to red. The Runes began to move and glow blue. She let the Light in. She cast the spell. Bone to Stone!

'BETRAYER!' He roared and lunged for her. She met his lunge and embraced him. Her hand reaching deeper into his chest.

The water held fast and the horses sped towards the ships. The ships began to circle, faster and faster. A great whirlpool formed. Sinking into the depths of Loch Fyne. The Vortex circling ever faster down into the depths of the loch, taking the ships with it.

'Do not stop.' Roared Gideon. He looked back. James was on the shore protecting the Mages who were now running towards the ships.

'Brothers, hold. Grab the Mages and carry them to the ships.' Gideon commanded and the Brothers pulled their mounts to a stop. When the Mages reach them, each pulled one onto their mount and continued their desperate race to ships.

'BONE TO STONE.' Amy screamed and called the souls, called the Light. She pushed the Darkness out and claimed back the Light of The Forevermore. With a strength beyond her female form she ripped the Cardinal's black heart from his body and pulled him to her embrace. He would not die from loss of his fetid heart, but she would hold it her prisoner for all eternity if she had to.

To his horror, he watched as his beating, black heart ripped from his chest. Slowly she opened her mouth and devoured his heart. 'Now Dark Mage I carry your heart within me. Trapped and bound to me. For I am The Grey Mage. I hold Light and Dark both in my power. I bind you to me Priest, Dark Mage. Only by our Mother and Father's hand will we be judged.

His howl reverberated in the crypt.

'BETRAYER, WITCH!' He screamed at her. She held fast.

BONE TO STONE, BONE TO STONE.' All those souls answered her. We bind you Priest, Lord of Dark. Bound by the Earth, bound by the Light.

'NO, YOU CANNOT DO THIS!'

But The Grey Mage could, the spell was cast.

The whirlpool began to drag the ships down into the dark depths. The men on board watched as horse after horse leapt on board. As soon as hoof landed the rider was pulled from its back. Others pulled the rider and strapped them to the sides of the ship. The horses were harnessed and lifted so they would not be injured. Blue lightening hit the water, exploding. Thunder boomed throughout the valley. Patrick watched as a bolt hit his home. Soon flames climbed up his castle.

'Jed, is Arabeth fine?' asked a terror-struck Elizabeth who was now tethered to the ship's hull.

'She is fine, do not worry?' Said a calm Jed

'Do not worry, do not worry.' Elizabeth growled. 'We spin as if we are a child's whip and top. We fall into the very depths of the ocean and you say do not worry.'

'Trust in the Mages.'

'I would batter you myself, husband. If I were not tied to the very side of this ship.'

The walls of the crypt began to crack. But still she held him in tight embrace.

'You will not leave this place. Welcome to your tomb, Priest.'

He did not comprehend at first. He could no longer move his feet. Then pain, unimaginable pain.

She threw her head back and reached a hand to the ceiling of their icy tomb.

'Kydan. Hear me. I cannot hold him.'

Kydan heard her plea and travelled to her aid. He knew the price he would pay for this. He would pay it. She was sacrificing all, and he would follow. He would be condemned for intervening. As he passed through the Vortex to the Earth Realm, he made offering to The Fates and surrendered his Forevermore Soul. For Love. The Fates heard his prayer.

James and Loach launched onto the deck. James jumped from his steed. He cleared Loach's his armour so the crew could put him in harness. One crew member getting a taste of Loach's steel shoes. The horse found the harness an infringement to his dignity.

'Loach.' James growled at his horse. 'Be still, they mean no harm. You will die if you do not go into the harness and be strapped to the ship.' As if his mount could comprehend his master's words, he stilled and accepted the indignity of the harness.

James made his way to the stern and stood. He saw the creatures racing across the water made road. 'Release the ships.' The Mages stood on the bows of the ships; James ran to the bow of his ship. Every man, woman and horse were now strapped and tied to those ships. None could move. Those with blades drew them. For they knew some of those creatures would make it on board.

Those ten ships began to circle the whirlpool. Every rotation faster. Prayers could be heard. All the time the Mages and James held position at the bow. The Vortex began to swallow them.

'Elementals of Earth. Hear my prayer.' James yelled into the maelstrom. He pushed his magic into the Vortex and compelled the ships downwards, faster and faster.

The ships circled, as commanded by the magics of both James and the Mages. Spray blew over them. Lightening flashed blue and exploded into the salt water. The ships began to descend.

Kydan punched his way through the Keep. He found himself in a cell above the crypt. He could go no deeper. The crypt was bound and sealed. He knelt on one knee and his huge white feathered wings stretched out. He placed a hand on the floor and surrendered his Forevermore soul to Amy.

She felt him. As her hand reached upwards, she felt his soul pass to her. 'Kydan!'

'Take it, take my soul. It yours and only yours. For we are bound by love and our child.'

'No, you must not...'

'YOU BETRAY ME. I SEE YOU FOREVERMORE. I WILL BREAK FREE AND BRING THE DARKNESS TO YOUR VERY DOOR.' His voice filled with rage and despair at the betrayal of Amy and the rise of this Knight. He had truly thought that in the days he had spent with Amy, he had won her over. That she had come to understand him, had found reason in all he did and all he had shown her of himself. And now he knew. She had simply played his game. She had smiled. Spoken soft words of understanding. He had thought he had been the cat chasing the mouse. He realised that she was the cat. It was he who had been toyed with. She had played for time. Time for this Knight of the Forevermore to rise. Time for her child to escape him, taking the Mother's heart with her. Now he was trapped!

He could speak no more. In his final thoughts he saw The Forevermore. The realm of First Creation. Charles du Gosse, Priest, Cardinal. The Deceiver who had been deceived! He could no longer move. He glanced down. Horror reached his soul. For the first time in all his long existence he felt the power of fear. Half his body was now black stone! It crept further.

'Bone to stone, so the curse is written.'

He understood and smiled. It was not over; he would find a way to break her spell. To end her curse. Soon his lungs stilled. His mind closed to eternal darkness. He became stone.

The creatures clawed their way onto the ships. Some of the passengers were torn apart where they sat. Others ripped with dagger. Kicked and crushed the creature's fetid bodies. James could not help. The ships roared downwards. Around the whirlpool the ships raced downwards. Deeper and deeper into the depths of the Loch.

The creatures in one moment turned to the mouldering corpses they had been. Gone. When their Dark Master has breathed his last so did the magic leave those creatures. The souls now unchained from this Dark Mage, passed back into The Nevermore. Those on board consumed with terror found relief as the fetid, rotting creatures were thrown out of their ships.

The cardinal stilled. Amy felt the searing pain of her body being crushed. Inch by inch her body turned to stone. Wave upon wave of pain seared through her mind. Soon her lungs breathed no more. And in her last moment she gave all her love to Kydan, then her mind stilled to darkness.

Kydan felt the curse reach up to him. It was only by his sacrifice that Amy had been able to hold the Runes that bound both her and the Cardinal to stone and eternal darkness. His price soon followed. His soul bound to Amy so the curse found him. Soon he too stilled. A final single tear formed and fell to the ground. A perfect pure white marble statue that was now Kydan, a Watcher of The Forevermore. An angel of stone, kneeling. Wings spread. One hand reaching as if to Hell. The other raised to Heaven. His head raised to Heaven, as if seeking forgiveness. A diamond glittered on the floor. A tear of a love that held a great Evil at bay.

All became silent.

Below Amy became the same perfect pure white marble statue. Her eyes gazing upwards towards her love. Her hand reaching to the heavens and to his hand which rested directly above her on the floor of his tomb.

The souls of those that had come to her aid now a writhing mass of stone human forms. Grasping at a black form that was The Priest.

The Runes dimed and faded.

All became silent.

The ships soon hit the sea floor and levelled. An unseen power pushed them forward, faster and faster along the Vortex. James and the Mages called the elemental of Water to keep open the Vortex and to push the ships along. As they moved through the depths of the Atlantic Ocean the Vortex collapsed behind them. The ships climbed high up the side of tunnel of water that had formed then fell down. Only to rise again on the other side. Ever moving forward.

Soon stomachs began to object and most heaved and wretched in the swaying ships. Still the Mages and James held their posts. Eyes closed; body fixed as if made part of the very oak that had been felled to craft the ships.

The Water Elemental fed the power into the Mages and into The God of War. All for the babe Arabeth!

The ships began to climb. Steeper. Climbing upwards.

'See, Elizabeth, see.' Jed laughed as the ship swayed and climbed.

'See what, you old fool.'

'See, do you see light above?'

'I am too busy praying with eyes closed, fool.'

Those ten ships rose from the depths. Higher and higher. They began to circle, still rising from the depths. One after the other leapt into the light of the day. As the last ship was spat from the whirlpool, it faded and all became calm.

All became silent.

The Age of Man

The cool autumn sun rose on the morning after the storm that had raged through Whitby harbour. Townsfolk quietly crept from the safety of their homes. Many gathered that morning on the docks. Two fishing boats had been cast from the sea onto the dockside, smashed and broken. Everywhere there were broken timbers, pots and roof-tiles. Many of the holy sisters came down from the abbey. Bringing food and comfort. It brought little comfort as the townsfolk truly believed Lucifer had called on them that night. Those ten ships gone from sight.

There was one on that morning, cloaked and shrouded from sight. He mounted his horse and fled the town, in silent thoughts of a new age that had come that night. The Nubian warrior that had been sent by his master to watch on the Brotherhood's ships, slipped out of the town and set path back to his master. He knew only that the Old God's had paid visit that night. For in those days on the road back, he knew only fear. The Earth had begun war on man.

It would be many centuries later that this tale of the Devil's visit and His theft of those ships would become one of those tales to tell on dark winter's nights. To scare and turn blood to ice. And to call the storyteller a daft old bugger, telling fanciful tales! A tale of Lucifer calling and stealing those ten ships and every soul on board, bound no doubt for Hell.

The town of Tickhill fared just as bad as Whitby that night. Those of that town lived through another storm-laden night. Truly they believed that God had called his Four Horsemen and End of Days had come. As on that same Autumn morning, as the sun rose as it did over Whitby did those townsfolk emerge and see what the Devil had been at play that night.

'It seems our Cardinal has fought his last battle.'

'Aye, Mayor. We have searched the rubble and found nothing.'

St. Mary's Croft was not more. As all cowered in their homes, they had left their Godly Cardinal to do battle with the very Devil himself. Every last stone of the great manor house had been shattered and scorched. As the townsfolk had prayed by their fires that night, as lightening, wind and rain had ravaged their town once more, the Cardinal had sacrificed all.

'We must send message to Rome by all haste.'

'Aye, I will see it done this day, Mayor.'

'I pray that in his sacrifice that he has sent Lucifer's children back to Hell and has brought our Lord's forgiveness and shining light back upon this town. Call all the townsfolk to the church. The Rector must lead in prayers and we must give blessings to our Lord God for sending us our Cardinal.'

No one spoke of the graves that had opened or of the missing corpses that should have rested in those graves. The mayor quietly filled them in and made those privy to the sight swear oath not to speak of the matter.

Many did keep their oath, but those filled with ale and wanting to tell a good tall tale, gave witness to the Devil's night and of tales of the dead rising from their tombs. Of Witches and a Godly Cardinal that sacrificed all. In the new age of man soon such tales became nought but fancies of simple, ale filled minds of fairy-tale and children's bedtime stories. But in all folklore, in all legends there lies truth. A truth that man turned away from, for man was God of this Realm, so he believed. He was wrong.

The Nubian Warrior soon came upon the town and found his brother, alive and living in the sanctuary of the Church. They made one final attempt to find out the fate of their other two brothers. They found only an empty York Road and an Abbey that knew nothing of soldiers or warriors that had been lost on that fateful road. Both on one quiet evening left for Southampton. They would venture back to their homeland. Their story told down the generations of a Dark Mage that sleeps in Albion. Waiting. Silent. Filled with rage and darkness.

Soon as all things do, the townsfolk forgot their Cardinal. Forgot were those days of demons and witches. St Mary's Croft was rebuilt. And so, it stands today, standing by the church on Church Lane, holding its secret. For the Devil had had its fun and left the pretty town of Tickhill in peace. For it was after all, nought but fairy-tales in The Age of Man.

On the shores of Loch Fyne did the last of the Brotherhood and Mages leave the land of Albion. Lachlan castle was left in ruins. Patrick Maclachlan and all his clansmen vanished in history and time. Tales of a great beast rising from the depths came to live along those shores. A beast spitting flames and swallowing all those that dared to take to a boat on a full moon. A tale of a wife, taking every night to the ramparts of the broken castle. Searching for her husband, The Laird of Maclachlan, until time took her to her grave, bereft and heartbroken. The monster of the Loch making for foreboding tales to the young ones. The Beastie that would snatch you to Hell for fishing at the midnight hour.

The Maclachan clan carried its secret down the ages. Rosslyn was sealed and bound. The Brothers of the Knights Templars become more legend than truth. The truth being more than the legend could ever imagine.

ALL IS NOW SILENT

Let Us Sleep Until End of Days

The ships settled on the now still ocean. Those on board began to stir from the horror of the night. The sun was already high. Time had shifted. The horses were silent.

James was knelt, exhausted. As were all the Mages. The powers they had summoned that night had taken all they had. Now was still.

'Come, Elizabeth. Free yourself.' Jed spoke. Elizabeth was battered and bruises would form, but in all was in good health.

'Oh, Jed.' Cried Elizabeth. 'Martha!'

Jed turned to seek out Martha. Horror awaited his eyes. A creature that had leapt onto the ship had torn her apart. Flesh had been clawed from her face and limbs. Her wretched corpse was broken and cleaved of flesh. Martha's last thoughts were of the Dream Realm and the image of her and Samuel living in a new land, happy together. 'You should not have betrayed us, Samuel. The Fates now bring justice to our door.' Her eyes met two gleaming black diamonds and she saw the huge jaws open, stinking, drooling, filled with yellow sharp teeth. Death!

As he lifted his head, he saw others that had met the same misfortune. Two horses had met similar fate. He heard a snuffle and a quiet whimper. Arabeth began to struggle against the swaddling that had fastened her tightly to his chest.

'Ssh, little one.' Jed hushed the tiny mite. He loosened the swaddling and lifted the flustered babe from her prison. Her eyes glowed red for a moment then faded to the rich amber of her mother and of all those females in her line. 'She is well, are you not little one?' The babe gurgled and a tiny hand pinched at his nose. He laughed.

Soon the crew began to untie those still alive. Many pale and green from retching and fear. When all had found their legs again, they began to stare at the new lands before them. With the last of their ebbing magics the Mages pushed the ships towards a sandy beach. The sun was high and warm. All stared at the never-ending forests and the snow-capped mountains in the far horizon.

'Drop anchor!' The captain's voice boomed. Soon the ships stilled and settled on the calm shore waters. Many simply dropped off the side of the ships and swam ashore.

'Perhaps they need bath.' Jed laughed at Elizabeth. 'I think stomach and bowel may have emptied on our journey!'

'Jed, how can you speak so.' Cried Elizabeth.

'We are alive, wife. We have seen magics beyond anything I could have imagined. The Fates move with us the day.'

'And what of our Fate now?' She whimpered.' 'What of Amy?'

Jed's smiled faded.

'She is alive in some form, The Grey Mage.' Said James as he loomed over them. 'She has given all and now we must make our final journey.'

'In some form?'

'She has forsaken her soul and trapped the Cardinal, that vile priest of the one God in her embrace, forever. Man cannot even take the word of a prophet of the light and not corrupt his words. They forsake the old Gods and corrupt the words of new prophets. This is your realm now. This is the age of man. You may rule as you see fit. Until The Fates return your Mother and Father, the realm of Earth is yours.'

'He speaks in riddles, as with all Forevermore kind.' Said Elizabeth.

'Come, let us concern ourselves with making this world our home. I am tired of dark priests, and those of The Forevermore. I just wish to live. Live as our ancestors did. A life in balance.' Said Jed, more to himself than to his wife.

'Aye, husband. For we have nothing but this land now....'

'Wife, I think you speak too soon, see on the shore.'

Many of the passengers were now on the beach. Grateful for the clean salt water to cleanse their clothes and body. Even the horses, once free and a gangplank had been lowered into the sea found the cool salt water preferable to the blood-soaked decks of the ships. For all the ships had fell fowl to the risen dead that had manage to board them. Loach and Hector had leapt with joy to wash battle from the coats and had soon found lush grasses to feast on. But it was not the chaos of men and horses that Jed looked upon.

Out of the dense forest came the Mi'kmaq people. It seemed to Jed that they had seen travellers such as them before. Many of the Brothers smiled and greeted the strong, muscular dark-haired men who had emerged from the forest. Soon women and children ran to the shore, creating a melee of strong arm shakes between men and hugs from the young children.

'They are the Mi'kmaq people. Our Brothers down the ages have travelled to these vast lands.' Gideon spoke to Jed and Elizabeth who were standing on the bloodied deck watching the strange and fierce looking people. Gideon reached out and rubbed a finger down little Arabeth's cheek. 'She seems none the worse for her journey.'

'Aye, it seems nothing much causes her concern....'

'Apart from a messy rear and an empty belly....' Smiled Elizabeth at the babe as she gurgled at Gideon.

'You have nothing to fear from these people. They are fierce warrior clans, but the most noble of peoples you could wish to abide with.'

'Are we to dwell with them?' Asked Jed.

'Aye, you and Elizabeth will be made welcome. A ship was sent as soon as we began our journey North. They will have made arrangements. It will be strange but by my oath they are good and worthy people.'

'You say Elizabeth and I?'

'There will be a few others that will remain with you. Most of all they await your babe. They are of the Earth, Jed. She will be protected here.'

'But you still avoid question?'

'Come, let us go ashore. Let us meet our new family, eat and rest. I will explain all.'

'Riddles, upon riddles.' Muttered Elizabeth. 'Will it ever become clear.'

The Mi'kmaq rounded up the horses, removing saddle and bridles. They found no need for them and duly sent them back to the ships to be stored. The crews soon unloaded blankets, knives, metal pots. Good cloth had also been brought and trinkets of silver and gold. These were gifted to the Mi'kmaq. Jed and Elizabeth smiled at the strange people, who smiled back. Some of the Brothers and Mages spoke their language and soon great dialogue was taking place.

'Jed, Elizabeth. Please meet Aiyana.' James spoke gently, as the young women looked in total terror of him. She was truly beautiful, and in much likeness to Amy, with her dark amber eyes and waist length raven hair. Her clothes were made from fine hide and had beautiful decorations of bead work about her simple dress. 'She has this spring lost her daughter to fever. She has made request that she would happily take you and Arabeth into their family home. She can feed the babe and Aiyana's father is their chief and spiritual guide, they would be good match for you.'

'You speak their words, no, I do not wish to know. They would welcome us?' Said Jed. 'Even they know us not.'

'They know of Arabeth. They know what she is and what she will mean to this Earth. They offer you home and your skills of farming and medicine will be welcome in their homestead.'

Elizabeth fell to her knees and began to weep. The young Aiyana knelt and placed her hand on her shoulder. She spoke words Elizabeth could not make sense of.

'She asks why you weep?' James asked.

'Their kindness is overwhelming and yet my heart breaks for all that we have left behind and lost, including you James.'

'All the sacrifice and loss has been for Arabeth. She must endure. Her bloodline must not be lost. As for myself. I am not lost; I am as I should be.'

'And your father?' Elizabeth asked.

'He made a pact to travel with us. He could have stayed in York and lived out his life with Martha and his kin. He chose to set the Cardinal upon us. He sent his brother, Geoffrey to his hearth and betrayed us to that Dark Mage. If it were not for Amy we would be lost to those creatures and Arabeth would be in her grave. They would have torn the Mother's beating heart from her breast and carried it to him....'

'If the Mother's heart is destroyed then the Darkness would have consumed the Earth in death. All creation would have become those undead that we saw. There would be no journey of souls to The Nevermore, no rebirth, no end to our suffering and sorrow of mortal life....' Jed continued. 'We are at the beginning of a new age. All we can do is live.'

'And we will, husband. James, can you explain why I weep. May I ask of Ayiana one thing. That she will become mother to our babe. For we grow old and Arabeth will need a family.'

James asked the young Ayiana, who then embraced Elizabeth and spoke of the gift she was giving to her family. It was that day on those distant shores that the babe Arabeth passed to the Mi'kmaq tribe and was named as Citlali, meaning star.

They camped for a few days, so all could recover. Friendships were made. The Mages cast spells and soon all could speak as Mi'kmaq. Jed and Elizabeth began to settle with their new family. Citlali took to Ayiana. They soon became mother and daughter. Ayiana's husband fierce and strong, but soon tiny Citlali stole his heart and some of the pain of their lost daughter faded. Jed sometimes caught Elizabeth watching the new family together. Tears would tumble and Jed would hold her. He hoped the terrible, heart-wrenching loss would ease in his beloved wife's breast. Time fades suffering. It never leaves, but loses its bite as each year passes.

'Raise the anchors.' Yelled Gideon. All the Brothers, Mages and crew had come aboard the ships. The Mi'kmaq were on the shore line. 'Mages, cast your spell.'

The ships slowly made their way to the mouth of a vast river that fed into the ocean. The Mi'kmaq, watched as those ships made their way, against the flow, upstream. Those on board spoke little. James made his way to the bow and remained there. Guiding those ships up the great river. To journey's end.

Each night the tribe would camp. The ships and all on board would remain silent.

'Citlali grows strong.' Chetanzi said as he sat beside the fire. The warrior chief and father to Ayiana had become fascinated with the couple their tribe had welcomed into their family. Jed, quiet and strong. Elizabeth, with her fiery spirit and eyes of sorrow. He wanted nothing more each evening than for Jed to talk of his homeland. The strange men who he called Priests and this God. Of how his kind, medicine and spirit guide kind were taken by these people and sacrificed to their God. He could not understand that such people, people who knew herbs and could heal. Those who could bring the child from the mother's womb in safety. Those who spoke to the ancestors, the Earth Spirits could be treated so.

Elizabeth and Ayiana took to leaving the two to their deep conversations. 'I think they will be both in their graves long before they finish their nightly discussions.' Elizabeth smiled as she looked at the two men. Their faces animated in discussion, glowing in the fire.

'Women have too little time to take up such worries.' Ayiana said, tutting at the men. Elizabeth found a kindred spirit in the young women. For she also booked no nonsense from her father or husband. Their simple home was ordered and always well kept. Each morning the simple round home of skin and wood packed away and each night quickly set. It seemed to Elizabeth that these, hers and this tribe, two peoples that were so divided by the great ocean but yet were so similar. She prayed that the world she had left behind would never find these lands. That man would never cross the great ocean. The Mi'kmaq left no mark on the land they lived. Moving with the seasons. Taking only what they needed. They felt no need to put stone upon stone. It was life in balance. The life of her ancestors.

'What is that sound, it sounds if the very land roars?' Jed asked Chetanzi.

'You will see my friend.' Chetanzi smiled.

'You lead to intrigue. I have never seen such trees. These woodlands, filled with game and fish. And those strange swimming rats that build dams.' Jed said. 'It is truly a wonderous land you abide in.'

'Perhaps once your lands were like this, before you built these towns and cities.'

'Maybe, but land like this is gone now.'

'My friend, leave behind your past. Move forward, for those that dwell on their past cannot see truly what lies before them.'

'You speak wise words.'

'Now see.' Said Chetanzi. 'See this land, feel it. Find yourself, for you are of an old bloodline, rooted in the Earth.'

Jed quietened. He breathed in the cool, rich damp forest air. Felt the last of the Autumn sun. Listened to the creatures that moved. He felt a steady roar, growing louder as the tribe moved ever deeper into the forest and nearer to the mountains.

The path grew steeper, soon the forest thinned and a mist settled over them. The roar grew and grew. The ships continued their silent journey up river. Soon Jed could only look down upon them from the steepening cliffs.

One frosty, clear bright morning the rounded a steep gully.

'By all in the heavens. Do you see that Elizabeth?' Said Jed as he stood at the head of a cliff. Staring at a huge pool far below him.

'I have never seen such beauty.' Said Elizabeth. 'I have never seen such water. Such a waterfall.'

'It is Sokanon Achak Odina.' Said Ayiana

'Rain Spirit Mountain Falls.' Jed said. 'They are wonderous.'

'More than you can imagine.' Said Chatenzi. 'Come there is a trail to the very edge of the falls. Tread with care for the pathway now becomes dangerous.'

The tribe slipped into single file and silence. Each concentrating on the perilous narrow trail they climbed to the very head of the falls. They made camp at the highest point on flat grass land that lay beside the head of the falls. Water thundered over the cliffs. The very ground rumbled at its power. As the sun set behind the mountains the tribe gathered at the head of the falls. Fires were lit and a heavy brew of herbs were smoked. Drums began and a rhythmic chant echoed into the huge basin that the falls plummeted into.

Jed could see the ships rolling in the foaming waters in the basin.

The roar that was the falls began to lessen.

Jed and Elizabeth watched in silence as the river ceased to flow.

The Sokanon Achak Odina became still. The basin below become smooth in the moonlight. The steady beat and rhythmic chant continued.

'My eyes deceive me.' Jed spoke quietly to Elizabeth.

'My husband, it they deceive you then so do my eyes.'

The ships came closer. Soon they could see James and the Mages on the bows of the ships. The Brothers, in full Templar Armour stood in rows upon the decks. Silent.

The basin continued to pull water ever higher. The whole gorge continued to be filled, the river water now pulled from down-stream.

Chetanzi walked and stood beside the couple, now staring at the wonder before them. Sokanon Achak, the Rain Spirit lives in this mountain. Our people call upon her to open the great cave. Come.'

Chetanzi led them down a path that suddenly appeared. As before the raging falls had covered it. The way down began in terror as the steep rock steps were slippery and there was nought but sheer drop to one side.

'Chetanzi, that water climbs near. It will drown us.' Jed said.

'No fear. See that flat stone there. Stand there and wait.' Chetanzi laughed lightly. Jed and Elizabeth carried on and soon stood on a flat balcony. The water ever climbed. The ships grew nearer. The water seeped over the balcony. It froze their feet. Panic gripped the couple. Then the water stopped.

Behind them the cliff rumbled. Chetanzi shouted. 'Move to the side where I stand.' As the moonlight touched the cliff face the rumble grew louder. A great wall of stone moved away into the cliff face. 'Sokanon Gaho, the home of the Rain Mother.'

The ten ships glided past the trio and into the black darkness of the cave. Chetanzi guided them into the cave. He took out his battle axe and in the darkness of the cave, he struck what seemed to be a huge piece of rock, jutting out into the cave.

A steady hum, became an ear-piercing ringing. Light burst into the cave. Jed and Elizabeth covered their eyes. 'The light will settle soon.' They heard Chetanzi say. Soon as he said the blinding light faded to a beautiful incandescent glow.

'See, my friends.' Chetanzi said and Jed and Elizabeth unshielded their eyes.

Their eyes beheld a true wonder of creation. Huge crystals lined the walls and ceiling of not merely a cave, but a cavern that seem to have no end. The crystals hummed and glowed with white light. A sight of untold beauty. They looked upon a lake. And stared as if they had lost their minds.

Ships. Everywhere. Of every kind, of every time and of every nation floated silently.

'The Forevermore Army of our Mother.' Chetanzi whispered. 'Sleeping and waiting.'

'I, I do not comprehend what my eyes see.' Stammered Jed.

'Throughout the ages of men our people have guarded this place. When we are called, we guide these warriors or Knights as you call them to this place.'

The ships glided slowly and stopped. In silence the anchors were dropped. The trio walked on the sandy shore.

Egyptian. Phoenician. Viking. Polynesian. Chinese. Spartan. Roman. And more, tribes long forgotten. Tribes un-named by this age of man. Thousands of warriors.

The Forevermore Army.

Gideon and James stood on the bow. Their journey was coming to an end.

'You speak less each day.' Gideon said, watching the Forevermore.

'I set mind to journey's end. Soon we will join our Brothers.' James said, staring at the basin that lay before them. The great falls pounding into it.

'How do you know all this?'

'My soul has lived many times, in many realms. My time on this river has allowed much of my many lives memories to begin to return. I was last here as Anhur. A great battle was fought and the darkness swallowed my army in the dessert. I gave great battle to that un-creation. It allowed for our great queen to be spirited away....'

'How could you die. You are Anhur, God of War.'

James chuckled. 'Humankind and their Gods. I am simply a Forevermore. We are reborn. We are always sacrificed. Amy has given sacrifice so her child may carry our Mother's heart away....'

'But she remembers not her past lives. My mind boils as this water.'

'I believe The Fates play many games with Creation. I was born same. Born of humankind, but my soul was of the Forevermore. It is only now that memory returns. My mind speaks that our past sacrifices gave us freedom from memory of past lives...'

'I do not understand.'

'When a creation dies, as all creations do their life-force passes into The Nevermore. Perhaps Heaven seems better word to you. The Father gathers all those that have died on Samhain and guides them onto their rebirth. Sorrow, love, hate, greed, pain, suffering. All mortal life left behind. Passing into the Light of The Nevermore, pure once more. Reborn into Creation.'

'And The Forevermore....'

'It is the house of Creation. Our life-force returns there, whole. We bear all our past lives, the joy, sorrow, pain and happiness that is life. My friend, my Lord Commander, immortality is not a gift. We are bound in service of The Fates and Creation.'

'I think I choose mortality. God's I am weary of this world.'

'Your mortal life is not done yet, my friend. Nor that of your Brotherhood and Mages.'

'I know, but Brother, my friend I am sore weary.' Sighed Gideon, his heart heavy, his mind in turmoil. Creation was a strange creature, if that what it was. There seemed no rhyme or reason to life. Only mortality and death. And immortality, servitude and sacrifice. None seemed to have good outcome.

'And The Darkness, un-creation.'

'God's do I forget you see into our thoughts.' Said Gideon, smiling. 'I think I will leave The Darkness to your kind. I see enough of the cruelty of my own kind.'

The ship shuddered to a halt. It began to creak and groan as if alive.

'Are all ready?' James asked

'It is time?'

'Yes, Lord Commander. It is time.' James said and Gideon left to instruct his Brothers and Mages that their time was upon them.

Soon all stood on deck. Silent warriors. Silent Mages of the Earth Realm.

The ships began to rise. Slowly. The waters lifted them ever higher. Soon the drums and ritual chants could be heard from the Mi'kmaq. Cliff face disappeared under the tower of water that formed. The songs calling the Rain Spirit. The Rain Spirit had answered.

James saw Jed and Elizabeth with Chetanzi standing on a ledge. He smiled. He had promised to tell all, but knew as they settled into their new home the people of the Mi'kmaq would speak of all they knew. Citlani was safe. He could feel her heartbeat and just underneath the ever-steady beat of the Mother's heart too.

He opened his soul and accepted his fate.

Gideon stood once again beside him, he also put mind to rest. 'What lies ahead, so be it.'

The cavern was beautiful. The hum soothing. The huge crystals glowing. Gideon stared in wonder at all the ships. At all the warriors now laid on the decks, sleeping. Thousands upon thousands. Sleeping, waiting.

Quietly the ships halted. He saw his other Brothers, who had made previous journey. At peace. 'We come as called. My Brothers, warriors of the Army of The Forevermore, we come.'

All those on board now laid fur on the decks. The Brothers removed their swords. They laid down and place their sword on their chests, crossings hands on them. Gideon took one last look at James, Anhur, God of War. 'See you on the other side my Brother.'

James turned and smiled at Gideon. 'Yes, Brother. Let the Age of Man rise and The Fall begin.'

Gideon left the bow. He took his place and let his weary mind settle.

On the bow, his Brothers had made a fine bed. Covered in fine fur. James called his armour. The sharp scales grew and glowed. His face glowed with Runes. In his mind he was sure he heard the distant whiney of Loach. 'Live well and long. But show mercy to these people, no hoof to arse Loach. Be good.'

He thought of Amy and sent out a single thought to her. 'Sleep well, Grey Mage. We will meet again.' He felt her stir and also the black heart of the Cardinal within her. 'For we are Trinity, and we will meet again.'

With that he lay down, he pulled his sword onto his chest and clasped his hands over it. The runes glowed ever brighter.

As the last of the Mages also lay to rest, Sokanon Gaho passed over them. The light wind of her breathe whispered over their life-force.

Soon all memory faded to darkness.

The Great Sleep began. As those warriors began their rest a great blue globe of light float down. It hovered at the foot of James' resting place. As it settled it took corporeal form. Adam. The Book of Shadows of the family of the Grey Mage had come to its rest too.

The Age of Men had risen.

The three watched as the ships fell silent. 'Come, all is done this night.'

'What....' Jed started to say.

'They sleep. That is all the Mi'kmaq know. We protect this scared place and now we protect our Mother's heart. That is all.'

Jed asked no more and led Elizabeth out of the cavern. Maybe it is time just to live, he thought. He had seen enough of magic and wished to live. So, he would. 'Did you see our book?'

'Yes, husband. I did.' Said Elizabeth and smiled. This time the smile held no sorrow. 'All is at rest now, husband. It is now our time to live.'

The great stone doorway rumbled shut. As they climbed back to the camp the tower of water receded and the waters once more began their relentless fall over the cliff.

As morning came, they left the great falls and headed for their winter camp.

Final Words

'My brother, what did you do?' Michael looked upon Kydan. The perfection of him. The huge wings stretched out, the very tips touching the jail cell roof. Each feather perfectly carved and a flawless white marble, that it seemed to glow the faintest of blue. The perfection of his sculptured and muscled body replicated in this marble. The way he kneeled, on one knee. His head lifted to the heavens and his arm reaching farther. His other hand resting on the floor. Michael knew that Amy was directly below that hand. He could feel their connection. A quiet vibration. He saw the light from the jail window catch something on the floor. He knelt and found a tear-shaped diamond.

'You gave her everything. Everything for her and your child. Our Mother's heart. The Fates heard you, my Brother. They heard you.' He whispered gently into his hand and the diamond became a perfect red rose. He stood and placed it in Kydan's upturned hand. Slowly the hand moved and grasped the fragile flower. Michael smiled. 'It will bloom and keep you both safe until our Mother and Father return. It is a gift from The Fates.'

'I have never seen anything so....' Said Raphael as he appeared at the side of Michael. 'It seems love has transcended us again.'

'It would seem so. It seems even us Watchers cannot escape that Fate.' Michael laughed. 'Have you managed to go below, to the tomb?'

'No, whatever creature sealed it, it cannot be broken.'

'Then we must seal this too so they may all rest until The Fall.'

The two Watchers cast the Runes. Soon the jail under the Keep was lost and forgotten. The new builders of St Mary's Croft filled in the cellars to build a new modern home for the new incumbent Priest.

Prophecy of The Fall

'Fallen, fallen is Babylon the great. She has become a dwelling place for demons, a haunt for every unclean spirit, a haunt for every unclean bird, a haunt for every unclean and detestable beast. For all nations have drunk the wine of passion of Her sexual immorality and the kings of the Earth have committed immorality with Her and the merchants of the Earth have grown rich from the power of Her luxurious living.'

Revelations, Ch.18 V.2-3.

'For in a single hour your judgement has come.'

Revelations, Ch.18, V.10

So be it.

Author's note.

Thank you for reading, my hope is that you have enjoyed reading this first book of The Forevermore.

The beautiful town of Tickhill near Doncaster, South Yorkshire is a small, vibrant place not only to live in but to visit. St Mary's Croft is real. The church is truly worth a visit. The castle and pond are there to see. And you will find good pubs and restaurants too. I lived there for six months. Living in St Mary's Croft held a fascination for me and seemed to be a house of secrets and was the beginning of the inspiration for this story. Don't pass through, stop and pay a visit.

Roche Abbey is nearby Tickhill and is a beautiful and tranquil place to spend an afternoon. The caves at Creswell take you back to our ancient ancestors and again is another place to visit and enjoy.

Lachlan castle is off the beaten track on the Western Coast of Scotland. Tucked away on Loch Fyne it is well worth a detour. A short walk from the carpark you will find the old, now derelict castle, sat on the shores. The views are spectacular and the place is peaceful and perfect to picnic or get away from the more popular tourist attractions. Patrick MacLachlan existed, but did not disappear!

The Mi'kmaq people are a First Nations People, indigenous to Canada's Atlantic provinces and have a rich cultural history.

Printed in Great Britain
by Amazon